99 Erics

a Kat Cataclysm faux novel

by julia serano

Switch Hitter Press
Oakland, California

Published by Switch Hitter Press
PO Box 11133, Oakland, CA 94611-1133
www.switchhitter.net

book cover design by Delphine Sevrain at Mean Child Studio
book layout & design by Julia Serano

Publisher's Cataloging-in-Publication Data
(provided by Five Rainbows Cataloging Services)

Names: Serano, Julia, author.
Title: 99 Erics : a Kat Cataclysm faux novel / Julia Serano.
Description: Oakland, CA : Switch Hitter Press, 2020. | Also available in
      audiobook format.
Identifiers: LCCN 2019918543 (print) | ISBN 978-0-9968810-4-3 (paperback) |
      ISBN 978-0-9968810-5-0 (ebook)
Subjects: LCSH: Dating (Social customs)--Fiction. | Bisexual women--Fiction. |
      Sexual minorities--Fiction. | Satire. | Humorous fiction. | BISAC: FICTION /
      LGBT / Bisexual. | FICTION / Women. | FICTION / Humorous /
      General. | FICTION / Absurdist. | GSAFD: Humorous fiction.
Classification: LCC PS3619.E73 A12 2020 (print) | LCC PS3619.E73 (ebook) |
      DDC 813/.6--dc23.

9 8 7 6 5 4 3 2 1 BLAST OFF!!!

Dedication

In loving memory of Buddy
my dear Nanday Conure
who passed away in March 2018
just as I was finishing up this manuscript

She was the sweetest entity I have ever known
my best friend and my constant companion
for thirteen-plus years

Whenever I would write
Buddy was almost always perched on my right shoulder as I typed

Losing her was like losing a part of me
so now I am lying on my proverbial bed like a lump
waiting for my body to physiologically change

I miss her so much
and I will forever cherish the shards of memories
that I still have of her
and I won't be the same person without her

Table of Contents

1. Eric Number One

I always wanted to be a novelist. Like, ever since I was twenty-six. I even bought all these how-to books on the subject, and they all said the same thing: Put your characters into conflict! And not just once or twice. But like, in *every single chapter!*

And I am the queen of conflict avoidance. When my friends suggest trying out some new German restaurant, I'll cheerily say "sure," and I will actually sit there and eat the red cabbage and spätzle just to avoid a potential disagreement. So I couldn't possibly fathom spending hours upon hours creating complex characters with well-fleshed-out backstories only to perpetually make their lives miserable. I simply couldn't do it.

This is why I write absurdist short fiction. So I can tell the tale of the woman who has kidneys the size of kidney beans, or the scientists searching for a cure for "sad cow disease," or the mountain climber who ascended their way out of the uncanny valley, without having to delve into the whole "conflict thing."

But the problem is, when you tell people you're a writer, they always ask the follow up, "So what do you write?" They do this because they fancy themselves as readers. And they are inevitably disappointed when you tell them you write absurdist short fiction. They're all like, "What the hell is *that?*" They don't even seem to care when you mention that you won the 2014 *Absurdist Weekly Review* Flash Fiction Award.

Then I got a brilliant idea: Perhaps if I sought out a bad relationship—like a *really* bad one—it would force me to deal with conflict in my real life, which in turn might help me with novel writing. After much consideration, I decided my best bet was to seek out an indie rock guitarist, since guitarists are notoriously egotistical, and indie rockers are all emotionally detached and unbearably ironic. The plan seemed foolproof.

After paging through the listings of the local alternative weekly music section, I decided to target a band called The Orange Dolphin Puppet Revival, for obvious reasons. At their show, before they took the stage, I saw this guy with disheveled hair painstakingly tuning like four or five guitars. I figured he had to be the one. So I went up to him and I kissed him, completely out of the blue. He asked me my name and I said Kat. He told me his was Eric. I asked him if he felt like his name was some kind of underlying cause of him becoming an indie rocker—perhaps if his parents had named him "Rick" he might be playing rockabilly or speed metal instead? Eric didn't find this funny. But he still seemed interested in me. Probably because I was all flirty: I bit my lip, fidgeted with my sweater, giggled a lot. Basically, I acted like an insecure ninth-grader. Many supposedly grown men seem to like this.

After the show, I took Eric home with me. I was hoping he would, you know, fuck me, then ignore me, then say mean things to me when I asked why he wasn't returning my calls. Not because I'm a masochist. (Okay, maybe a little bit because I'm a masochist.) But mostly, as part of my self-imposed experimental overcoming-conflict-avoidance therapy. But that didn't happen with Eric. Instead, he just sort of followed me around like a lost puppy for a week or two. He opened doors for me, did my dishes, and so on, when what I actually needed was for him to treat me really really badly. So that I could become a novelist.

Finally, I told Eric I wasn't interested in him. He was crushed. As he was sobbing on my shoulder, I expressed my surprise, because indie rockers are supposed to be aloof hipsters detached from real-life human emotions. This only made him cry more, because according to Eric, The Orange Dolphin Puppet Revival are not an indie rock band after all. They're an *emo* band, which is apparently a totally different thing.

Everything turned out okay though. Eric wrote a song called "Kat" about how I broke his heart, and it reached as high as number twenty-three on the college radio charts. And my new book *99 Erics*—about dating ninety-nine different pathetic guys named Eric—is currently ranked 25,097 on Amazon, which is like pretty good for a collection of absurdist short stories.

2. Materials and Methods

Remember way back, when you first moved to the city where you now currently live. And how everything seemed so new and shiny and exciting—it was an untainted place, chock-full of possibilities. And shortly after moving there, you met the most amazing person, and the two of you soon became inseparable: You were lovers and best friends, and together you explored every nook and cranny of this place. You ended up being together for a long time—like almost four years. But eventually, you both wanted different things out of life, so you split up, as people sometimes do.

They have since moved away, but you still remain in this city that is no longer new and shiny. And every day, you pass by places that conjure up memories from that special time in your life: "There's the apartment building where we first moved in together, the one with the uneven floor." "There's the laundromat-slash-comedy-venue where we went on our second date." "There's that weird blob-like statue that we always used to make fun of." And even though many years have passed, and you have had numerous lovers and a few significant others since, long-lost moments from that once special relationship still haunt you wherever you go.

Do you know that feeling?

Well that's how I feel all the time. But only with Erics.

Like, whenever I walk by that trendy restaurant in the Mission—the one that is way too expensive for a place that features sliders and mac & cheese on their menu—but Eric #23 insisted we go, because money means nothing to him, because he's not barely scraping by a living as a writer. And during the meal, he just goes on and on about the supposedly environmentally friendly start-up company he recently started up. And he is so proud of himself—you know, for being both an environmentalist and a highly successful capitalist, which in his mind are somehow not contradictory things—that he didn't even once ask me what I do. Not once! Then afterwards, when we split the bill, he boasted about how he would write off his half of the meal as a business expense since he talked about his start-up during dinner.

And now, I can't help but think about Eric #23 every time I walk down that particular block of Valencia Street.

Or that craft beer bar near Jack London Square, where I met Eric #59. And I have to say that I hate the term "craft" almost as much as I hate the word "artisanal," but they really do have tons of amazing beers at this place, no joke. Before meeting in person, this particular Eric and I had chatted about our mutual appreciation of IPAs, and knowing this place would have a great selection, I suggested it. But upon meeting there, he immediately started complaining about how the place was a bit too "divey" for his tastes, even though there was no piss all over the bathroom floors, or lonely old men in the corner of the bar drinking themselves into oblivion. In fact, it was a bar full of relatively happy people in the primes of their lives paying seven dollars and up for difficult-to-find craft beers that they immensely enjoyed. Seriously, Charles Bukowski wouldn't be caught dead in a place like this! If he wasn't dead already, I mean. And then it dawns on me: Eric #59 probably thinks this place is divey because of the punk music they're playing on the stereo. So now I'm trying really hard not to judge this Eric based on his stereotyping of an entire genre of music, when he suddenly starts coughing and gesturing toward his neck. He's choking on the complimentary bar nuts, so it becomes my duty to perform the Heimlich maneuver. Which scares me shitless—I've never done this before. What if I hurt him? But I do it anyway, and everything turns out okay. Except for our date, of course, which completely sucked.

And now, every time I pass that craft beer bar on my way to Buttercup, I can't help but think of Eric #59.

Or the Ruby Room, which is where I met several Erics, although Eric #47 was a standout. We had an awesome long rambling conversation. We talked at great length about the differences between introverted extroverts and extroverted introverts. He laughed at my story about Eric number one's emo band, and I laughed at his story about a San Diego-based black metal band who purposefully consumed rancid foods and mild poisons in order to make themselves ill (under the assumption that this was an especially Satanic thing to do), but then had to cancel their tour because they were all too sick to perform. Eventually, we started making out right there at the bar. (Me and Eric #47, not me and the San Diego-based black metal band, that is.) At one point, while sucking face, his dental crown came loose. He was really concerned at first. But he smiled when I apologized on behalf of my tongue. Later that night, we both cracked up when I called that moment one of my "crowning achievements," even though we both knew that it was the *worst pun ever*.

And now, every time I walk past that bar on my way to Lake Merritt, I can't help but think of Eric #47.

So let's get one thing straight: This is not a memoir. Okay? This book is not about overcoming adversity, nor have I gone on some Eat-Pray-Sleep type of journey. I just dated ninety-nine people named Eric, that's all. And unsurprisingly, I did not grow as a human being nor did I learn anything about myself in the process. Also, memoirs are supposedly based upon "real life" experiences, whereas these stories are heavily embellished, and frankly, some things are completely made up. Most writers wouldn't tell you that, but I just did. Just being honest here. About my making shit up.

And even though this venture began as part of my desperate attempt to become a novelist, this isn't really a novel. I've given up on all that. In addition to not being able to put my characters into conflict, I am also not a very visual person. So I'm no good at describing . . . things. Like, I would envision a scene with two characters, and all this amazing dialogue would spring to mind—the exchange would be funny and clever and weird, but in a good way. (Although none of it would help to move the story forward, which I suppose is another strike against me becoming a novelist.) But before I could actually sit down and write up this wonderful digression, I would get stuck on all the visual details: What do these people look like? How do I describe the room they are in? Is there a table in the room? Is there a tablecloth on the table? If so, what color is it? Which of these details are important to share and which are superfluous?

So I have given up. In this book, you will not be getting any passages like, "Kat brushed back her shoulder-length reddish-brown hair that would sometimes turn almost strawberry-blonde in the summertime, as she contemplated the leopard-print tablecloth. Its many leopard spots resembled a mad mob of amorphous eyeballs that seemed to be staring at her ominously, relentlessly." I promise.

Another problem I have is that I first honed my writing chops in grad school (before I dropped out, but that's a whole 'nother story). It wasn't some sort of MFA program where your graduate thesis is an actual creative writing project. No, my thesis was in linguistics, which is like the hardest of all the soft sciences. And unlike creative writing, where breaking conventions is often celebrated (e.g., "Wow, the book begins at the end of the story and then works its way backwards!"; "Amazing, it is a series of six nested stories that initially appear to be unrelated, but over time you realize that they are all interconnected!"; "Egads, this is the best novel written from a second-person limited point of view that

I have ever read!"), academic papers have set-in-stone formats. And they always begin with an "abstract," which is basically a one-paragraph summary where you tell readers what will happen over the course of the article. In other words, *you have to give away the ending right from the start*—no plot twists or unexpected turns of events allowed.

Unfortunately, these writing tendencies have become deeply ingrained in me. Take the title of this book for instance: *99 Erics*. See, I have already given away the total number of Erics that there will be. If I was a real novelist, I would have come up with a better title, something like: *An as of yet Undetermined Number of Erics*. Now that would really keep readers in suspense.

I have reluctantly come to accept that I am not, nor will I ever be, a real novelist. I am merely a faux novelist, and I am embracing that. And this right here—the very book that you are reading right now, at this very moment—is my first faux novel. It's about the eponymous protagonist's experiences writing a book about her supposed experiences dating ninety-nine different people named Eric. It will be more surreal than slutty. Not that there is anything wrong with slutty.

Now it's time for me to preemptively address the three most common questions that I routinely receive with regards to this particular project:

1) Where did you meet all these Erics?

Well, I met a few of them serendipitously over the course of my day-to-day life. But given that only 0.068% of the U.S. population is named Eric (yes, I looked it up), resulting in a Meeting Erics by Random Chance (MERC) index of approximately 0.27 per year, this project would likely have taken about 400 years to complete if I left it up to happenstance. So for the most part, I placed personal ads on various online dating sites. Specifically looking for Erics.

2) I can't believe you fucked ninety-nine guys named Eric!

So the operative criterion here is dating, not fucking. And

Merriam-Webster defines a date as "the oblong edible fruit of a palm (*Phoenix dactylifera*)." Oops, that's no good. Wait a minute . . . okay, here: *Wikipedia* defines dating as "part of the human mating process whereby two people meet socially for companionship, beyond the level of friendship, or with the aim of each assessing the other's suitability as a partner." See, it says nothing about fucking. I merely dated an inordinate number of Erics in order to "assess their suitability." And also, as part of this literary endeavor.

Although I did fuck a few of them.

3) Really? How many Erics did you fuck?

None of your fucking business! This is my faux novel, not yours. So shut up and let me do the talking . . .

3. Lady Parts

So upon deciding that I would date a multitude of Erics, my first stop was to my local sex toy store. Not because I envisioned requiring sex toys for my dating of Erics. But rather to visit my friend Eric, who works there. He is one of two Erics that I previously personally knew at the onset of this project, and he will subsequently be referred to as Eric #3.

For those of you who have never lived in a fairly progressive urban setting, I should make clear that this isn't one of those skeevy "adult stores" that you used to see along the sides of highways, where embarrassed-looking middle-aged men would slink into to buy their porn VHS tapes way back before all that shit became downloadable. No, this place is called Lady Parts, and it is a female-owned, sex-positive, all-genders-and-sexualities-welcome store where, as soon as you walk in, you are greeted by a smiling and completely non-judgmental person who will ask you if you need any help. They are always totally disarming and super-informed, and the next thing you know, you are having an intimate conversation with this stranger about how you hate the vibrators that have those weird pulse settings because you find them too distracting. Or how whenever you use those rabbit-style vibrators, instead of experiencing clitoral and vaginal stimulation simultaneously, you mostly just end up thinking about real-life bunny rabbits, which totally takes you out of the moment.

And sometimes you reminisce about how revelatory Lady Parts

seemed to you back when you were a young twenty-something who just moved to the big city. When you first entered the place, you were enthralled with the store's shelved walls covered with dildos and vibrators in all shapes and sizes, books about all aspects of sexuality, plus erotica and porn DVDs, and so on. And you were like a kid in a candy store! (Except that in reality, you were an adult in a sex toy store. Which is very different.) You so badly wanted to try out *all the things*. But of course, as a young person who only recently (and rather hastily) moved to this high-cost-of-living city, you were pretty much broke. So you were perpetually in the process of saving up to buy new toys and new books, although not the porn—not because you are philosophically opposed to pornography, but rather because you are simply not a very visual person.

Anyway, Lady Parts used to be this magical place full of endless exploration. But over time, you slowly but surely absorbed all the information and tried out many of the toys. You began to figure out what reliably works for you and what does not. And eventually you realized that, vibrator-wise, all you really ever need is your Hitachi Magic Wand, plus a small egg for when you travel. And you and your partner have already found the dildos and strap-on harnesses that work best for you. And between the two of you, you now have a pleasure chest full of sex toys and accessories that you both accumulated over years of sexual exploration and previous relationships. But you never really use most of these toys anymore because, frankly, they just are not as good as your favorites. It's the sex toy equivalent of when you discover a wonderful new restaurant, and each time you go there you excitedly try a new dish, until eventually you settle on the one or two favorite dishes that you wind up getting all the time, despite the fact that they have an entire menu full of other stuff.

Sometimes you and your partner talk about getting rid of all the toys you don't use, but you never do, because it's not like you can just drop them off at Goodwill. No, you have to boil them all, then call up all your sex-positive friends and actively try to find new homes them, as if they were pets that you are no longer able to care for. Such as real-life bunny rabbits.

So nowadays, as a sexually experienced woman, when I go to Lady Parts, I do not feel at all like a kid in a candy store. I feel more like an adult doing her grocery shopping. I have a mental list of the few staples that I regularly procure: that specific brand of condoms or dental dams, my preferred lube, and on rare occasions, a new Magic Wand when my current one is starting to sound like a dying car engine. Which is even more distracting than those pulse vibrators.

But on this particular day, there is only one thing on my shopping list: Eric #3. And maybe that sounds sort of creepy, like I am objectifying this guy because of his name. But I have found that most men tend not to mind it too much if you objectify them. Probably because they are not objectified on a regular basis, so it comes across as more unexpected than disturbing to them.

Upon walking into the store, I approach Eric #3 and he smiles. We exchange hugs and hellos. He asks about Matilda, and I say she's fine. Then I ask about David, and Eric says he's fine too. Eric then asks me if I am going to the reading tomorrow—which is how I know Eric #3, from the local literary scene. I say maybe. Then he asks, "So what brings you to the store today? Is there anything I can help you with?"

Me: You can help me by going out on a date with me.

Eric: Seriously?

Me: Seriously.

Eric: Sorry, I'm just a bit taken aback. I mean, you know I'm gay. Plus people almost always read me as gay, so I usually don't get asked out by women.

Me: Actually, most straight men don't get asked out by women either.

Eric: Well, I'm flattered. But can't you see how me being exclusively attracted to men might represent an impediment to us dating?

Me: Not dating plural. Just one date. For literature's sake.

I went on to tell him about my *99 Erics* project, and to stress that all we would have to do is "assess one another's suitability" (without actually having to do anything physical) in order for us to formally call it a date. I also mentioned that it would be my treat. He agreed, and we decided to meet up for a couple drinks after his shift.

After seating ourselves at the bar, Eric #3 glanced around the fairly crowded room and remarked: I thought this was a queer bar?

Me: It is.

Eric: Then what are all these straight people doing here?

Me: Well, a lot of the techies and newbies who've moved into this neighborhood in recent years didn't know that it was a queer bar. Or didn't care. So now they hang out here too.

Eric: Why doesn't someone just kick them out?

Me: On what basis? Because they *look* straight? I mean, as a woman and man sharing a drink together, we probably strike some people as a straight couple. What's to stop them from kicking us out?

Eric: Well, you look straight-ish enough, but I seriously doubt that anyone would ever read me as straight.

Me: Oh yes, of course, because you are *so much more queer than me!* [I said extremely sarcastically, even though, as a writer, I know that it's considered poor form to use adverbs to describe dialogue.] Anyway, nowadays it's against the law to kick someone out of your establishment because of their sexual orientation. And heterosexuality just so happens to be a sexual orientation.

Eric: Great, so they are taking over our bars and our laws.

Me: Funny thing is, this was never a problem ten or fifteen

years ago, because most straight folks wouldn't be caught dead anywhere near a queer bar. But nowadays, they are no longer afraid of us, I fear. In fact, I wouldn't be surprised if they thought that hanging out at a queer bar gives them some hipster cred.

Eric: Fucking hipsters . . . [he muttered, as he took a sip of his whiskey sour.]

Me: You know, for a long time, I thought that I hated hipsters too. But then one day, I was at a bar, writing in my journal and nursing my IPA, when these two guys sat down next to me. And they struck me as hipsters due to their vintage clothing and beards of notable length. And I couldn't help but overhear what they were saying—not because they were especially loud, but because as a writer, most of my best material comes from listening in on random people's conversations. And I heard one of them say to the other, "God, this place is crawling with hipsters." And I began to wonder who they were talking about. Was it the guy at the bar with the thick-framed glasses who was staring into his mobile device? Or the woman with all the piercings and dyed-purple punk haircut? Or the table of twenty-somethings who brought board games with them to play at the bar? Or maybe—just maybe—I was one of the hipsters they were talking about! I mean, I don't think that I look particularly hipster-ish. But perhaps these guys assume that people who write in their journals in dark bars whilst drinking pints of good beer are hipsters? Or maybe it's my liberal use of the word "whilst" that qualifies me as a hipster in their eyes?

And the more that I considered it, the more that I became convinced that "hipster" is merely a contemporary manifestation of what philosophers call the constitutive Other. Whenever we come across people who seem superficially different from us with regards to fashion sense, or taste in food or art, we reflexively label them "hipsters" as part of an ongoing social identity formation process, one that allows us to establish our own identities as unique and authentic individuals in contrast to this inauthentic hipster Other.

Eric: Could be . . . [he said as he stroked his handlebar moustache.] Or maybe it's just that you are a hipster who doesn't understand what the word hipster means?

Me: Actually, that would be perfect, because now everyone in the bar will likely view us as not just a straight couple, but a straight hipster couple!

I raised my beer for a toast, but Eric #3 didn't reciprocate. Instead, he countered with a disgruntled smirk.

Just like a hipster, I thought.

4. Bomb

Okay, so now I feel like there is this bomb just sitting here in the pages of this book. Because in the last chapter, I casually introduced the fact that I am queer, mentioned my partner Matilda, and alluded (albeit via second-person point of view) to us sharing a large assortment of infrequently used sex toys. And let's be honest, this shouldn't really be a bomb; it should just be a small info drop—like in Chapter 2, when I briefly mentioned dropping out of grad school. Your reaction should be, "Okay, now we have learned a little bit more about this protagonist who we are only now just starting to get to know."

In a perfect world, the whole thing would be just that: a small info drop. But we don't live in that world. Rather, we live in one with a long history of unscrupulous writers who purposefully treat their character's sexual minority status as though it were a time bomb that they set to detonate well into the story for maximum effect. "Oh my god, it turns out he's gay!" "Holy cow, she used to be a man!" "Criminy, this changes everything!"

But here's the thing: We all know that people who are gay, or transgender, or kinky, or sex workers, and so on, exist. In fact, if you sit down and actually do the math (as I have, because I *love* math!), each of these groups is more prevalent in the U.S. population than plumbers, stamp collectors, or people from Wyoming. Not to mention people who drop out of graduate-level linguistics programs. But if I were to mention that a character in this book falls into one of these latter categories, you probably wouldn't blink an eye. At the very most, you might be mildly surprised. But you certainly wouldn't consider it to be a "plot twist."

If, over the course of this book, I ever reveal to you that one of the characters is a time traveler, or has superpowers, or is a cloned version of another human being, then by all means, feel free to be surprised, as none of these things are known to exist in real life. If I mention that one of the Erics used to be six-foot-five, but has since become five-foot-three, you will have every right to be shocked, as dramatic shrinking is not a part of the human experience. But sexual minorities are. We are part of the fabric of life, which, if you were to touch it, would probably feel like velour, or perhaps corduroy.

Anyway, unscrupulous writers craft time bombs out of their characters' sexual histories and proclivities. But not me. I am a one-woman bomb squad! And I am here to defuse these assumptions-in-the-form-of-time-bombs one by one. So here we go:

Assumption #1: Oh, you're a lesbian. But then why are you dating all these men named Eric?

Okay, see, there is this word called "bisexual." And it's a fairly common word, one that almost everyone knows. Your next-door neighbor knows it. Your grandmother knows it. Your teenaged nieces and nephews know it. And so on. But unfortunately, despite knowing the word, many people tend to be really bad at applying this knowledge to actual real-life situations. For instance, in response to me describing myself as bisexual, some straight people will say, "No, I think you must really be a lesbian who's too afraid to fully own it"—as if their heterosexuality somehow gives them piercing insight into the lesbian experience. And some gay people will say, "No, you're merely a heterosexual who is sexually experimenting"—despite the obvious fact that they live in a you're-not-gay-it's-just-a-phase glass house themselves, and they really shouldn't be throwing stones.

So to be clear, I am bisexual: I don't limit my dating pool to members of a single gender. And you don't have to relate to or understand that experience in order to accept that fact. Personally, I don't understand why anyone would become a plumber, or stamp collector, or Wyomingite (yes, that's what they're called, I looked it up), but I will never doubt these people's existences, nor do their proclivities drive me into a frenzy of consternation.

Assumption #2: But wait, if Matilda is your partner, then you must be cheating on her. With Erics, no less!

So Matilda and I are ethically non-monogamous. Or polyamorous, if you prefer that term. Which can mean different things to different people. But in our case, it means that we are primary partners, but we can also be romantic or sexual with other people within certain parameters that we have established together.

Being ethically non-monogamous suits us, in part, because we both have aspects of our sexuality that we cannot readily explore with one another. Being bisexual, I sometimes enjoy dating and fooling around with men. And while I can be somewhat kinky at times, Matilda is into more hardcore BDSM and role-play, which is not my thing. Like, for me personally, sexual arousal and pain exist at opposite ends of the enjoy/not-enjoy experiential continuum. And role-playing doesn't work for me because I am not a good actor—I can only play the part of Kat Cataclysm. On top of that, I like making jokes during sex, which isn't conducive to creating a supposedly serious scene.

Assumption #3: But Matilda must be dismayed by the prospect of you dating all these Erics!

Actually, she is somewhat amused by it. She thinks it's weird, but then again, she likes the fact that I am weird. She finds it endearing. Probably because she's weird too.

To be honest, Matilda is far more concerned about the fact that I am a writer than she is about the fact that I am dating a plethora of Erics. She worries that I will mine all of our most precious moments together and/or all the sordid and not-so-glamorous parts of our relationship, and like, fashion stories out of them. As writers often do. So she made me promise not to write in depth about our relationship. Which is why you will never stumble upon a book called *1 Matilda*. At least not written by me.

I should also mention that Matilda isn't even her real name. She won't let me use her real name because she is a Democratic operative—seriously, that's what people who work for the Democratic party call themselves—"operatives"—as if they were fucking spies or some shit. And all her coworkers, who fancy themselves as open-minded liberals, and who often pat themselves on the back for being so accepting of gay people such as Matilda, would hypocritically freak out if they were to learn that she was in an ethically non-monogamous relationship with a bisexual woman who dates lots of Erics. Not to mention all the BDSM and role-playing on her part.

Assumption #4: I heard that bisexuals are really promiscuous and unable to commit to relationships, so it makes sense that you are polyamorous and seeking out lots of men named Eric.

Fuck you. And fuck your stereotype trap.

What is a "stereotype trap," you ask? Well, it's a logical fallacy that goes something like this:

A) Negative stereotype exists about minority group X.

B) Minority person Y seems to fit that stereotype.

C) Therefore, the stereotype about group X must be true.

(Alternately, if you're an "upstanding" member of group X, then you might accuse person Y of "reinforcing" those stereotypes, thereby holding back the entire group.)

Here's the thing though: Everybody is different. And even within relatively small minority groups, people will fall all over the map, and have all sorts of different personalities. That's why I call it a stereotype trap: because some members of the group will inevitably resemble the stereotype. But that doesn't make the stereotype true.

So when confronted by peddlers of stereotypes, rather than engage them in the pointless this-stereotype-is-true-versus-false game, the most effective and emotionally rewarding response is to simply say "fuck you."

Which is why I said "fuck you" just a moment ago. In response to those stereotypes.

Okay, I am done holding your hand and walking you through all this now.

5. Patronizing

Sorry if I came on a bit strong last chapter. And I know that as soon as I say that, some people will immediately rush to my defense and assure me that it's totally valid for me to express my anger and frustration as an oppressed polyamorous bisexual person, and that it's not my job to placate people in the monogamous monosexual majority. In theory, I totally get this. But at the same time, it's not really my personality to confront other people. Remember: I am the same Kat Cataclysm who failed at being a novelist because I am the queen of conflict avoidance (plus all those other reasons). And as a writer, I know how crucial it is to not have your characters do anything out of character. Such as having your character confront her readers about assumptions they may or may not be making about her, when her modus operandi is avoiding conflict. Especially when that character is you! (By which I mean me.)

Also, while I don't like it when people make incorrect assumptions about me, I have to admit that I often make incorrect assumptions about other people. Much to their chagrin. For instance, the first time that I heard someone say, "There's more than one way to skin a cat," I assumed this person knew this to be true from their own hands-on experiences flaying felines. And for a long time, I presumed that people who listen to techno music were only doing it in order to purposefully annoy me. Because *why on earth would you listen to techno music?!* But then Eric #3 told me that he really (and somewhat stereotypically) enjoys techno music. So I have since stopped making these assumptions about people.

So I guess the sad truth is that incorrect assumptions are going to happen from time to time. The important thing is to own them when they happen: "Oops, my bad, I have made a proverbial ass-out-of-you-and-me, my sincerest apologies." And the worst thing you can do in such situations is to refuse to believe the person when they tell you that your initial assumption is wrong. Because then you're just being patronizing. And not in a good way—you know, when you are patronizing a person's establishment, thereby helping them earn a living. But rather, patronizing in a bad way: speaking down to them in a condescending manner, as if you know better than they do.

Some men speak down to women in a patronizing manner, so I can tell you firsthand how annoying this is. Like, I'll meet some guy at a party and he'll ask me what I do for a living. And I'll tell him that I am an absurdist short fiction writer turned faux novelist who's writing a book called *99 Erics* about the writing process behind writing the faux novel *99 Erics*, although I am not really making any kind of living doing this. But then, rather than ask me about or express interest in my project, this guy will just lecture me about some article he recently read in *Harper's Magazine* about thirteenth-century absurdist short fiction, or some NPR story he heard about the collapse of the traditional publishing industry, or how he recently read *The Complete Book of Baby Names* and learned that Eric is derived from the old Norse name Eríkr, which translates to "forever ruler."

And of course I know all these things! Intimately! Far more than this guy does! But even when I share this knowledge with him—for instance, by listing old Norse "forever rulers" such as Erik the Red, Leif Erikson, and Eric the vampire from that old HBO show *True Blood*, who was like 1,000 years old, which isn't forever, but it's *pretty darn close*—this guy will still act like he knows more about these things than me. It's so patronizing! And definitely not in a good way.

But then last summer, I was on a day trip to Stinson Beach with my friend Gabriella and her family, and her daughter asked me a simple question about whether it was high tide or not. But rather than answer her question, I went into a big spiel about how the tides are caused by the moon orbiting the earth. And when tides are high, it's because the moon's gravitational pull is literally lifting the water upward toward it. And after telling her all this, she gave me a frustrated look and said, "I know, I learned all about that last year in school."

Then it hit me: Oh my god, what I just did was so patronizing! And I don't want to be a patron. Not in a bad way.

Since then, I've tried to really commit myself to not speaking in a patronizing manner to anyone. Which is difficult to do. But after considering the problem at great length, I think I found a helpful solution: Rather than assume that your knowledge and expertise are superior to that of other people you encounter, instead try treating them as your equals. In other words, speak to them as though they already know everything that you know.

And just as I was refining my how-not-to-be-patronizing skill set, I went on a date with Eric #5, who I met through the usual personal ad channels. We had very little in common, which often happens when your one and only dating criterion is having been given the given name Eric. But we both liked baseball, so we went to a local sports bar to watch the Bay Bridge series: the Oakland A's versus the San Francisco Giants. Turns out, Eric #5 is one of those guys who gets all of his baseball information from those AM radio sports shows, where the host is this loudmouth who constantly barks and rants about everything. Whereas I get my baseball information from websites like *Fangraphs* and *Baseball Prospectus*, where they use advanced statistical analyses to garner insight into the game and its plethora of players.

So when Eric #5 started boasting about the defensive acumen of the Giants' rookie infielder, I (for obvious reasons) responded,

"Actually, he is rated as one of the worst defenders this season according to both UZR and DRS. Although, as we both know, defensive statistics typically take more than one season to stabilize." And when Eric #5 mentioned that another Giants player was having a career year at the plate, I (for obvious reasons) countered: "The guy's BABIP is a whopping .457, so his batting average is bound to regress in a big way. And given his poor plate discipline, I doubt he'll end the year with an OBP over .300. So I am not particularly impressed."

Suddenly, Eric #5 stood up and said, "Aren't you the little miss brainy pants with all of your numbers, and showing off how much smarter you are than me. How fucking patronizing!" Then he swigged back the last sip of his beer and stomped out of the sports bar.

I just sat there in shock. Not because Eric walked out on me. But because it never occurred to me that one can be patronizing by both assuming that you are smarter than someone else, as well as by assuming that they know as much as you do.

Not to mention the fact that the word "patronizing" can be both a good and bad thing.

It's like, *what the hell are you "patronizing"? Make up your fucking mind!*

6. Benevolent Dictator

I met Eric #7 at a Noam Chomsky college lecture. It was one of those special annual talks named after some guy who used to be an esteemed professor at this particular university, but then the professor died, so his former colleagues established this posthumous eponymous lecture series to commemorate him. And they really try to make it a hoity-toity affair—they even host a reception afterward, with wine and cheese and shit. And it all seems somewhat fancy at first, until you consider that they are serving the wine in plastic cups, and then you notice the wine label and it's "two-buck Chuck," which was admittedly a catchy gimmick until Trader Joe's raised the price to $2.50 per bottle. But hey, it's all free, and I am a writer who is barely making ends meet, so of course I queue up in line for some food and wine.

And I'm sure that some people actually think of this process as "waiting in line"—you know, you're just biding your time in a linear fashion until you eventually get the stuff you want. But I prefer to think of this process as "becoming a sitting duck." Because if you are a relatively youngish woman who is by herself in a public space, and especially if you are waiting to be served some sort of alcohol, some men will take this as a sign that you must be absolutely dying to have a conversation with them.

So I was not at all surprised when the guy standing behind me said, "Great talk, huh?"

"I suppose . . ." I didn't even look at him when I said it. And I assumed that he would assume that I presume that I am too good for him. Many men seem to come to this conclusion when women rebuff their advances. But in actuality, I just had things on my mind—specifically, the whole confusing matter regarding the word "patronizing," which *no, I'm still not over yet!*—and I just didn't want to be bothered right then. It's as simple as that.

But some guys are persistent. And I totally blame Hollywood for this. Because many movies have some sort of male lead who is super-forward and relentless in pursuing the female love interest. And she is resistant at first, but over time he woos her—whatever the fuck "woo" means. Somehow, she goes from contemplating filing a restraining order to eventually falling in love with this guy over the course of like, ninety minutes. And teenage boys, who tend to think of girls as some sort of mystery—even though we are like *half the fucking people on earth*—will watch these films and conclude that girls must want them to be really aggressive and to not take "no" for an answer. And that, in a nutshell, is rape culture.

Anyway, the guy in line behind me was not easily deterred. "Hi, my name is Eric."

And he had me at Eric.

So we shared some small talk over mediocre Cabernet (me) and sparkling water (him). He turned out to be a decent enough guy, so as the reception started winding down, I asked if he wanted to go out and grab a drink, you know, to assess one another's suitability. He gave me a puzzled look, but then said yes, so long as by drinks I meant coffee, because he's straight edge.

So we went to Caffè Strada, which (as usual) was teeming with students buried in their work. Or perhaps they were just goofing off on their laptops—how am I to know the difference? But we were able to find a table anyway. Once we were seated, Eric #7 returned to his initial inquiry: "So what *did* you think of Chomsky's talk? You seemed annoyed when I first asked you."

Me: Oh, that's just because I was trying to rebuff you. Although it didn't work. Anyway, I thought his talk was fine. Just fine.

Eric: You sound disappointed.

Me: It's just that I am really into linguistics, so I was hoping he might talk a bit about his thoughts on the origin and nature of language.

Eric: But the very title of his talk was "Neoliberalism and Manufacturing Consent in the Twenty-First Century."

Me: I know, but a girl can dream, can't she?

Eric: Personally, I think that exposing the fact that the U.S. is merely a corporate oligarchy disguised as a democracy is far more important than any theory about the evolution of language.

Me: But language is important too! Like, you couldn't have said what you just said without language. Also, it's not as if dismantling the corporate oligarchy requires people to only focus on that one task, to the exclusion of all other matters. That is, if it were even possible to dismantle the corporate oligarchy.

Eric: You sound really apolitical.

Me: No, I'm definitely on the progressive side of the spectrum. But I'm a depressive progressive, in that, while I will vote and such, for the life of me I can't see things ever getting any better in my lifetime. So if I think too much about politics, I just end up feeling powerless and depressed all the time. So I try not to think about it. That's my coping mechanism.

Eric: That's exactly how the corporate oligarchy wants you to feel.

Me: I know. My partner Matilda reminds me of that all the time—she's a Democratic operative.

Eric: That's so weird.

Me: What's weird, the fact that I have a female life partner and just mentioned her while on a date with you?

Eric: No, I just took that as a small info drop. I'd imagine that you are probably polyamorous and pansexual given that you are partnered to her but on a date with me. Although, I wouldn't dare to presume, as that would be patronizing.

Me: Yes, in a bad way. Although you presumed correctly in this case.

Eric: When I said "weird" just then, I was referring to the fact that they call themselves "operatives." And also that she thinks that positive change can ever be achieved by working within the current political system.

Me: I take it that you're an anarchist then.

Eric: Yes. Why, do you have something against anarchism?

Me: In theory, no. A world with no authority or hierarchies, where everyone voluntarily participates in society, sounds quite lovely, really. My main concern has to do with how we get there from here. Like, as soon as we abolish the government, what's to stop people from engaging in all sorts of nefarious activities? Such as gang rape.

Eric: There doesn't have to be gang rape.

Me: No, but there probably would be. And I really don't ever want to be gang raped.

Eric: Then what's your suggestion? What political alternative do you favor?

Me: I'm not sure. Frankly, most political ideologies presume that there is one way of doing things that will work best for everybody. But the problem is, everybody is different with regards to their desires and tendencies. For every act you can think of, there will be some people who will love it and others who hate it with a passion. This is why political ideologies are always doomed to fail. Communism doesn't work because some people simply will not want to be a proletariat doing work for the greater good of society. And capitalism doesn't work because not everybody lauds competition and prioritizes making money. Some people lead simple or ascetic lives, while others enjoy indulgence and extravagance. And while some people tend to be altruistic and egalitarian, others will inevitably be greedy egotistical assholes who crave power over other people. And these latter people will inevitably exist in, and screw up, your beautiful anarchic utopia.

So basically, I don't think any single political system could ever really work. Which is why I'd happily settle for one of those Scandinavian-type governments, where they have capitalism to appease all the wealth-seekers, but also have lots of regulations that reign in the power they can wield and havoc they can wreak. Then you tax these wealthy people very progressively in order to fund all the basic needs of life—housing, healthcare, food, education, and so on—so that all the simple, altruistic, and egalitarian folks can thrive as well.

Eric: So you want a social democracy? Is that your answer? That would satisfy you?

Me: Yeah, I guess.

There was an awkward pause after that. Eric #7 stared down at the foamy remnants of his cappuccino. He had a disappointed yet contemplative look on his face, like that of a parent who has no idea what to do with their wayward child. So I took a sip of my coffee. Then another sip. But his expression still hadn't changed. Apparently, I broke the conversation. So I tried to start it up again.

Me: You know, they say that the absolute best form of government would be a benevolent dictatorship.

Eric: I most certainly do *not* agree with that. Power corrupts. And absolute power corrupts absolutely. Even if you start out benevolent.

Me: But what if you were the one who was appointed benevolent dictator?

Eric: I wouldn't accept that position.

Me: But if you did accept it, what would you call yourself? Like, what title would you want your subjects to refer to you by?

Eric: This is a silly question. I refuse to answer it.

Me: Actually, the masses could simply call you Eric, since your name is derived from the old Norse word for "forever ruler."

Eric: Really?

Me: Really. Do you know what title I would choose if I was a benevolent dictator? I would call myself "God Empress of The Known Universe." Do you know why?

Eric: No.

Me: Because I am not so arrogant as to believe that I could rule over regions of the universe that I am not yet personally aware of.

[Another long and awkward pause, insufficiently filled by coffee sips.]

Eric: Okay, I've made my decision.

Me: About what?

Eric: I have assessed your suitability. And the answer is no. You are not suitable for me. I mean, you're a nice enough person, but we're too politically incompatible for us to ever be partners.

Me: But James Carville and Mary Matalin have made it work all these years!

Eric: Sure, but one is a Democrat and the other a Republican. Which are pretty much the same thing. In my eyes, at least.

Me: Well, let's agree to disagree on that.

Eric: No. I disagree with agreeing to disagree about that. Because I know I'm right.

Me: Okay, well let's agree to agree then. About us not being suitable for one another.

Eric: Agreed.

7. My Very First Blog Post

You can't just be a writer anymore. All the websites say so. The days of being an Emily Dickinson or J. D. Salinger—just locking yourself away in a room somewhere, and writing writing writing for the pure unadulterated joy of writing!—are like totally over now.

Writing is not enough anymore. This is what all the websites say. On top of writing, the twenty-first century writer needs to create and sustain a "platform," which may include (but is not necessarily limited to) a website and a blog, numerous social media accounts, regular public speaking appearances, and so on. And it is upon this writer's platform that the contemporary writer must metaphorically perch if we wish to develop an online "presence" and to establish our "brand."

And the websites go on to tell us that it is this very online presence and personal branding that will help us get "noticed" by the publishers who, upon noticing us, may or may not publish the book that we've been meaning to write, but haven't quite gotten around to just yet, because we've been too busy learning HTML and web analytics in our efforts to create and sustain our burgeoning writer's platform.

This is what all the websites are saying.

Well, not all the websites. Just the ones whose stated purpose is to help writers with their writing careers. And while these writer-focused websites are generally sincere and often quite helpful, I cannot help but notice that they are also invariably written by writers. Specifically, by writers who write about helping writers with their writing careers. In other words, helping writers with their careers is *their career*. Nay, it is their brand! The brand that will help get them noticed by publishers!

And by reading their extremely helpful blog posts about creating my own writer's platform so that I can develop my own online presence, I am simultaneously helping them establish their online presence. It is a win-win situation. For the both of us.

And now, by reading this—my very first blog post—you, dear reader, are presently participating in my newly acquired online presence. So thank you for the present of your presence!

And if you just so happen to appreciate this blog post—wherein I blog about people who are blogging about blogging—then by all means, feel free to blog about it.

8. Why the Internet Is Like the Worst Thing Ever

I have a roll of duct tape. Just one. I've had it since college, when I bought it because I needed to repair my dorm-room bookshelf after a bizarre accident involving the book *Atlas Shrugged*. I know what you're thinking: "*Atlas Shrugged*, Kat? What were you, like, a young Republican?" To which the answer is no.

The reason why I had *Atlas Shrugged* was simply because I was really into Rush as a teenager—the band, not the conservative radio host. See, I grew up during a time when people were still heavily reliant on FM radio, and in a place where all the radio stations were either Christian-themed or exclusively played classic rock. Since that was all there was, I gravitated toward the weirdest possible music that falls under the latter category. Namely, progressive rock (or "prog rock") of the 1970s: bands like Yes, King Crimson, Emerson Lake & Palmer, Genesis (before Peter Gabriel left the band and they let that twerp Phil Collins take over), and of course, Rush. Their drummer wrote all their lyrics, and they were the type of lyrics that sound so philosophical and profound when your only life experiences are isolated teenaged ones. And in tenth grade, when I heard that some of their lyrics were inspired by Ayn Rand, I went out and bought all her books: *Atlas Shrugged, The Fountainhead,* and . . . actually, I can't remember if she wrote any other books. But if she did, I probably had them. I'm pretty sure of it.

So anyway, *Atlas Shrugged* is not only a dense tome of unadulterated and melodramatic individualism, but it also provoked an incident that broke my bookshelf. Which I fixed with duct tape. And I've had it ever since. Not the book, nor the bookshelf, nor the incident, but the roll of duct tape. And it's still almost full. Because unless you're a handyman and/or one of those crafty-types who make duct tape purses that you sell on Etsy, you will only ever need one roll of duct tape for your whole entire life.

I noticed that roll of duct tape today while rummaging through my "odds and ends" desk drawer in search of my tube of lidocaine. And upon seeing it, it struck me that this roll of duct tape will probably outlive me. And the prospect that I will most likely not live my life fully enough to have consumed an entire roll of duct tape suddenly filled me with ennui.

But then I thought to myself: What if I *did* take the time to watch all those YouTube videos and internet tutorials that instruct you on how to make duct tape purses? Perhaps that could become my new hobby and/or non-lucrative entrepreneurial venture, thereby allowing me to live my life to the fullest as demonstrably demonstrated by the countless empty rolls of duct tape that I would leave in my wake!

But then I remembered that I am not a creative person. Not when it comes to visual . . . things. I cannot make art. Or crafts. Art and/or crafts. I can only be creative with words.

And that's when it hit me: I am a writer! And this whole roll-of-duct-tape-as-a-metaphor-for-the-passage-of-time isn't necessarily an indication that my life sucks, but rather it is a wonderful story idea! For instance, what if it wasn't me who felt like my life was slipping into oblivion, but rather some other person named . . . Steven. No, Stephan—but it's still pronounced "Steven." And the story begins with Stephan reading his horoscope, and he's one of these guys who takes astrology very very seriously. And one day, he checks online to read his favorite astrologist . . . let's call her

Cassandra Roseannadanna. And she says that Geminis (Stephan's sign) needed to (and I quote): ". . . wrap up their entire bodies in duct tape and await next week's horoscope for further instructions."

So Stephan, being a die-hard believer in astrology and everything Cassandra Roseannadanna says, does her bidding, only slightly reluctantly. He placed his laptop on the floor along with a bowl of water and another bowl full of Ritz crackers (for sustenance). Then he slowly but meticulously began wrapping the duct tape around his legs. Then torso. Then finally his arms.

(Pro tip: Most writers would be concerned about describing the visuals here: How does Stephan bind his arms in duct tape without using his arms? But being an absurdist-inclined and not-especially-visual writer frees me from having to consider such trivial and potentially unrealistic details.)

Then Stephan waits. For like a week. Until Cassandra's next column comes out.

While he's waiting, he wonders whether every Gemini in the world is doing the exact same thing right now. He imagines the possible economic ramifications of one-twelfth of the world's workforce suddenly not showing up to work for a whole week, all at once. Because of duct tape. The president is likely addressing a concerned nation right now, but Stephan can't watch it, because he has found that it's too difficult to type anything into his computer with just his nose. Plus he needs to stay glued to Cassandra's webpage. For further instructions.

Having an inordinate amount of time to think, Stephan starts to question whether following Cassandra's instructions was a good idea. After all, her name is Cassandra. For Christ's sake, she is named after a mythological figure who knew the future before it happened—sure, I'll grant you that—but at the same time, nobody believed a word that she said. So, by the transitive property of given names, maybe Stephan shouldn't have believed this Cassandra either?

And for the first time in his life, Stephan began to question whether following his horoscope was a good idea. Perhaps horoscopes are like the Bible, or stuff politicians say: not to be taken literally. Maybe astrology isn't even real? Or maybe, if it is real, Stephan's not actually a Gemini. In fact, now that he thinks about it, his birthday is right on the cusp of Gemini: June 20th.

"Hey wait a minute," Stephan exclaimed within the confines of his own mind, "I was a Cesarean baby. I remember my mother telling me that I wasn't due for a few more days, but then due to complications, the doctor induced her to give birth. What if that means that I'm not a Gemini after all? Perhaps I was supposed to be born a Cancer? Fuck! I don't know anything at all about being a Cancer! In fact, the only thing that I *do* know about Cancers is that Cassandra never told them to wrap themselves up in duct tape!"

As Stephan lay still on the floor, contemplating his likely demise due to lack of water and Ritz crackers (which he had already consumed by that point), he began to laugh. At first, a small chuckle, but then evolving into an uproarious howl. It wasn't Stephan's impending death that he found so amusing. Rather, it was the fact that he never in a million years would have imagined that he would finally use up that entire role of duct tape.

The end.

Whatd'ya think? Not bad for a first draft? Initially, I considered calling the story "Horrorscope," but a quick internet search revealed that many people have used that title before me. As I kept searching, I also found that others prior to me have made jokes about how C-sections and induced births might hypothetically screw up a person's astrological profile. I also came across astrology-themed message boards where real-life soon-to-be parents seriously discussed the possibility of inducing their child's birth on a particular day and time in order to create the most zodiacally optimal outcome possible. Which was even more depressing to me than finding out that somebody already came up with a particular astrology-themed joke before I did.

This is why the internet is like the worst thing ever. And perhaps that sounds like hyperbole to you. Because it is. But at the same time, the internet does often suck for writers.

Here's another example: One of the very first absurdist short stories that I ever wrote began like this:

The fire wasn't my fault. I mean, yes, I started it, but I refuse to take responsibility for it. I tell you, the English language is to blame. After all, "inexpensive" means not expensive. And "inorganic" means not organic. I could go on and on. So naturally I assumed that "inflammable" means not flammable. But apparently it doesn't. In fact, it means the opposite of "not flammable"—that is to say, "flammable."

And the entire story is set in a courtroom, where this particular guy is on trial for arson and fire insurance fraud. And the expert witnesses are not cops, firemen, nor their forensic teams (as you'd expect), but rather linguists and philosophers of language, and famous ones at that: Wittgenstein, Saussure, Chomsky, Derrida, and the entire Prague school. And rather than argue over the fire-related evidence, they instead debate the very nature of language. And at the very end, this guy is deemed "not guilty" because, during cross examination, the prosecuting attorney accidentally used the word "defensible" when he meant "indefensible," thereby undermining his own case by demonstrably demonstrating how easy it is to confuse two words that are almost identical, except for the prefix *in–*.

But when I submitted this piece to the editors of the anthology *Ceci n'est pas une surréaliste histoire courte collection*, they rejected it. And in their rejection letter, they said they searched the internet and found that *The Simpsons* had already used the flammable/inflammable joke in an episode back in 2001. So now my entire short story is rendered irrelevant (which is very different from relevant), even though their take on flammable/inflammable most likely did not invoke famous linguists nor parody courtroom procedurals.

So the internet clearly sucks. Not just for writers, but for all creative types. Seriously: just search the web using any common word or phrase, followed by "band," and you will inevitably find a band with that name. It almost makes me empathize with Eric number one's emo band's arcane name: The Orange Dolphin Puppet Revival.

Almost.

Anyway, I'm not the only person who hates the internet. Eric #11 hates it too. In the middle of our date, I asked him if he is on Twitter. And he said no. And I asked Facebook? Instagram? And he said no. And I asked MySpace? Friendster? And he was like, "I don't use social media. Not at all. Not anymore"

And I asked, "Why not?"

He paused for a moment. Took a sip of his drink. All dramatic-like. Then he answered: "It's because I am an ardent liar."

And this is the moment in the conversation where most of his dates would likely flee. But not me. No siree. I am not dating this Eric because I hope he might be potential husband material, or even a reliable boyfriend. I'm just hoping to get a book chapter out of him.

So I responded with a sincere, "Do go on . . ."

He took another sip of his drink, albeit not quite as dramatic this time. Then he told me: "Well, the truth is that I find the truth to be just so . . . boring. Frankly, telling the truth all the time is like having to eat the same bowl of Cheerios every single morning for breakfast. Nay, for every single meal! It's so mundane. Trite. Banal. And similar synonyms. Whereas lies—little white lies that wouldn't hurt a fly—they are like the blueberries that you add to the bowl of cereal to make it more interesting and enjoyable. Then the next day, you add strawberries instead, to mix things up. Or bananas, or kiwis, and so on . . ."

"Kiwis on Cheerios?" I questioned. But Eric #11 was in the midst of a confessional tell-all. And he wasn't about to engage me in my digression about which fruits pair best (or worst) with which brands of cereal.

Eric #11 continued: So when I was in high school way back, my mom would ask me how my day was, and I'd say I was out playing ultimate frisbee with friends. And I'd tell my ultimate frisbee friends that I was hanging out with my girlfriend. And I'd tell my girlfriend that I was helping my mom with some chores around the house.

Me: But where were you really?

Eric: It depends. A lot of times I would go on these really long walks in the woods nearby our house, where I would contemplate life. And count the plant life. And invent new lies. Mostly about fake things that I supposedly did.

Me: Wow. What is the most outrageous lie you ever told?

Eric: Well actually, none of them were outrageous. They were all completely believable. That's rule number #17 of being a lying enthusiast: Never tell unbelievable lies.

Me: That sounds reasonable.

Eric: Glad to hear that you think so. That's how I saw it too. Until the internet happened. At first things were fine, as the internet was mostly emails and message boards back then, so it was easy to compartmentalize everything and everyone in my life. But then social media happened, and everyone I knew started friending and following me. My mom. My girlfriend (who was a new girlfriend by this point). Not my ultimate frisbee friends because by then I had outgrown them. But I had more mature rock climbing friends. And my co-workers. And boss. And so on.

And then all of a sudden, when someone asked me how my day was, and I'd reply "I spent a quiet day alone, tending to my garden," they'd be like, "No you didn't, you went out to see the latest Wes Anderson film, and I know because you complained about how unrealistic the film's characters and plot were on social media." At that point, I realized that there were two potential life paths ahead of me: I could constantly get called out by people in my life for lying, or I could completely disconnect myself from all social media. And I gallantly chose the latter.

Me: Great. Great story.

Eric: So you don't think that it's weird that I'm an ardent liar?

Me: No.

Eric: No?

Me: No. Because I don't believe you. I don't believe that you're a liar.

Eric: But it's true!

Me: If it were true that you're a liar, then it follows that you must be lying right now about being a liar.

Eric: But I'm not *always* a liar. Only when I choose to be. Which I am most certainly not doing at this very moment.

Me: But if you *are* a liar, then you are probably lying about not lying at this very moment.

Eric: Your line of reasoning makes no sense. Your are selectively choosing when to accuse me of being a liar, and when to accuse me of lying about being a liar. Which I suppose would make me a slightly different type of liar.

Me: Well, you just told me that you selectively choose when to lie and when not to lie. How is that any different from me selectively choosing between believing that you are lying and believing you are lying about lying?

We were both tired and confused at that point. I stared at my cell phone most of the rest of the evening, scrolling through my Twitter feed, and reading all the anonymous angry comments that my very first blog post received. And Eric #11, lacking any social media outlets, blankly stared at his phone waiting for a phone call or text message to suddenly materialize. I imagined that he was imagining being by himself, on a long walk, inventing new lies to tell people. Most of which likely involved lying about lying.

By the way, I should be honest with you. This chapter—the

one that you are still reading—didn't actually happen. It's all made up. One giant lie. Except for the part about lying about lying. And also parts of the part of the story about duct tape.

9. Like

So you've probably noticed that I like to use the word "like." It's a generational thing, I suppose: If you lived any part of your childhood in the '80s, '90s, or '00s, then you have simply been socialized to say words like "like," like, fairly often.

As a writer, I find the word "like" to be quite useful, as it can help make whatever follows more pronounced or emphatic, much like the brief pause before the punchline of a joke. And when I am talking, sometimes I will still be formulating how to phrase what I am going to say, and I'll drop in a "like" to give my neurons an few extra microseconds to construct the most thoughtful and judicious sentence possible. No harm, no foul.

While "like" seems completely harmless to me, many people really and truly dislike "like." In fact, they downright hate it. And they will make fun of your speech patterns and dissect your usage of "like" in a patronizing manner. Like, in a bad way. For example, about twenty minutes into our date, Eric #13 (the one who liked to collect sand dollars) said to me: Boy, you sure do use the word "like" a lot.

Me: First, I'm a girl, not a boy. Second, yes, I like "like." Is that a problem?

Eric: Well, it makes you sound unintelligent and unsure of yourself.

Me: Actually, I am quite smart and sure of myself, thank you very much. Perhaps the problem is not my use of the word "like" per se, but rather people like you who automatically assume that people who use the word "like" must be insecure or unintelligent.

Eric: Look, I'm just trying to be helpful here. Many people simply find it annoying when people abuse the word "like." It's a bad verbal habit, much like how people abuse the word "literally."

Me: You just used the word "like" in your last sentence.

Eric. It was a simile. That's how you are supposed to use "like." To compare things to one another.

Me: But fruit flies like bananas.

Eric: What?

Me: "Time flies like an arrow, but fruit flies like bananas." It's a classic sentence that demonstrates syntactic ambiguity. Both the words "flies" and "like" have multiple meanings, but people generally have no problems understanding which meanings are relevant based upon how they are used and the surrounding words. Similarly, if I were to say: "Your understanding of how language works is, like, really poor," most people will comprehend that I am simply using the word "like" in a third different way, namely, to emphasize how poor your understanding of language is.

Eric: But you can't just go around making up new meanings for words willy-nilly. Language has rules!

Me: But people have been using the word "like" to emphasize what follows for several decades now. And on top of that, definitions are always changing, because language is flexible and always evolving. Take the word "literally": It used to mean "in a literal or strict sense." But now people use it in a second way that is more figurative or metaphorical. So now, much like most words in the English language, "literally" has more than one meaning. Some words have, like, a dozen or more different meanings depending on the context. So what's the big deal?

Eric: It is needlessly confusing.

Me: No it isn't, you're just acting needlessly confused.

Eric: Okay, this date is literally over.

He stood up from his chair and reached for his backpack,

which was literally filled with sand dollars. Then he reached into his back pocket, pulled out his wallet, and rummaged through it for actual dollars to cover his half of the bill. This being the second date where an Eric walked out on me in a huff, I was literally beside myself. So I kinda sorta lashed out at him as he was preparing to leave:

Fine, be that way! Leave why don't you, Mister Inflexible Language Sand Dollar Guy. See if I care. Because I literally do not care—not one iota! But obviously I do care, given that I am raising my voice in the middle of a crowded restaurant right now. I was just so-called "abusing" the word "literally" just then, just to troll you! And I refuse to stop there. In fact, now that the word literally has been destroyed in your eyes, I plan to make it my life's ambition to destroy the word "verbatim" next! So five years from now, whenever you hear that somebody somewhere said something "verbatim," you will have no idea whether the person in question literally said it, insinuated it, and/ or whether the person recounting the story is merely paraphrasing or parodying what they said.

So there!

10. Publishers Clearing House

When I speak to other writers about my book *99 Erics*, one of the first things they often ask is, "So, who's your agent?" Because according to writers' lore, agents fulfill the mythical "gatekeeper" role. They supposedly recognize your true genius and passionately believe in you, so much so that they do all the things that you would rather not be bothered with: They shop your book around to publishers, negotiate your contract, contact media on your behalf, etcetera, so that you don't have to worry your pretty little head about such trivial matters. Because you are a genius! And you need to focus 100 percent of your energy and attention on your next groundbreaking artistic endeavor, which is most likely a Young Adult novel wherein the protagonist befriends a wizard, or vampire, or angel, or something of that ilk, who ultimately helps them unlock their true potential and enables them to save the world.

Because wizards are to insecure teenagers as agents are to hopeful writers.

So unsurprisingly, these waiting-to-be-discovered writers are always shocked when I tell them that I don't have an agent. Nor do I need one, because I am totally D.I.Y. Nor do I bother indiscriminately sending off my manuscripts to publishers in the hopes that they will become interested in my work—such an approach is pointless, as your manuscript merely becomes one stack of papers on top of a much larger stack of other stacks of papers. No, what you really need to do is to make yourself stand out from all the other wannabe writers out there.

So here's what I do to stand out: I carefully research book publishers in order to find one or two who seem to be a perfect match for my work. Then I seek out the home address for the acquisitions editor for that publishing house. Then I put together an impromptu poetry slam for them on their front lawn.

For those readers not in the know: Poetry slams are basically open mic poetry readings, except for the fact that several random members of the audience are chosen to judge the poets' performances Olympic-style on a scale from one-to-ten. Of course, this means that I furiously have to promote the event in order to wrangle enough performers and audience members to make it an unforgettable show. But it's worth all that work, because it really does get me noticed!

Now, I know some of you are likely thinking: "Kat, isn't that kind of creepy and stalkery to show up at a publisher's home with a poetry-slam-sized contingent of people?" I really don't think so. It's not like I go around peeking in prospective publishers' windows or following them around from place to place. I am simply giving them a gift. The gift of poetry slam.

Some have suggested to me that, even if said poetry slam does not strictly constitute stalking, it is nevertheless non-consensual. And I'm like, but of course: Poetry slams are supposed to be non-consensual. It's in their very nature. I cannot tell you how many times I've been at my local bar, drinking an IPA and writing in my journal (as you do), when all of a sudden all these people come pouring in and they start setting up for a poetry slam *without even asking my permission!*

But hey, when at the bar, do as the bar does, so of course I sign up to read. And I start getting all excited about reading my newest thing—you know, that "fresh piece"—the one that's super intense and visceral and confessional and like *totally fucking real*. But unfortunately, it is also super-duper in need of major edits.

After all, I just wrote it today—literally only moments ago as the non-consensual poetry slam organizers were first barging into this bar without even asking me first. And naturally, I can't see how blatantly in need of editing this hand-scrawled behemoth of raw literature is, because it is my *fresh piece*, the one that expresses all the emotions that I am currently feeling. And *don't you dare try to edit the emotions that I am currently feeling right now at this very moment!*

At most open mics—the ones that are not poetry slams—this is no big deal. You can just read the fresh piece and people will solemnly listen to you. This is probably because they are just biding their time until it's their turn to read *their* fresh piece. But at poetry slams, it is different because of the fucking judges, who will give you like five-point-eights and six-point-twos for your work—work which, in your heart of hearts, you know really and truly deserves a ten. Or at the very least, a nine-point-two.

And the kicker is that these so-called judges may not even be writers like yourself. In fact, they are likely to be, like, fucking laypeople.

Like the guy who gave me the five-point-eight is probably some dude-bro who just so happened to be in the bar before the slam even started, just drinking an IPA, but sans writer's journal. Hell, it probably wasn't even an IPA—it was most likely a Budweiser or Coors or some shit. Come to think of it, I'll bet you this guy showed up at the bar with his dude-bro pals to watch the football game that was on TV earlier—the one where the team named after a subpopulation of Northern Europeans infamous for their conquering and pillaging metaphorically slaughtered a football team named after indigenous people who in real life were slaughtered, conquered, and pillaged by a more historically-recent subpopulation of Northern Europeans. Not to mention the fact that the latter team's name is totally racist!

So how is this half-drunk dude-bro, who only moments ago was metaphorically rooting for Northern Europeans to slaughter Native Americans, ever possibly going to understand my sex-positive-feminism-rooted absurdist yet highly confessional fresh piece? Not a chance.

Of course, my slam score probably would have been higher if it weren't for the fact that the woman who went on before me was like the most polished poet ever. She not only had her piece memorized, but she was making all these grand gestures with her hands, and her facial expressions were really emotive, and by the end of the piece there was this whole call-and-response thing that just organically developed between her and the audience. And you find yourself joining in the call-and-response, and you're like totally loving this woman! Until you realize *holy crap*, I have to go on immediately after her. And in the wake of all the call-and-responses, and laughter, and cheers, not to mention all the spontaneous snapping that poet generated, my fresh piece ends up being greeted with absolute unadulterated silence—a silence that feels so respectful and makes you feel like the audience is really intently listening when it happens at non-poetry-slam open mics, but which is a clear sign that your fresh piece is going over like a lead balloon when it happens at a poetry slam.

So then you decide to seriously commit yourself, and you start memorizing and choreographing all of your pieces. Even the mediocre ones. And you start going to slams all the time: the San Francisco Slam on Sundays, the Berkeley Slam on Wednesdays, the Oakland Slam on Thursdays, and so on, plus going to other occasional non-poetry-slam open mics, where you suddenly totally shine, because now *you* are the polished performer. And at the poetry slams, your scores definitely improve quite a bit.

But you eventually come to realize that there is an upper limit for you—a poetry slam glass ceiling, if you will. Because it turns out that slam audiences only want to hear one of three types of poem: the really funny one, the righteous political one, and the overcoming adversity one. And you don't like to talk about politics anymore (because you're a depressive progressive). And your life-coping mechanism is to *not* talk about the adversity you have faced. And you think your poems are really funny, but they're more surreal and subversive, and the audience only seems to get straightforward vanilla humor.

And your most hilarious piece is the one wherein you casually mention that time when you were at a party having a conversation with your ex, her current partner, your current partner, and your current partner's other partner. And you make your former U.S. Surgeon General C. Everett Koop joke about how when he said, "When you have sex with someone, you are having sex with everyone they have had sex with for the last ten years, and everyone they and their partners have had sex with for the last ten years." And how, when he said that, he probably never imagined all of you hanging out at the same party talking and laughing with one another.

And it's a pretty funny joke, you think, except that a big chunk of the audience has no idea who C. Everett Koop is. And on top of that, you start to notice that the audience, who had been laughing along quite boisterously to your piece, are not laughing so much anymore. And you realize that this is because you have just invoked polyamory. And the audience is now thinking, "Oh my god, this person is not like me after all! I can no longer relate to them as a normal human being!" Or maybe they are thinking, "This is hilarious, but if I laugh along too loudly, my friends will suspect that I am polyamorous myself." Either way, the response is tepid from then on out.

And at that moment, it becomes crystal clear that you have just wasted two years of your life honing your poetry slam skills, when what you always wanted all along was to be a novelist (albeit one who eventually settles for being a critically acclaimed absurdist short fiction writer and self-proclaimed faux novelist). And poetry slam has not helped you at all toward this end goal.

I mean, at the slams, some people will cheer you on and appreciate your work. So it's easy to presume that you are building a following there. But the truth is, these people are not really your fans. They follow the poetry slam, not you. And when you stop showing up to the slams, and instead you become the *featured* reader at some absurdist-focused and/or polyamory-friendly literary event, these people will not show up. Believe me, I know firsthand.

So you can spend the next three or four months crying into your IPA, lamenting those two wasted poetry slam years of your life. Or, if you are clever and marginally entrepreneurial like me, you can *exploit* poetry slam instead. How? By becoming a poetry slam organizer yourself! That way, those slam-goers become *your* followers. And if you strategically coordinate your poetry slams to occur on the front lawns of your potential future publishers—as a gift, not in a creepy stalkery sort of way—well then, the more power to you.

This is how I met my editor Mario. He loved my gift of poetry slam—even called it a hoot! Impressed, he asked to read a copy of my *99 Erics* manuscript-in-progress. I didn't hear back from him for four weeks, which was a complete mind-fuck. I mean, the first week was no big deal, you know, because he has to read the damned thing. During week two, I was constantly checking my email and voicemail, to no avail. By week three, I was starting to think: Oh my god, I must be a sucky writer who has written the worst faux-novel-in-progress ever. And of course, this triggers an existential crisis, and I decide to just quit writing and go back to grad school to finally get my PhD in linguistics. I even began applying to grad schools. And the applications invariably asked me to write an essay about a time in my life when I experienced failure, and what I learned from that experience. And I really really wanted to write about my experience failing at poetry slams because of the polyamorous content of my poems, and how from that experience, I learned how to exploit the genre of poetry slam in order to obtain a publishing deal for myself. But then I realized that I had seemingly failed at getting said publishing deal. And I wasn't sure that I had learned any lesson from that. At least not yet.

But then thankfully, during week number four, after I had already made peace with the fact that I was a failed slam poet and failed author who would never get back into grad school again after failing at it the first time, Mario called to invite me out to lunch to discuss my manuscript.

At that lunch, Mario spoke glowingly about *99 Erics*—he absolutely loved it! But then he suggested that I re-work it to be more of a Young Adult novel. You know, set in some post-apocalyptic future world, where the population is divided up into five or so factions, or districts, or divisions—that's it, divisions! And perhaps these houses—I mean, divisions—could be based on . . . the five senses! They could have names like the Retinals, Auditors, Olfactors, Gustators, and the Tactiles. And each division has a specialized role in society based on the one sense that they are most proficient at. And our teenage protagonist (who has a vaguely exotic name, perhaps something like "Katnip") is born into the Tactiles, who are the least respected division because they are all so touchy-feely. And of course, there is some sort of ritual that young people of every division must participate in, during which young Katnip begins to realize that she transcends these divisions somehow. Perhaps because she has some sort of "sixth sense." Like a sense of humor? Or timing? Or fashion sense? Who knows, the possibilities are endless! And over the course of the trilogy (because it *has* to be a trilogy, if not longer), it becomes clear that Katnip is the chosen one who overthrows the dystopian overlords and unites all the divisions!

After Mario's spiel, I stared blankly at him for a minute before asking: But what about the whole dating ninety-nine people named Eric part?

Mario: Well, maybe there could be just one Eric. Maybe he is a boy from another faction—I mean, division—and he and Katnip fall in love? You know, a chaste sort of romantic love. No sex of course, since it's a YA novel.

Me: That's fucking inane! Sex is a vital part of life for many of us, like eating or breathing or thinking and the like. Why would I want to write a YA novel if I'm not allowed to discuss sex at all?

Mario: Well, because YA novels sell far better than absurdist faux novels about dating an inordinate number of men who just so happen to have the name Eric. Plus, imagine the film rights!

Me: But whatever happened to "sex sells"?

Mario: Sex does sell, but only if it's done in a sensationalistic or scandalous way. Believe me, the audience wants to feel dirty and ashamed after reading about sex. But Kat, when you write about sex, you make it sound like a mundane part of every-day life that we shouldn't be ashamed of. And that particular angle on sex doesn't sell so much.

Me: Hmmm. Well, if I agree to write a YA novel without the sex, could I at least use profanity?

Mario: No. Of course not. Don't be silly.

Me: How about killing people. Could my protagonist kill people? Like lots of people?

Mario: Sure, no problem!

So Mario and I eventually compromised. I signed a two-book publishing deal: *99 Erics* by Kat Cataclysm (in its uncensored form), followed by my forthcoming YA novel *The Senses Ceremony*, published under the pen name Kathleen Kennings.

Almost forgot: Between those two book releases, I plan to self-publish a chapbook of all of my old slam poems, tentatively titled *General Surgery and Surgeons General.*

11. Laypeople

Okay, so I really want to apologize for using the term "laypeople" in a derogatory manner in the last chapter. Because I know how that makes laypeople sound all slothful and lazy, as if they are literally just laying in bed or on their sofas all day, while the rest of us supposedly "non-laypeople" are presumably hard at work, utilizing our highly specialized knowledge and skill sets in order to help make the world a better place. I'm mean, it really is quite classist! Or perhaps elitist is a better word for it? I'm not quite sure. But there definitely is some kind of "ism" out there that is totally oppressing the so-called laypeople.

And the more that I think about it, the more it's like, well, aren't we all laypeople? I mean, there are some things that I know intimately well—such as absurdist short fiction, sex-positive feminism, sabermetrics, linguistics, and of course, the inane banality that is dating ninety-nine Erics in a sad attempt to generate material for a faux novel. But at the same time, I don't know shit about astrophysics, or the tax code, or how carburetors work, or bartending, or roller derby, or that opening chord progression to John Coltrane's "Giant Steps," and countless other things.

Like the other day, I was at the supermarket, and there was this woman who was knocking on the pumpkins and sniffing the cantaloupes, and I was thinking, "What's her deal?" But then I realized that she must have some highly specialized knowledge about these forms of produce that I utterly lack. And it made me feel so small and insignificant.

I guess what I'm saying is that we all have extensive knowledge about some things but not others. So every single one of us is both a layperson and a non-layperson, simultaneously. When you really really think about it.

I'm sure that some people might protest me calling myself a layperson. Such people will likely point out that I am writing this book, and it's all about things that I have either directly experienced and/or completely made up out of the thin air that is my brain. Which basically means that, for all intents and purposes, I am omniscient. Whereas you, dear reader, have no idea what's going to happen next. You may not even know what is happening right now at this very moment in Chapter 11 with this whole "laypeople" digression. And frankly, I wouldn't blame you.

So given all this—the argument would go—isn't it appropriative for me, the omniscient narrator and the only person who knows what this book is all about (inasmuch as anyone can fathom what this book is about), to claim a layperson identity?

I admit, this a really good point. I will have to give this some thought.

12. Fan Fiction

Eric #17 pretty much fell right into my lap. He emailed me out of the blue to tell me that he's been enjoying my *99 Erics* blog (which I started up back in Chapter 7, in order to help build up my "brand"). He's also read a few of my absurdist short stories, and it turns out that he's a writer too, so he suggested that we meet up for lunch sometime. While he seemed nice enough, I was a bit hesitant to get together with him at first, as I usually avoid getting involved with people who are fans of my work. Because they obviously have such horrible taste!

Just joking. (Although I suppose there's a grain of imposter syndrome in every self-deprecating joke.) No, the real reason that I was concerned about going out with Eric #17 is that I simply can't trust my own stories to save my life.

Allow me to explain. Back when I was regularly doing poetry slams, I'd often have people come up to me and say, "Hey, I saw you perform the other night and I loved your piece!" And I'd say thanks, and then we'd chat, and it would always be a wonderful low-key conversation. Even though I was technically the "artist" and they were in the "audience," there were never any weird power dynamics between us. Because there is this whole communal aspect to live performance. The two of us had shared an evening together, and our lives became briefly intertwined in that moment. So it was easy for us to bond over that mutual experience, despite our differing perspectives.

But the written word is an entirely different beast. Whenever I write a story, it is an intensely solitary experience. I will grapple with it for days, weeks, even months, all by my lonesome. And once it's finally completed, I am relieved to be free of it, and I will eagerly move on to other endeavors. But this story that I've created—my Frankenstein's monster, if you will—has a mind of its own. And once it is published, it will go out into the universe and interact with other people. It might make these people feel amused, amazed, aroused, ashamed, angry, afraid, or annoyed. This story of mine might fuck with readers' minds, open up new worlds for them, stick with them for years to come, or simply make them pissed off that they wasted an evening reading the damned thing.

And all of this will happen without me even being there!

So then, when I eventually come across one of these readers, sometimes there will be a strange asymmetry between us. Because they feel as though we've shared this intensely intimate journey together. When in reality, while they were curling up in bed with my story, I was likely alone at home clipping my toenails, flossing my teeth, or obsessing about some new growth on my face that's probably just a zit, but I'm freaking out that it may be a recurrence of skin cancer.

And readers who strongly identify with the characters I create, and who see themselves reflected back to them in the stories I tell, might assume that the two of us share much in common. When in actuality, my characters and stories are nothing like me! Sure, they may possess some of my traits, tendencies, and true-life tales, but they are almost always a gross exaggeration: far more funny, or witty, or attractive, or compelling than I could ever be in person. So I fear that, if these readers were to ever get to know the real me, they would inevitably be disappointed.

That's a long explanation as to why I was initially reluctant to go out on a date with Eric #17. But then I figured that there are only so many Erics out there in the world. And as the saying goes, beggars can't be choosers—which, oh my god, I just realized as I was typing that that that's such a fucked up saying! Much like "laypeople," that phrase is classist and/or elitist. And I refuse to be a party to denying anyone's freedom of choice. Beggars can totally be choosers! Just as I had the freedom of choice to *not* date this particular Eric. But I decided to go ahead with it anyway, for literature's sake. And here's how it went:

Eric: So as I was saying over email, I love your absurdist short stories! "Smells Like Teen Dystopia" is hilarious, especially the part where you poke fun at post-apocalyptic universes where citizens mysteriously forget the historical names of the cities they inhabit. Oh, and what's the story that mentions Bruce Willis and has all those allusions to *The Scarlet Letter?*

Me: "Stephanie's Secret."

Eric: Yeah, that's great too!

Me: Thanks, glad to hear you liked them.

Eric: And all of your *99 Erics* blog posts are excellent as well. Like, the one about the Eric who took off his shirt in the middle of the restaurant in order to show you his new nipple piercings. Or the one about the Eric who suddenly broke into song, as if you were in some kind of musical. How clever! How did you come up with those stories?

Me: Um, well, I just went out on dates with those Erics. Then I wrote down what happened. With some embellishments, of course.

Eric: What?! Are you telling me that those were all real-life situations? I had no idea. I figured they were just more of your absurdist short stories.

Me: Nope, they are all for real. For the most part.

Eric: Even the Eric who didn't know who Orson Welles was? I mean, how could you possibly not have heard of Orson Welles?

Me: In his defense, that Eric wasn't much of a film buff. Also, he was pretty young. Like, barely over nineteen. Which is way younger than I prefer my dates, but it's hard to find people who are both named Eric and willing to date you. And beggars can't be choosers . . . oops. Um, anyhow, I suppose that his lack of awareness about Orson Welles might not have seemed so strange if I hadn't left all those details out. My bad.

Eric: No, the story is great as is, don't change a thing. I loved all the sledding references, and the part toward the end where you ordered rosebud tea!

Me: Well, the sledding jokes really happened, but that last bit was an embellishment. We weren't even at a tea house. And I'm not sure that rosebud tea is even a thing.

Eric: Actually it is. It helps boost the immune system. It's also good for digestive issues.

Me: Oh. Good to know. Anyway, we've talked about me for a while, so why don't you tell me a bit about yourself? You mentioned you're a writer, correct?

Eric: Sure, I dabble. I've been trying to write my own absurdist fiction for some time now. But it hasn't really panned out, as I find it too difficult to create interesting and complex characters, only to put them into conflict and make their lives miserable.

Me: I can totally relate to that.

Eric: That's why I've turned to writing fan fiction lately, so that I can borrow other people's characters, and then place them into all sorts of adventures and misadventures of my own choosing.

Me: That makes sense. So what type of fan fiction do you write? *Star Trek*-themed? Or based on some Marvel or anime character? Or Harry Potter? Buffy? Doctor Who?

Eric: Actually, I've taken to writing Kat Cataclysm fan fiction.

Me: *What?!* But that's me. I'm Kat Cataclysm! And I'm not even a fictional character!

Eric: But how could I have possibly known that? I just assumed Kat Cataclysm was your protagonist, and that you were penning fictional stories under her name. I mean, seriously, it doesn't even sound like a real name! How did you get it?

Me: That's a story for another chapter. But now you have me curious. What sorts of stories did you invent for her? By which I mean me.

Eric: Well, I basically stick to your "dating Erics" motif, but then I try to make them as unusual or comical as possible. Like, in one story, you go out with an Eric who is unduly concerned about the sun eventually turning into a red giant and devouring the Earth, even though that won't happen for over a billion years. Then there's the one about the Eric who cut himself shaving with Occam's razor. And the Eric who was suing the English language because he believed that alphabetization is discriminatory toward people whose names begin with the letters "P" through "Z."

Me: Wow, those all sound fun! Now I wish that I *was* writing fiction, so that could borrow a few of those ideas for myself.

Eric: I'll tell you what, if you ever get the chance to turn *99 Erics* into a TV series, and you're looking for more Eric stories, please consider hiring me as a writer. I'd be happy to turn some of my better pieces into teleplays.

Me: I'm flattered that you think *99 Erics* is television-worthy. But honestly, I'm not sure that I'd want it turned into a TV show. Because I know that the first thing the producers and network higher-ups would do is to make Kat Cataclysm as conventionally attractive as possible. Which means that they'd probably make her a blonde and way thinner than I am. And I'm sure they'd disappear some of my other traits, like my freckles, A-cup breasts, the scar on my face from skin cancer . . .

Eric: But that scar is barely noticeable.

Me: Which is to say that you noticed it! Don't worry, I used to be self-conscious about it, but I've come around to thinking that it's pretty fucking badass that I have a scar on my face. Even if it isn't especially noticeable. So where was I? Oh yeah, they would definitely erase my bisexuality too. If someone is straight or gay, people tend to see that as central to their character. But if the character is bisexual, producers will view that as superfluous, or they'll worry that it will confuse audiences. Even though audiences wouldn't be so confused if the media regularly depicted bisexual characters.

Eric: Preach!

Me: And while they're at it, I'd bet the producers would also erase your disability.

Eric: Hmmm, I'm not so sure about that. They might consider my cane to be an interesting "distinguishing characteristic." But what they *would* do is cast an able-bodied person to play me.

Me: You're right. And it would be total Emmy bait.

Eric: To be sure. Hey, wait a minute. Are you suggesting that I'm a character in your *99 Erics* series? Like, are you planning to write about our lunch meeting here?

Me: Lunch meeting? I thought we were on a date! After all, you're the one who asked me out. Plus you've read my blog, so you had to know that dating Erics was a "thing" for me.

Eric: No I didn't! I thought that Kat Cataclysm was merely a character you created, and that the dates in your stories were all fictional. I was simply trying to network with other writers, as that's what all the How to Become a Successful Author websites say to do. That's why I initially reached out to you. And upon reading your stories, it seemed like we had quite a bit in common too. Although I'm not so sure about that now.

Me: How so?

Eric: Well, you seem to have a fetish for people named Eric, whereas I do not.

Me: *I don't have an Eric fetish!* It's just a literary conceit. Besides, the very notion of "fetishes" is classist and/or elitist. Like, if someone is attracted to white, blonde, super-thin, young, cisgender women with larger than A-cup breasts and no facial scars—aka, the type of actor who would be cast to play me in a hypothetical

99 Erics TV show—no one would ever call that person's attraction a "fetish." But as soon as you're attracted to someone who is a minority, or anyone who is construed as having some kind of defect or deformity, then people will dismiss that attraction as a mere "fetish." It's basically a psychobabble way of saying that you consider those groups to be undesirable. Ergo, by suggesting that I have an "Eric fetish," you are basically insinuating that there is something fundamentally wrong with being attracted to people named Eric. Such as yourself.

Eric: I admit, this a really good point. I will have to give this some thought.

Me: So do you have any other objections to me including you as one of my ninety-nine Erics?

Eric: Well, perhaps it's a technicality, but my name isn't actually Eric.

Me: It isn't?!

Eric: No. It's Frederic. I just use Eric as my pen name because I recently learned that there's already an established author who goes by my actual name.

Me: Holy crap, that must have totally screwed up your "brand."

Eric: Yes. Yes, it did.

Me: In any case, I think we can make it work. After all, "Frederic" has the name "Eric" subsumed within it.

Eric: Although the two names have completely different roots.

Me: True. Eric is derived from the old Norse name for "forever ruler." But Frederic is an English name of Germanic origin meaning "peaceful ruler." You have to admit they are pretty close, both being rulers and all. Given all this, I'm going to take some poetic license here and declare you an official Eric.

Eric: Wow, you're a real Flexible Flyer, aren't you?

Me: Come again?

Eric: Flexible Flyer. It's a brand of sled. If you're going to turn our little get-together into a story, then I thought it might be nice to end with me tying things back to the Orson Welles bit from earlier.

Me: Sorry, I guess I sort of blew that.

Eric: No worries. By the way, if I am going to be one of your ninety-nine Erics, can I ask what number I will be?

Me: You are Eric #17.

Eric: But I don't identify with the number seventeen! Can't I be sixteen?

Me: You don't have the music chops to be Eric number sixteen. Besides, it's not up to me. It's all chronological. Them's the rules. Anyways, what's so special about the number sixteen?

Eric: It's highly divisible. It's two to the fourth power. Or four squared. Not to mention the square root of 256!

Me: I find it odd that you are so into even numbers.

Eric: Really, that's how you're going to end this chapter? With a math joke?

13. Socially Constructed Ice Cream

When my editor Mario read the last chapter, he voiced his concerns that Eric #17's voice sounded a little too much like my own. Or in his words, "Kat, it sounds like you're having a conversation with yourself in that chapter." So he suggested that I implement a fanciful plot-twist, wherein we later learn that Eric #17 and I are clones, although he is transgender, and he transitioned to become a man prior to our meeting. But other than the whole gender identity thing, we are somehow exactly identical in every possible way. Especially in our conversational styles.

And (Mario continued) perhaps Eric #17 and I could decide to team up together to solve crimes? Maybe, instead of a faux novel, this could be a mystery series? Because (as he so eloquently put it): mystery series + human clones + transgender people = profit!

I told Mario no way. For one thing, transgender people have it bad enough without writers like me evoking their existence for the sole purpose of creating supposedly interesting plot twists which, let's face it, are not very interesting or surprising—not if you actually know actual transgender people. And I am not about to turn my transgender friends into bombs! On top of that, the TV series *Orphan Black* already did the whole they-are-clones-but-one-of-them-is-transgender thing. Plus, if you actually sit down and watch that show, you'll see that all the *Orphan Black* clones end up being completely different in their personalities, aptitudes, and almost every other possible way. Because nurture trumps nature!

Well, except for the disease that the clones are all genetically predisposed to. Which is totally nature.

Plus, I think that Eric #17 and I sharing similar speech patterns is totally realistic. But not because two people who have never met before, but who have all the same vocal cadences and quirks, is ever likely to happen. Rather, it is realistic with regards to how cognitively sucky we humans are at remembering things as they actually occurred.

Let's face it: Our memories are super-duper distorted. People will often say, "I remember it like it was only yesterday." But no, we don't remember it like yesterday. We don't even remember yesterday like it was yesterday!

For one thing, there is not enough room in our brains to store everything that happens. And the things that we do quote-unquote "remember" aren't perfect film footage of what actually took place. Rather, they are usually a few mental snapshots that we associate with certain sounds and smells and emotions. And we assemble these shards of memory together, and craft a narrative around them. And we come to believe the narrative that we create as though it were the unadulterated truth, when in reality, it is simply a partial or complete fabrication.

Like, I remember this one time during my sophomore year of college, when my best friend Gabriella and I skipped class to go grab some ice cream. And while we were eating it, she kept trolling me about this guy I had just started dating—like, it had only been two or three dates or so at that point—but she nevertheless starting singing that "K-I-S-S-I-N-G" song that children taunt one another with. So much like a child might have reacted, I spontaneously smashed my ice cream cone on her face, and we both couldn't stop laughing for like ten minutes straight. And we both vividly remember and often reminisce about that moment together. Except that in Gabriella's mind, we were at a Dairy Queen and the ice cream in question was vanilla with jimmies. Whereas I remembered it being a Baskin-Robbins, and I'm pretty sure that I didn't start appreciating vanilla until my mid-twenties, plus I *never in a million years would have ordered jimmies!* No amount of arguing will ever make us agree on what actually went down that day. Other than the smashing ice cream in Gabriella's face part.

So you can see why all the philosophers say that our reality is entirely socially constructed. And I pretty much agree with them. Except when I am actually eating the ice cream, and I'm like, *"Oh my god, this is an amazingly real experience—I can firsthand taste the ice cream in my own fucking mouth, with my own fucking taste buds!"* Then I'll get all philosophically turned around and start identifying as a "materialist" rather than a "constructivist." At least as far as ice cream is concerned.

Anyway, that's why Eric #17's voice likely sounds like my voice in the last chapter. Because I wasn't able to write about our date until several weeks after it actually happened. And that date is even further back in time now, because you are reading this in the future. Or my future, at least. So I had to take the conversation we had—which I can no longer remember verbatim (which I suppose is okay, because as I've previously established, the word "verbatim" can now also mean "paraphrased")—and reconstitute it from just a few shards of memory. Which is another way of saying that I simply made a lot of it up. Which is probably why Eric #17 sounds like me.

Sorry about that.

14. Children of the Corndog

I remember a time, not so long ago, when food was primarily about . . . well, food. Sustenance and gustatory enjoyment! There was typical American fare aplenty at various diners, pubs, fast food joints, and other eateries. Or, if your palate was a bit more adventurous, you could instead opt for one of a variety of ethnic cuisines—Italian, Chinese, Mexican, Indian, Ethiopian, and so on—in small family-owned restaurants where the chefs grew up preparing food in that tradition. And if you wanted to try to recreate some of these tasty items at home, you could tune into the Food Network, which once upon a time actually aired cooking shows: celebrity chefs in simplistic kitchen sets teaching viewers how to make Duck a l'Orange or Chicken Teryaki in the classic style.

But then Guy Fieri happened. And *Top Chef* and *Iron Chef America*. And the next thing you know, good food simply wasn't good enough. It needed to be louder and weirder and more intense! Put some Sriracha on that pizza! Put gorgonzola on those nachos! Instead of teaching the audience how to cook, let's dazzle them with a reality TV cook-off where wannabe celebrity chefs have thirty minutes to prepare a three-course meal out of daikon root, ground turkey, and cashew nuts! Why bother passing recipes down from generation to generation when you can just make shit up as you go along! Fuck traditional pots and pans—all you need is a tank of liquid nitrogen, a thermal immersion circulator, and a 100 gram package of transglutaminase!

And before any of us knew what was happening, our entire dining landscape had forever changed. Suddenly, it is no longer acceptable to open up a straightforward Vietnamese restaurant or Philly Cheesesteak shop. You need an angle. A shtick. Like, how about Philly cheesesteaks, but served Bánh mì style? Or spring rolls that, instead of being filled with tofu and rice vermicelli, contain the Italian lunchmeats and provolone cheese one normally finds in a hoagie? Hey, what about scrapple phở? If you can fill up a menu with these sorts of concoctions, then your new Vietnamese-Philadelphian fusion restaurant will get written up in all the culinary magazines, and people will flock to your place even though you charge twice as much as you could get away with if you owned a traditional Vietnamese or Philly Cheesesteak restaurant.

This is what has become of food.

And I'm mentioning all this now because of Eric #19. Eric #3 (my friend from Lady Parts and the local literary scene) set the two of us up together. Usually when friends set you up on a date, it's because they fancy themselves as relationship prognosticators, and they are somehow convinced that the two of you will, as they say, "hit it off." Eric #3 wasn't so sure about that. But he thought that, at the very least, we'd be able to help one another with our ongoing projects. In my case, obviously he could fulfill the role of one of my ninety-nine Erics. As for Eric #19, he was a semi-famous filmmaker working on the screenplay for his next film, wherein one of the main characters was slated to be an absurdist short story writer. Since Eric #19 did not personally know any real-life absurdist short fiction writers, perhaps meeting me could provide him with some material or ideas to help him flesh out his character.

I say Eric #19 was a "semi-famous" filmmaker because I'm sure that most of you wouldn't know his name if I told you. But if you are familiar with his work, then that means that you are likely a humongous horror-fantasy buff. Eric #19's films are all cult classics, the type that inspire legions of fans to produce an endless stream of blog posts, Reddit threads, and YouTube videos dissecting and discussing the mysteries and theories surrounding his latest films, *The Trepanation* and *Microcosm II: Half the Battle.*

While Eric #19 is clearly not a household name, he nevertheless is one of those extremely rare birds: an artist who is not only making a living off his art, but a very good one at that. And during our pre-meet-up phone call, he insisted that he wanted to take me to his latest favorite restaurant in San Francisco. And that it would be his treat.

The restaurant is called Lazy Fair, and they specialize in an updated California-cuisine take on county fair food. Like, they have corndogs, but the "corn" part is honeyed polenta and the "dog" part is rosemary wild boar sausage. And they serve funnel cakes, but with one of two toppings: truffle or niçoise olive tapenade. And on top of all the ridiculously expensive yet admittedly tasty food items, they play carnival music in the background, and they hire child actors to run around with balloons, in order to give the space an authentic county fair feel.

So the waitperson serves us our meals. Eric #19 ordered the Lazy Fair Deep-Fry Pu Pu Platter™, which comes with a variety of panko-encrusted food items (e.g., Kumamoto oysters, Dungeness crab cakes, mint chutney lamb dumplings, "venison fingers," and miniature sticks of sage-infused butter) that you then cook yourself in the small personal-sized deep-fryer that comes with the meal. Being less extravagant, I just ordered a burger, but of course it wasn't "just a burger": It was a duck and brandied fig burger with heirloom tomato and pâté "special sauce." Oh, and it came with a side of tarragon vinegar French fries and scallion aioli.

After taking a bite of my burger and washing it down with a sip of the restaurant's home-brewed "Petting Zoo" IPA, I asked Eric #19: So your new film, what's it about?

Eric: Well, it's a zombie film. But not just any old zombie film. It's a zombie film based in science. The protagonist is a geneticist who is studying a virulent epidemic that is starting to spread throughout New York City. But it's not just any old disease; it's one that . . .

Me: Turns people into zombies?

Eric: Yes, exactly! And our geneticist protagonist identifies a family of prions associated with the disease which, once they infiltrate human cells, hijack the mitochondria to significantly lower metabolism rates—which is why the zombies move so slow and why they seemingly live forever, albeit in an undead sort of way. And the prions also force the mitochondria to produce the zombie-specific prion-like proteins that can then infect other people.

Me: I don't think mitochondria make proteins. I think that's ribosomes.

Eric: Apparently mitochondria have their own ribosomes. Or at least that's what *Wikipedia* says. Hey, wait a minute, how do you know so much about biology?

Me: I don't know a whole lot, really. But I was once in a relationship with a biologist, so I guess I picked up a little along the way. But anyway, then what happens?

Eric: Well, while doing internet searches looking for similar cases, the geneticist discovers that, somewhere out there, there is an award-winning absurdist short story writer who is in the process of writing her first faux novel. And the plot of her faux-novel-in-progress is that a mitochondria-hacking-prion-zombie-disease breaks out in New York City—events virtually identical to the ones the geneticist has encountered. And the main character in her faux novel just so happens to be a geneticist who, over the course of the book, discovers that he and the disease are not real, but merely plot devices in somebody else's absurdist short story. So then he (the film geneticist, not the book geneticist) goes on a quest to find this absurdist short story writer, because he fears that the faux novel she is writing is coming to life in the real world, and he needs to convince her to write a happy ending to her book-in-progress in order to save humanity, even though he knows how difficult the task will likely be given that absurdist writers are typically extremely averse to traditional happy endings. But in addition to that dilemma, while on his quest, the geneticist has to grapple with the distinct possibility that he is merely a character in somebody else's book, rather than a real-life person who has the free will and the agency necessary to save the world and . . . I'm sorry, am I boring you?

Me: No. Your story sounds great. Great story.

Eric: But you have a disconcerted look on your face.

Me: Disconcerted? Me? No. Never. Unsettled, maybe.

Eric: What's unsettling you?

Me: Well, the carnival music for starters.

Eric: You mean the ambience. Just pretend that you are at an actual authentic county fair.

Me: But I'm not. I'm in San Francisco. Like, a twenty-minute BART ride from my apartment. And I'm eating a $26 burger—I don't think they have those at county fairs.

Eric: I told you, this is my treat, so don't worry about the price tag on that burger.

Me: I'm not sure what I hate more about carnival music: the relentless organ and accordion, or the fact that it's all in 3/4. Which is like the worst of all time signatures.

Eric: Well, it's not as bad as 11/8.

Me: Hey, watch it buddy, three of my top ten favorite songs of all time are written in 11/8! Oh, wait, one of those is actually in 13/8. My bad. But aside from the music, there are all these children running about the place.

Eric: They're not children. They are professional child actors. There is a notable difference.

Me: What difference?

Eric: They're acting! Plus, they are also part of the ambience.

Me: Yeah, but I still don't like it. Children are too unpredictable. Because they are all drunk.

Eric: Drunk? I highly doubt that these child actors have consumed any alcohol. That would be so unlike child actors.

Me: I'm not insinuating that they are raiding their parents' liquor cabinets or anything. I'm just saying that children are naturally drunk. Like, it's in their very biology.

Eric: This seems highly unlikely—what's your evidence?

Me: Do you know how parents usually have a hard time getting their children to eat vegetables?

Eric: Yeah, so?

Me: Well, when I'm sober, I will cook myself vegetable stir fry, or make myself a salad. But when I'm drunk, I have no desire to eat vegetables—I'd rather have "drunk food": things like pizza or French fries or ice cream—not coincidentally, the very same foods that kids like the most!

Eric: But that's hardly . . .

Me: Here's another example: Children are always doing things they know they shouldn't do. And afterward, when their parents ask them why they did it, they'll inevitably reply: "I don't know." And their parents will continue to interrogate them, searching for some kind of underlying logic or ulterior motive. But there isn't one. Their kid is simply drunk. And we adults should be able to relate to this, because we often ask ourselves: "Why did I stay up partying so late when I knew I had to get up for work early the next day?" Or "Oh my god, why did I sleep with so-and-so last night?" And the answer to those hypothetical questions is simply, "I don't know." Because "I don't know" is a euphemism for "I was drunk."

Eric had a dumfounded look on his face. It seemed clear that I was totally winning the argument. So I went forward with my concluding remarks: Look, I'm not suggesting that children are alcoholics per se. Rather, I am suggesting that we are all born drunk. Like super-fucking drunk—which explains why babies are always vomiting, and shitting in their pants, and can't even hold their own heads up. That's why none of us can remember the first few years of our lives—we have literally blacked them out. And growing up is like one long sobering up process, where you get a little less drunk with every day, with every year. As younglings begin to sober up, they eventually gain the ability to walk, and to talk coherently. And when they turn sixteen, we let them get their driver's license, because they are finally sober enough to operate a vehicle.

At this point, the waitperson interrupted us. They collected our dishes and asked if we wanted any dessert. Eric #19 ordered the porcini and caramelized onion kettle corn, whereas I selected the crème brûlée cotton candy.

Me: So, if you don't mind me asking, are you considering basing your absurdist short fiction writer character on me then?

Eric: Well, I was considering it. But now that I've gotten to know you, the answer is definitely no.

Me: Why not? I'm interesting. And personable. Interesting and/or personable.

Eric: Don't take this the wrong way, but you are a bit too much of a "Manic Pixie Dream Girl" stereotype for my taste.

Me: What? I am nothing like a Manic Pixie Dream Girl!

Eric: Well, let's face it, you are quirky, whimsical, and bubbly. You have an almost child-like sense of playfulness . . .

Me: Hey, are you insinuating that I play like a drunk person?

Eric: . . . You have idiosyncratic interests, unconventional tastes in music, and are constantly spouting off all sorts of odd facts. Plus, you have bangs.

Me: I have bangs because I have a high forehead is all!

Eric: It's just that I envisioned my absurdist short story writer to be a serious, fully-fleshed-out, and well-rounded character.

Me: But I am fully-fleshed-out! I have an entire backstory! It's just that you're not privy to it all yet because we're only about a third of the way into this book. And plenty of serious things have happened to me over the course of my life, it's just that I prefer not to dwell on them—that is my coping mechanism! And I am most certainly a well-rounded character—I am the protagonist after all, and readers are constantly subjected to my inner thoughts, desires, motives, etcetera. In fact, I am not only the protagonist, but I am the author of this book as well. Which means that I am omniscient! And omnipotent! Whereas you are just . . . *a layperson.*

Eric: Sorry, but you still seem like a two-dimensional stereotype to me.

Me: Oh yeah, well, can a two-dimensional stereotype do this:

Suddenly, all the child actors stopped dead in their tracks, letting go of their balloons. Simultaneously, their eyes turned a deep blood red, and they began chanting "cir-el-lik, cir-el-lik, cir-el-lik," while weirdly moving their index fingers. Then they each grabbed the nearest knife and walked toward Eric #19 in a slow-yet-determined zombie-like fashion. I could tell that Eric #19 desperately wanted to scream, but he couldn't, because I refused to write him any more dialogue. Realizing his fate as a helpless character in my faux novel, he closed his eyes and awaited his gory demise.

The camera cuts to me, a few minutes later. I am finishing off my crème brûlée cotton candy, which is fantastic by the way. As the camera pans back, it becomes clear that I am surrounded by the zombie-like child actors, who are still clutching their bloodied knives. I look at them all and ask: "Why did you all just stab Eric #19 to death?"

In unison, they respond: "I don't know."

Fade to black.

FIN

15. Easter Eggs

Okay, I've put this off way too long, so now I'm going to have to tell you the story about Eric #2. He probably wasn't the first Eric that I ever met in my life. But he was the first Eric that I ever dated, and the only one that I ever agreed to have a child with. This was all many years ago, long before I had the idea to write this book. And if any of you Freudian wannabes are anxiously speculating as to whether this past history subconsciously influenced my decision to write a book called *99 Erics* (as opposed to *99 Evans,* or *99 Emilios,* or *99 Erins)*, well, I'd be lying if I said that this possibility has never crossed my mind.

Eric #2 and I met back in college—it was one of those long-established sleepy-college-town universities that litter the northeastern U.S., and where many of the professors and students carry themselves as though it were an Ivy League school, even though it isn't. It definitely wasn't my first choice for college, but they offered me a scholarship to play softball, and no one else did. So there I was.

Eric #2 and I started dating during our sophomore year, and were fairly serious by the time we were juniors. During our senior year, he suggested that we apply to all the same graduate schools together (genetics departments for him, linguistics departments for me) so we wouldn't have to be apart from one another. Part of me was hoping that grad school could be a whole new exciting adventure, rather than a mere continuation of my college life. But on the other hand, Eric and I got along pretty well together, and most everybody in my life seemed to love him—after all, he was smart and funny and attractive, at least as far as guys go. And he had one of those BOOMING MAN VOICES that is super-fucking annoying when you're in the airport waiting to board your flight and he's the person sitting next to you making business call after business call on his cell phone, but which probably sounds super-duper confident and reassuring if you just so happen to be the dupe on the other end of said business call.

Anyway, I guess you could say that I was the dupe in this scenario. Eric had strong opinions, while I am the God Empress of Conflict Avoidance and one of the most ambivalent people I know. Staying together was the path of least resistance for me, so I reluctantly agreed. When we both were accepted to the same university for grad school, we got an apartment together. Then we settled into a new normal: He spent his days and nights working in the lab, and I spent mine buried in books and writing. At the end of the day, or early the next morning, we'd catch up on how our projects were going. We'd maybe go out to dinner or see a film together on the weekends. But that was it. We shared a really stereotypically boring academic life.

Then came Easter, which is one of those holidays that pass without you even noticing when you're agnostic and your partner is atheist, but which I remember in this instance because of what happened that day and how ironic it was in retrospect. It started out normal enough: After working through most of the day, we shared take out. He told me about the progress he was making on his genomic imprinting project. I talked about a paper I was writing on Jakobsonian markedness. Then, out of the blue, Eric told me that he wanted us to have a child. Sooner rather than later.

And this was the first time the subject ever came up in a serious way. And I immediately said no.

He asked me why. So I stated the obvious: Children are drunk. Like, all the time! And frankly, I didn't want to spend the next sixteen years of my life taking care of a drunk person until they are finally sober enough to drive.

But then Eric #2 picked apart my argument as being "unscientific," citing statistics about childhood alcohol dehydrogenase levels and discussing the specifics of human neurological development.

So I countered with how we were both relatively broke grad students who never in a million years could afford a child.

He countered with platitudes about how having a child would bring us closer together. Plus somehow, we'd find a way, he assured me in his soothing yet BOOMING MAN VOICE.

Then I pointed out how this would certainly impact my career far more than his. After all, I'd be the one dealing with pregnancy, breastfeeding, etcetera. Plus the lion's share of parenting almost always falls upon the mother, despite some fathers' best intentions.

He replied that he would use his burgeoning expertise in genetics to clone me, so that I could pursue my linguistics career while my clone would raise our child. And we both laughed at the ridiculousness of that proposition. We made jokes about what we would name my clone, and how we would dress her (to the best of my recollection, we named her Anastasia and agreed she should wear one of those oversized "Frankie Say Relax" t-shirts with lederhosen). And all the laughter eased the tension between us. We cuddled for a while. We agreed to sleep on it.

And a few days later, I agreed to have Eric #2's baby.

This is where the part of my brain that relentlessly attempts to construct overarching life narratives really wants to play the Young and Impressionable card (which comes with +3 points for optimism, but -2 points for critical thinking), as a way of making sense of that arguably inadvisable and life-altering decision on my part. But for now, I will hold onto that card and instead play the Bubble of Couplehood card (which comes with +3 alliance points, but -5 for critical thinking). Even if you've never heard of the Bubble of Couplehood before, I'm sure you are aware of its effects: By spending the vast majority of your intimate and unguarded moments with this one particular person, the two of you wind up creating your own alternate reality with its own bizarre rules and customs. Like, the long-established societal axiom that states that it is absolutely not okay to walk into the bathroom and start flossing your teeth while another person is on the toilet urinating goes straight out the window. Or despite longstanding conventions regarding the meanings of words and the grammar of language, the two of you are somehow able to sustain a twenty-minute-long conversation that consists almost entirely of inside jokes, endearments, and silly voices.

There is a French phrase—*folie à deux*—to describe when two people who are close with one another start sharing the same delusions. And that, in essence, is what the Bubble of Couplehood is. And within that Bubble, notions like, "Hey, wouldn't it be so much fun to buy a house together?" or "Having a baby will bring us closer together!" will make perfect sense to the two of you, even though many outsiders will interpret those very same premises as being fraught with misconceptions and potential peril.

So that is my long-winded way of saying that, for better or worse, the week following that Easter evening, Eric and I hatched our plan to become pregnant together. Except, of course, that I would be the designated pregnant person.

For the first time since college, I went off the pill. And over the next several months, whenever I reached the point in my cycle that was most likely to be peak ovulation, we scheduled penetration sex for that evening. Afterward, Eric #2 would sleep like a baby (pun unintended). And while he was fast asleep, I would just lay there in bed with insomnia.

It was the same insomnia that plagued me back when I was just about to reach puberty, when my mother and other adults in my life let me in on the highly guarded secret that is the miracle of the female reproductive system. (Although it's not actually a miracle, it's just biology, and seriously, it really shouldn't be such a secret.) My mother, family doctor, health teacher at school, and so on, all stressed how special my eggs were, because I only had like a few hundred of them total. I was told that my body would release one per month, and the rest would just get old and stale and crinkly relatively soon enough. These adults made it sound as though my eggs were already tiny little people just waiting for the right circumstances to blossom into beautiful bouncing babies.

And because my eggs were supposedly super-duper precious—like Fabergé eggs or some shit—I had to take really good care of my body, and not do any fun stuff like drink alcohol, take drugs, or sleep with the "wrong guys," and so forth. All the conversations that I was exposed to about being a young developing woman made it seem like I wasn't even a person per se, but rather just a fucking Fabergé egg bus driver, constantly transporting all these microscopic precious potential people from one destination to another. And if I drove off the road, I'd be responsible for several hundred microscopic deaths. I'm pretty sure nobody talks this way to boys about their sperm. If they did, I bet boys wouldn't cum into their dirty socks so much, because like, what a horrible way to slaughter millions of potential little people!

The Fabergé egg thing totally fucked with my head as a teenager. I'd lay awake at night and imagine one of my microscopic eggs being released. And I would name each and every one of them: Rachel. Bob. Lydia. Jackson. And so on. And I'd envision my fallopian tubes as being like a giant water slide, and Bob, or Lydia, or whoever the egg-of-the-month was, would be shouting "weeeeeee" in absolute joyful exuberance, because after all, waterslides are hella fun, especially when you've been cooped up in an ovary your entire life. And they'd be expecting to land safely in the big pool of water that is the uterus, but little did they know that nobody filled the endometrium with blood vessels that morning, and they'd just land with a big horrible SPLAT! When my period would come, I couldn't help but imagine that this was Rachel's blood, or Jackson's, or whoever's turn it was to ride the fallopian waterslide of death that month.

And even though I was now old enough to know better, these very same daydreams-slash-nightmares continued to haunt me. Each and every single night. For about six months. At which point Eric #2 started to seem concerned that we weren't pregnant yet. By which he meant me. So we scheduled simultaneous fertility tests, which is the sort of thing that you do when you live in the Bubble of Couplehood.

And when we received our results, we were both ecstatic: Eric because he wasn't sterile, and me because I was.

I know that most people prefer the word "infertile" to "sterile." And that's perfectly fine for them. But I actually like "sterile" because I felt so completely cleansed after hearing that news—I was fucking Fabergé egg-free! I could finally live my life without constantly thinking about the consequences for all those precious potential people that I thought were living and dying horrible deaths inside my belly. It was so fucking liberating. Like, now I could drink all the IPAs that I wanted, and smoke weed, and do mushrooms, and date all the wrong guys (a few of whom have turned out to be named Eric).

But I have found that you cannot readily share this joy with others. Because when the subject comes up—which in my experience, often happens when a first-time mother or mother-to-be finally realizes that they have just been monopolizing the entire conversation with tales about their baby or pregnancy, so they want to bring you back into the conversation, but rather than ask, "So what's new in your life that currently excites you?" they instead keep things focused on their favorite topic by asking, "So do you have children?" or "So have you thought about having children yourself?"—and you respond, "No, I am sterile! Or infertile! Or whatever you wanna call it!" and you accompany your reply with a spontaneous and largely improvised happy dance, they will become extremely disconcerted. Because now they feel really really awful on your behalf, because in their mind, you will never experience the miracle of life, even though it's not a miracle, it's really just biology, and you already experience plenty of biology in your day-to-day life, thank you very much. And they really really want to say "I'm so sorry for your loss," because in their eyes, it really and truly is a devastating loss.

But from your perspective as a sterile lady amid happy dance, it seems clear that they are promoting a hierarchy here, one where biological mothers are super-duper special (because of "miracles" that aren't really miracles), and women who have not had that experience are by default "not-so-special" and "missing out" as a result. I mean, I could totally turn this around and say that most biological mothers are missing out on being a polyamorous bisexual woman, or an award-winning absurdist short fiction writer, or a human being who no longer has to worry about fucking Fabergé eggs. But that would imply that my life choices and experiences are superior to theirs. And I am not about to do that, because that would be patronizing. In a bad way.

Anyway, needless to say, Eric #2 was devastated, and didn't appreciate my happy dance at all. He immediately started running through all the possible plan Bs (once again, pun unintended) for us (by which he meant me). Maybe I could get a second opinion? Maybe we could look into infertility treatments? But as I was processing this brand new news about my body, and as Eric was listing possible courses of action, to be honest, all I could think about was one thing: Gabriella. My best friend from college. The one who I got into the ice cream fight with back in Chapter 13.

During freshman year, Gabriella and I were assigned to the same dorm room on account of us both being on the school's softball team. She was an oddball and I was a weirdo, and we quickly became inseparable. She introduced me to punk rock and sex-positive feminism, and I introduced her to Monty Python and agnosticism. When she complained about having to write a paper on Shakespeare, I turned her onto *Rosencrantz and Guildenstern Are Dead*. And when I naively spouted my prog-rock-inspired libertarian take on politics, she took her softball bat and attempted to destroy my entire collection of two Ayn Rand books, breaking my bookshelf in the process.

I was totally smitten with Gabriella. I can see that now. Although back then, the part of my brain that relentlessly churns out overarching life narratives couldn't make sense (or didn't want to make sense) of what I was feeling. That narrative-producing part of my brain insisted that we were just super-duper close friends, while completely ignoring how I often spent history class daydreaming about seeing Gabriella at softball practice afterward, even though I saw her just that morning on account of us sharing a dorm room together. Or how when I masturbated, sometimes I would think of boys, but other times I would think about Gabriella.

And my narrative brain, when confronted with the inescapable evidence that Gabriella and I made out on like a half-dozen or so occasions, insisted that it was merely homosocial behavior and not in any way sexual, because we never touched each other "down there." Even though "down there" was very very excited about all the mutual kissing and touching and such.

I met Eric #2 the following year, and he asked me out. I said yes. My narrative brain back then was all like, "See, I told you we are heterosexual! I was right all along!" But my narrative brain today, looking back on it all, makes sense of the situation this way: While I was authentically attracted to Eric #2, and eventually fell in love with him, part of the appeal of that relationship was admittedly not having to seriously confront the possibility that I might be queer.

But my narrative brain in between those two moments in time—specifically, just as after finding out that I was sterile, and listening to Eric #2 recite all the medical tests I would need to take in order to determine what infertility treatments would be best suited for me, so that we could ultimately get pregnant, by which he meant me—that narrative brain came to a third and rather different conclusion: "Holy shit, I was totally in love with Gabriella all throughout freshman year, but internalized homophobia got the best of me, and so for the last few years I've let this patriarchal dude with a BOOMING MAN VOICE talk me into doing all sorts of things that I never really wanted for myself in the first place!"

And in the wake of that epiphany, as Eric #2 was telling me what I should be doing with my body in order to make him happy, I simply said: "Eric, I'm a lesbian."

Then I walked out the door.

I wandered the streets around campus for god knows how long. My mind was reeling—the combination of life-altering information about my anatomy quickly followed by a life-altering realization about my sexual identity, made the world feel alive. Abuzz. It was as if my brain had released all of its neurotransmitters at once. I was awash in new thoughts, connections, sensations. Perhaps I wouldn't need to do mushrooms after all.

I wasn't really sure where to go. I needed to leave Eric #2— that much was obvious. And knowing how persistent of a person he was, I was pretty sure that if I stayed in school here, he would relentlessly try (and possibly succeed at) talking me into getting back together. And my parents and I were barely on speaking terms by this point, even without them knowing that I was queer, which would most certainly be the final nail in that coffin. So that ruled out going home to them.

I walked by a payphone—as this was back when payphones were still a thing—and dug through my purse for all the coins I could muster. I dialed the number that I had memorized from calling it on numerous previous occasions.

"Hi, Gabriella? It's Kat. Can I ask a favor?"

16. Posers

These days, it's really difficult to talk about being queer. Because there's this popular presumption that society is now totally a-okay with same-sex relationships, which ignores the fact that this is far from the truth, plus most of us grew up during a time when it most definitely was not okay to be queer. And many people seem to have drunk the "we're just like you except for our sexual orientation" kool-aid, so they don't even consider the possibility that the experience of being queer might be considerably different from what straight people experience.

"So Kat, what *is* it like being queer?" some of you may now be asking. Well, I would say that it is kind of like bicycling to Alameda.

But not just any old bicycle trip to Alameda. You are going to the west side of Alameda, for some inexplicable reason. And people will argue over whether you felt the need to go to west Alameda because it's in your genes, or poor parent-child dynamics, or because fetal hormones hardwired your brain that way. But you couldn't care less about these debates. All you know is that you *really need to get to west Alameda, and it doesn't matter why!* Plus to you, there's a clear double standard at work here, as nobody would ever question you if you told them that you were bicycling to downtown Alameda instead.

Now if you *were* going to downtown Alameda (as everybody expects of you), you could simply bike over either the Park Street or Fruitvale bridges—both totally safe—and you'd arrive at your destination. Easy squeezy. But for west Alameda, the most direct route for you is the Posey Tube, which was built back in 1927, long before urban planners worried their pretty little heads about bike lanes. All they left you is a one-person-wide pathway perched on one side of the tunnel, just above the racing cars below, with only a guardrail separating you from your impending death.

The signs tell you to walk your bike, but if you did that, you'd be in the tube all day. So you precariously pedal your way across the Oakland Estuary, albeit way underneath all the water. And it's outrageously loud in the tube due to the cavernous echoing of all the car and bus engines. And your eyes are peeled on the tight path that you are navigating, as one small slip-up could potentially cast you over the guardrail. So your senses are overloaded, and you are on the verge of freaking out, or screaming, or crying, or dying, or possibly some combination thereof. But you keep on going—not because you are brave or courageous (which I suppose are pretty much the same thing)—but because there is no other way to west Alameda. *And that's where you need to go!*

But then lo and behold, you see someone approaching you from the other direction. You have to get off your bike, and they need to do the same, because the path is so narrow. And you'd think this would be a huge inconvenience, having lost all the momentum you had built up. But strangely it's not. And as you squeeze past one another, the two of you make eye contact and smile—not the fake sorts of smiles that accompany the exchange of everyday pleasantries, but rather the genuine knowing smiles of people who share the same intense and potentially traumatic experience. And in that brief moment, the two of you make a profound human connection unlike anything you've felt before. Because only a moment ago, you were both completely alone in a dark tunnel, freaking out, and afraid of dying. But now you both realize that you're not really alone after all. And it's beautiful. But it's also a little sad that you had to experience all that fear and loneliness in the first place.

So that's what being queer is like. At least in my estimation.

Now queer communities are an entirely different thing. That would be like if you decided to round up all of the people who have ever bicycled through the Posey Tube and put them all in the same room together. At first, you would all bond over your shared experiences traversing and surviving the tunnel. There would be expressions of Posey Tube Pride abound, and it would no doubt be a wonderful affair. But fairly shortly after that, you would all start to realize that you have nothing in common with one another aside from this one thing. After all, you each come from different backgrounds and have different personal and political views. Not to mention different bicycles!

And factions would no doubt develop, for instance, between people who have bicycled through the tube in differing directions. Because let's face it, while the mainstream majority doesn't understand why anyone in their right mind would ride their bike through the Posey Tube, it is easier for them to accept people who desire to go to downtown Oakland than those who desire to go to west Alameda. Because *why would you want to go to west Alameda?!*

And people who cross the tube every day on their way to work would start to look down on the people who have only done it sporadically for occasional visits, or the people who used to do it all the time but no longer do so because they have since switched jobs or moved elsewhere. And of course, the former group would probably call these latter groups something demeaning yet pithy, like "Posers," in order to invalidate their experiences. Even though they did have those experiences—those special moments of fear and recognition and intimacy amidst that precarious cacophonous tunnel.

And this is why, even though I have plenty of queer people in my life, I tend to avoid queer communities like the plague.

But that wasn't always the case.

When I first arrived at Gabriella's place in San Francisco, with nothing but a backpack and a shopping bag full of whatever I could hastily pack, I was excited to finally immerse myself in all things queer. Gabriella lived in a railroad apartment that had a rotating cast of anywhere from four to six roommates at a time, all of them dykes. This was obviously back when people in their twenties who were not computer programmers making six-figure salaries could afford to live in the Mission District. I only had to crash on Gabriella's couch for a few weeks before one of the bedrooms became available for me to move into. I forget who it was who moved out, but I am 99 percent sure that it was for one of the three usual reasons: 1) she moved in with her partner, 2) she fled to someplace with a lower cost of living, most likely either Oakland or Portland, and/or 3) she could no longer tolerate the chaos and drama of living with roommates who were constantly dating (and often breaking up with) each others' friends, ex-lovers, friends' ex-lovers, ex-lovers' friends, and/or sometimes one another.

In case you're wondering, Gabriella and I never did get back together after I moved out to San Francisco. Not that we were ever actually together in the first place. When I first showed up, Gabriella was already in a semi-serious relationship. And by the time they split up, I was in a relationship with someone. And so on. But honestly, it was probably for the best, as the lack of lover-drama between us no doubt helped us to remain close to this day.

Anyway, there is so much to learn when you first come out as queer. I would imagine that some straight readers will imagine that I'm talking about sexual stuff here, because *gay sex is so weird, like what do these people do when there isn't precisely one penis and one vagina?!* But frankly, the sexual stuff comes pretty naturally. I mean, it's common knowledge how bodies and genitals work, and both straight and queer sex generally follow the same basic premise: You do things to pleasure your partner, and they do things to pleasure you. Nothing could be more simple! Sure, there are all sorts of "advanced" techniques that you can learn, but those kinds of special skill sets exist for heterosexual couples as well (if you're interested, just ask my friend Eric #3 from Lady Parts—he can recommend a few books for you!).

No, the queer learning curve isn't so much about sex as it is about culture. Because minority groups typically develop their own cultures: They have a unique history, customs, and perspectives, often shaped by the obstacles they face living in a majority-centered world. Most minorities are born into their particular culture, and so they learn everything they need to know from their families, neighbors, and so on, from day one. In contrast, almost all queer people are raised in straight families and communities. So when you finally realize "Oh my god, I'm queer!" at the ripe old age of twenty-three, it also strikes you that you don't know anything about being queer. Culturally, that is.

Having Gabriella as a friend was immensely helpful in this regard. She introduced me to all her queer friends and took me to all these awesome queer events. And over time, I learned that there is so much more to being a dyke than girl-on-girl romance and sex. For instance, there are all these bands that you are supposed to be listening to, because they are the only ones speaking directly to the lesbian experience. And there are specific haircuts, styles of dress, and even tattoos, that you can sport in order to signify to people "in the know" that you are "family."

All of Gabriella's friends seemed so cool, and they were so patient and unconditionally accepting of me. At least at first. In retrospect, it was probably because they viewed me as a "baby dyke," which is what they call someone who has just recently come out into the community. I probably reminded them of their younger baby-dyke selves during that magical and foundational period of their own lives. So they took me under their wings, showed me the ropes, and other mixed metaphors. If I said or did anything that they perceived to be incorrect or naive, they would let it slide on account of the fact that I was still in the throes of throwing off the chains of heteronormativity. And they weren't judgmental about my several-year-long relationship with Eric #2—they assumed that it was simply something that I had to do in order to survive in the straight world.

But after numerous months of enculturation, your baby-dyke status eventually fades, and you become a fully mature dyke in their eyes, one who has already seen all the ropes and knows the lay of the land. And at this point if, rather than listening to the usual lesbian bands—who are fine, but there is only so much folk music and punk rock you can take, and seriously lesbians, explore more genres of music!—you instead play classic '70s prog rock records like *Close to the Edge* or *The Lamb Lies Down on Broadway*, all of your dyke roommates are going to look at you weird. Like, disdainfully weird. Because the music you are playing is not in any way Sapphic. And you really ought to know better by now!

And if you choose *not* to get an androgynous or asymmetrical haircut (because your personal preference is for length and symmetry), or *not* to get a wrist star or labrys tattoo (because of your trypanophobia), then some people will question your queerness. Even though tattoos and haircuts have nothing to do with your sexual orientation! I mean, these things are merely signifiers. And as a recently dropped-out linguist, you are highly aware that the relationship between the signifier and the signified is completely arbitrary! Or at least that's what Saussure said. So why risk getting a rainbow tattoo when, twenty or thirty years from now, the signifier "rainbow" might mean "shopping cart" or "macadamia nut"? Or "the refraction of light via airborne water droplets"? You never know.

Your new queer friends will cut you some slack when it comes to your haircut, taste in music, and so forth. Until you meet that guy—the sweet and soft-spoken one who works at the bookstore a few blocks away. One day while there, you find a used copy of *Even Cowgirls Get the Blues*, and you start paging through it. And the bookstore guy asks you if you've read it before. And you say yes, back in tenth grade—it seemed so salacious and surreal, and it made quite an impression on you. But you're afraid to re-read it, because you're pretty sure that Sissy and the cowgirls are depicted through the male gaze, and that would totally ruin it for you. The bookstore guy replies sadly it's true, plus there are all these other stereotypes in it, like The Countess and The Chink. You laugh, because you totally forgot about those characters, all you remember are the lesbian cowgirls. And after a smattering of smart bantering, he mentions that he is going to an absurdist literary reading on Thursday, and would you like to come along? So of course you say yes.

And the two days between the bookstore and the reading, you find that you are having daydreams about him, similar to the ones that you used to have of Gabriella way back during your college history classes. And after the reading, you take him to your favorite dive bar on Valencia Street, the one with the velvet paintings and the good beer selection. And both of you order stouts (because that's what you were drinking back then, rather than IPAs) and then you have the most awesome conversation.

So of course you take him home with you.

And the next day, this becomes a big scandal, because your roommates saw him leave the following morning. And so they start interrogating you. And you're like, why does it matter who I sleep with? And someone asks, well, is he at least gay? Or trans? So you respond no, he's heterosexual and cisgender (but you didn't use the word "cisgender," because as far as you know, that word hadn't even been invented yet). But you did tell him that you're a lesbian and he was fine with it. And men who date lesbians have to be at least a little bit queer, don't they?

And someone says, date? As in more than once? And when you respond yes, the two of you are planning to go out again in a couple of days, one of your roommates says she doesn't feel safe with a straight man coming over on a regular basis. And a second roommate seconds that emotion. And you're trying to stress how sweet this guy is: He wouldn't hurt a fly, plus he's a minority himself, although not a sexual minority, other than the fact that he is now dating a lesbian, which in your mind is at least somewhat sexual-minority-ish, although your roommates aren't buying it.

And the conversation continues on and on, for almost an hour. But about halfway through, your mind starts to wander. First, you wish Gabriella was here, because you know she would totally stick up for you. Second, it strikes you that there is this word called "bisexual" and perhaps you should consider the possibility that maybe it applies to you.

And third, you think about how, ever since your earliest memories, you always felt like you were different from everyone else. You were someone who never really fit in, no matter where you were or who you were with. And before today happened, you temporarily thought that you finally solved that riddle: You never fit in before because you were a queer person in a straight world; now that you have found queer community, you finally fit in.

But now you realize that you don't fit in in queer communities either. Maybe it's not that you're queer. Perhaps your problem is that you are simply weird. Not just with regards to your sexual orientation. But in a more systemic way.

Perhaps you are someone who, for some inexplicable reason, simply needs to go to west Alameda. Nobody understands why. Just ignore them. And go to west Alameda!

Verbatim! By which I mean, in a figurative or metaphorical sense. Because seriously, there isn't a whole lot going on in west Alameda. They don't even have a BART station. So why not try moving to downtown Oakland instead?

17. Ethical Slut vs. Confused Slut

So then you go back to the world of dating men. Which superficially sounds way easier than dating women, if for no other reason than your dating pool becomes significantly larger. But the problem is, you are no longer the same person that you used to be way back when you were last actively dating members of the male persuasion. Because now you have a lesbian history—or "herstory," I suppose, if you're going to be a stickler about it. And that doesn't simply go away just because you identify as bisexual now. And you've learned so much from your previous immersion in queer culture—far more than the superficial signifiers of queerness that everybody else thinks are so important, but you and Saussure beg to differ.

For starters, by now you have read books by queer theorists who argue that gender is merely a social construct (much unlike ice cream). In other words, it's just a bunch of arbitrary rules and conventions that we all follow. But we don't have to. We can bend these rules. Or break them. Bend and/or break them. And you have also read books by sex-positive feminists who taught you to not be ashamed of your sexual body and desires, and that all forms of sexuality can be beautiful, provided that they are consensual.

To you, all of these ideas now seem like basic common sense. And when you date people of the female persuasion, they are generally queer, or at least queer-ish, and therefore likely already familiar with these concepts. So it will not be at all unusual if, over dessert on your first date, the two of you discuss sexual preferences, boundaries, kinks, and enthusiastic consent, before you've even shared your first kiss.

But the men you date, by and large, have not had a lesbian herstory like you have. In fact, many them haven't even been exposed to the aforementioned feminist and queer concepts that you now take for granted. And for this reason, they will often behave in ways that seem utterly illogical to you.

Take for instance, Eric #29. I immediately had reservations about our date when he showed up wearing a backwards baseball cap, polo shirt, and cargo shorts. He struck me as the type of guy who, a decade or two ago, would have never in a million years considered moving to San Francisco. But nowadays, these sorts of ex-fraternity business-major types flock here in droves due to all the tech company jobs and money to be made.

Eric #29 and I had very little in common, but since he was seemingly into sports, I brought up the subject of baseball. I knew there was going to be trouble when he asked: Wow, how did you learn so much about baseball?

Me: I don't know *that* much. I'm not an expert or anything.

Eric: Well, you sure do know a lot for a girl. So who taught you then?

Me: Um, no one. I just follow it. You know, I watch games. I read articles.

Eric: So who is your favorite player?

Me: Let's see. I like Bryce Harper . . .

Eric: That guy is a total cocksucker.

Me: Oh, so you like him then?

Eric: What? No! I'm just saying that that guy can go suck my dick.

Me: Which is a good thing, right?

Eric: God no!

Me: Oh, so you don't enjoy receiving oral sex then? Are you stone?

Eric: No, of course I like oral sex.

Me: Then why would you use "cocksucker" in a derogatory fashion? I mean, who's going to want to suck your dick if you make it sound like such a horrible thing? It seems like such a disincentive.

Eric: I was just saying that Bryce Harper is a pussy, is all.

Me: And that's a bad thing?

Eric: Yeah.

Me: Oh, so you must be gay then. Funny, I thought your online profile listed you as heterosexual.

Eric: I'm not fucking gay! I'm totally straight.

Me: But if you are attracted to women's bodies, and if women's genitals excite you in a pleasurable way, shouldn't "pussy" be like the highest compliment you could pay someone? Like, when your favorite football team scores a touchdown, shouldn't you be joyously shouting out "vagina!" at the TV?

Eric: What are you, some kind of feminist?

Me: Do you have a problem with feminists?

Eric: Yeah, of course I do. They're a bunch of man-haters.

Me: Sure, there are a few Valerie Solanas-types out there. But the majority of women who call themselves feminists actually partner and have sex with men. In other words, most of us are literally man-lovers, not man-haters. In fact, you could make the case that men like yourself—straight guys who wouldn't be caught dead making love to another man—are the real man-haters.

Eric: You call yourself a man-lover, but what you really mean is that you're a slut.

Me: Yes, I am a slut. An ethical one. And you are a confused slut.

Eric: What do you mean by that?

Me: I'll show you: Do you want to go back to my place and have sex?

Eric: Seriously?

Me: Seriously.

Eric: Sure.

Me: Okay, so a moment ago, when you called me a slut, you made it sound like this awful thing, like you were condemning me and all other women who enjoy having lots of sex. But then you jumped at the chance to have sex with me, which means that you secretly wish there were more women like me who were open to the possibility of having casual sex. You seem oblivious to the obvious fact that far more women would be open to having casual sex with men if it weren't for people like yourself going around slut-shaming us all the time!

Or, to put it a different way: You are a man who seemingly wants to have lots of sex on the one hand, but who simultaneously harbors highly negative attitudes toward genitals, sexual acts, and people who openly express their sexuality. Ergo, you are a confused slut.

Eric: So does this mean that we're not going to have sex then?

Me: "You get nothing! You lose! Good day, sir!"

18. I've Misplaced Chekhov's Gun

I am like the worst person to watch TV shows and movies with. It's because of all those damned how-to-write-a-novel books that I read way back when I thought that I could actually become a real novelist, rather than a faux one. See, those writer's books teach you all these supposed rules regarding how to tell a proper story. And it turns out that nearly everybody follows these rules to a T.

So when Matilda and I sit down in front of the TV to watch her favorite hospital procedural drama, she will be shocked by, and become highly concerned about, the huge argument that two of her favorite characters are having. She may even exclaim, "Oh no, I can't bear to watch!" In contrast, I will be all calm, cool, and collected, because I know that the writers have simply decided to put these two characters into conflict because (as those writer's books repeatedly insist) this is what needs to happen in order to move the plot forward.

And then the show will introduce us viewers to a twelve-year-old leukemia patient, and this child's story will be so tragic that Matilda will be on the verge of crying. But I know better than to become emotionally invested in this character. Because they are merely a "MacGuffin"—a term these writer's books use to describe an object that the main characters pursue or obsess over, but which is not important to the story in and of itself. In other words, it doesn't matter whether this character is a twelve-year-old child with cancer, or a thirty-six-year-old classical pianist who injured their hand in a horrible car accident, or a sixty-one-year-old librarian with a rare brain disease. If they die, then it's no big deal, because that hospital is literally filled to the brim with MacGuffins! All that matters is that Matilda's two favorite characters—while working together to cure one of these many MacGuffins—learn to resolve their differences, or alternatively, finally decide to break up once and for all.

Here's another thing that often happens: Early on in the show, some character will nonchalantly mention that they have a flight to catch later that day, and I'll blurt out: *They are going to die in a plane crash!* Or another character will say something unremarkable like, "Hey, I like your earrings," and I will exclaim: *She's going to find those earrings in so-and-so's apartment later in the show, and she will assume that the two of them are having an affair!* And these things will ultimately come to pass, and Matilda will be like, "How did you know that was going to happen?" And I'll assure her that it's not because I am prescient. It's simply because all those writer's books invariably instruct you to keep your story tight and to avoid any superfluous information. And while this may sound like sage advice on the surface, what often goes unmentioned is that strictly following this rule will inevitably make your story incredibly predictable. Because as soon as you mention that there is a gun hanging up on the wall, everybody like me—aka, those of us who have read all these writer's books and know all these rules—will be expecting that gun to be fired at some point later on.

One of the distinct advantages of being a faux novelist (rather than a real one) is that I am not bound by any of these writer's-book conventions. Take for instance that tube of lidocaine that I was searching for back in Chapter 8, when I ended up stumbling upon that old roll of duct tape. I'll bet you that all the writer's-book people have since been feverishly wondering about when and how I am going work that lidocaine back into the story. They may even envision some climactic scene wherein I eventually confront my arch nemesis (who is likely named Eric): He is pointing his gun at my head, but then I miraculously disarm him by pulling that tube of lidocaine out of my purse and squirting it into his eyes, thereby numbing his vision.

But the joke is on you, writer's-book people! Because that tube of lidocaine was superfluous information. And it is *not* making any reappearance in this book. No way, no how. No siree. Other than me referencing it again here in this chapter. Which I suppose is sort of a reappearance. Albeit a lackluster one.

And I'm sure that many of the writer's-book people have been trying to analyze this book using Joseph Campbell's concept of "monomyth" or "hero's journey," which has all these defined stages: The story always begins in an ordinary world, then there is a call to adventure, then after accepting said call our hero enters into an unknown world, where they find a mentor and some allies, then they go through all these various tests, leading up to some supreme ordeal, after which they return home with an elixir of some sort. And I can imagine all of these writer's-book people presuming that my inability to write a proper novel (as expressed in the first chapter of this book) was the so-called "call to action" that brought me into this unknown world of dating Erics. And they are likely to view Matilda, Eric #3, and Gabriella as my allies on this journey. And so on.

But guess what. Dating people named Eric is not some kind of unknown world—this is all taking place right here in the San Francisco Bay Area, where I have lived for many years. Plus, I already knew Matilda, Eric #3, and Gabriella well before I even embarked on this so-called journey. And if you scour the pages of this book, I can assure you that you will find absolutely no mentors whatsoever: I am perfectly capable of dating ninety-nine Erics without anyone else's help, much like I am able to understand baseball without requiring some sort of "father figure" to show me the way.

And the only elixirs in this story are the numerous pints of IPA that I mention over the course of this book. But I don't return home with them. Instead, I simply drink them in random chapters, whenever they are served to me.

I have nothing against plot. But I don't understand why all the other elements in a story—setting, character, point of view, theme, style, tone, and possibly other elements that I once learned in seventh-grade English class, but have since forgotten—have to take a backseat to the plot. Can't a character simply be interesting or entertaining *for the sake of being interesting or entertaining,* without being subjected to conflict in every chapter? Can't we appreciate our protagonist's witty dialogue and silly internal thought processes, even though she is simply sitting in some bar or restaurant talking to Eric-number-fill-in-the-blank, who is not in any way important to the story, because let's face it, *all of these Erics are MacGuffins!?* Can't we simply marvel at how effortlessly Kat Cataclysm slips into second-person-limited point of view from time to time, in a way that brings people into her world rather than alienating them?

Instead of dissecting the real or imagined "plot" of this book, can't we take a moment to consider its theme? Is the theme of this book Kat versus man? Or Kat versus nature? Or Kat versus self?

Wait a minute. All of those themes involve conflict. Which the writer's books claim moves the plot forward. Hmmm. It seems as though all of these story elements are somehow interconnected.

Who knew?

19. Shopping Carts, Part One

The best orgasm that I've ever experienced happened in a dream. Which probably sounds pretty depressing at first, as if all my real-life sexual experiences were so pathetic that they paled in comparison to this one dream. But in actuality, the opposite is true: The dream orgasm was so unbelievably intense that it lit off virtually every single nerve cell in my entire body! I woke up absolutely euphoric!

And from that point on, I committed myself to a singular life goal: More dream orgasms please!

But the problem is, you can't just conjure up dream orgasms at will. Because, by definition, they only happen when you are dreaming. And when you are dreaming, you are not quite the same person—you are "dream you" rather than "awake you." And while awake you is constantly scheming about how to create more fantastic dream orgasms, dream you is preoccupied with her face at the moment. Because once again, she has made the mistake of looking directly into the dream mirror. And by now, she really should know that whatever you see in the dream mirror will only ever get worse. This time, she has noticed a blemish on her face, and the longer she stared at it, the bigger it got, until ultimately it turned into this giant tumor. As if she needed skin cancer again! And now she's trying to figure out what doctor to call, because she can't quite remember words like "dermatologist" or "oncologist" at the moment, because she is not very smart, as evidenced by the fact that she doesn't have the basic common sense to *not* look directly into the dream mirror.

Dream you never learns.

So how do you teach dream you—who let's face it, is not the sharpest tool in the toolshed—to stop looking into dream mirrors, and start having more dream orgasms? Well, you can't really. Because dream you is really bad with setting and achieving goals. Like, really really bad. Like, way worse than awake you. And that's not saying much.

No, dream you cannot be trusted with this mission. It is far too important. You—by which I mean awake you—are going to have to take over mid-dream.

In other words, you need to become a lucid dreamer.

So you search the internet, hoping to find a few tips on how to become lucid in your dreams. And there's a deluge of information out there: all sorts of different methods you can try, and tricks to prevent yourself from automatically waking up once you do become lucid. And after consuming all this material, you decide to try what seems to be the easiest of all strategies, namely, "reality checks." Basically, you train yourself to regularly question whether what you are experiencing is really happening, or whether it's just a dream. And if you make this a habit—something you do a multitude of times on a daily basis—then dream you will habitually do this too. And once dream you realizes that her reality check has failed, and that she is actually in a dream, then she will become lucid—aka, she turns into awake you. And then awake you seeks out all the dream orgasms!

But like I said, dream you is not so bright. She could be sitting on the couch with Eric #2 (who awake you hasn't seen in a zillion years) in your old apartment (even though it doesn't look anything like your old apartment) with your current cat Flutie M'lar on her lap (even though Flutie didn't come into your life until you met Matilda years later), and upon taking in her surroundings, she'd probably come to the conclusion: "Yep, everything here seems pretty normal and real to me!" So what you need is a fool-proof reality test: one that gives a clear-cut yes-or-no answer to the "am

I dreaming?" question, one that not even not-so-bright dream you can ignore.

What you need is a piece of paper. That you keep with you at all times. With a distinct set of words on it that you know by heart. Because when we are dreaming, if we stare at words for more than a few seconds, they will automatically start to morph into different words. This is what the internet says. So if, upon examining your reality check paper, it ever says anything other than the words that you've committed to memory, well then you, my friend, are clearly in a dream.

So now, because of your quest for dream orgasms, you regularly keep a folded piece of paper in your back pocket. And every so often, you pull it out and look at it. And when you do, it always says the same thing: *It's like "The Gift of the Magi," but only with shopping carts.* Which might seem like an odd thing for a piece of paper to say. Especially to signify "you are still in reality." But you chose these words because you've been convinced (for quite some time now) that this is the *funniest punchline ever.* The only problem is that you have yet to write the joke or story that can provide the proper setup for this once-in-a-lifetime punchline to reach its full potential. So in the meantime, at least you can use it for your reality check.

A few weeks after starting to make this reality check part of my daily routine, I went out on a date with Eric #31. He is a stand-up comedian who has made a name for himself on the local scene. I tell him that I write absurdist short fiction, and that some of my work is possibly probably fairly funny. If you ask me.

Apparently intrigued that we seemingly share humor in common, Eric #31 asked: Have you ever considered doing stand-up comedy before?

Me: I've considered trying it on numerous occasions. I even worked up a five-minute act at one point. But I talked myself out of it, on account of the fact that my material is probably a little too esoteric for most audiences.

Eric: You never know. One thing I've learned is to never underestimate comedy audiences—they are smarter than most people give them credit for.

Me: I think you give them too much credit.

Eric: How about this, why don't you run a few of your jokes by me. And I will give you constructive criticism.

Me: Okay, I suppose. I wrote a whole bunch of "walks into a bar" jokes for my act—I could maybe share some of those?

Eric: Sure, go for it!

Me: [clears throat] An anthropomorphism walks into a bar. Get it?

Eric: Yeah, that's kinda funny.

Me: A solipsist walks into a bar. Or perhaps it was merely an internal mental projection of some sort.

Eric: What's a solipsist?

Me: A paraprosdokian walks into a bar and no one gets the joke.

Eric: You probably shouldn't make fun of Paraprosdokians—the younger crowds don't go for ethnic jokes so much these days.

Me: A malapropism walks into a barn.

Eric: And then what happens? Wait a minute, did you say bar or barn?

Me: A Freudian slip walks in on its parents having sex—I mean a bar! Walks into a bar.

Eric: These sound like the sort of jokes your dorky tenth grade English teacher would tell. What's with all the literary references?

Me: I'm an ex-linguist.

Eric: An ex-linguist? You really shouldn't completely give up on language like that.

Me: So what type of comedy do you do?

Eric: Well, for a long time, I did observational humor—which I know is kind of overdone these days, but I added my own twist. See, lots of comedians focus their efforts on making witty observations about the world. But me, I dedicated myself to making *all the observations*, not just the witty ones. For instance, I would say, "Hey look, a chair." Or "This thing in my hand appears to be a microphone." Or "It seems as though no one is laughing right now." And so on. I was really a comedy pioneer of sorts—*Laugh Tracks* magazine called me the first "omni-observational comic" and *The San Francisco Chronicle* described me as ". . . if you put Steven Wright and Proust together in a blender, but mostly Proust came out. Only not nearly as literary."

Me: Wow, that's really something.

Eric: Yeah, thanks. But being a comedy pioneer and all, I didn't want to rest on my laurels—whatever laurels are . . .

Me: Trees. Laurels are a type of tree.

Eric: Oh. Well, I don't have any of those. But I did have a modicum of success. And I didn't want to rest on it. So I am trying to invent another new genre of comedy. I was noticing how, in recent years, there have been a lot of books and movies about vampires, demons, and zombies. And I thought "why not combine horror with comedy?" So I am working on some new material that is simultaneously scary and funny. Like, I have this one bit about a haunted grocery store. It's still a work in progress, but it's kind of like Edgar Allen Poe's "The Tell-Tale Heart," only with shopping carts.

I was stunned. Literally—in the literal sense of the word. Eric #31 had just uttered a phrase almost identical to my punchline-turned-reality-check, albeit sans O. Henry. It seemed so improbable. Nay, impossible! Improbable and/or impossible. I mean, what is the likelihood that someone else in the known universe would make shopping carts a central element in their comedy-routine-in-progress? And even if someone else *did* come up with a shopping cart premise, what is the likelihood that I would be on a date with that person? And that his name would be Eric to boot! Although most people I've been dating lately are named Eric, so I suppose this last bit isn't so surprising. But the rest is!

Then it hit me: Perhaps this was all a dream? After all, it's all too bizarre. Plus, I am inordinately obsessed with shopping carts and dating Erics, so it makes sense that both of these elements might manifest in my dreams.

So I reached for my reality-check paper.

But it wasn't there. Because I wasn't wearing any pants.

Normally, not wearing any pants while out in public would be yet another indication that I was in a dream. But on this occasion, I wasn't sporting pants because I was wearing a dress. Because I had just come from a job interview. Or at least, I think I did? Perhaps it was merely a dream job interview? But not for a dream job, rather a regular old job, just inside of a dream. In any case, like most dresses, this dress had no back pockets. Which is why I didn't bring my reality-check paper with me today.

Then it occurred to me that, without my reality check paper, I had absolutely no way of knowing for sure whether this was a dream or real life! And if it was a dream, then that would mean that I am dream me (not awake me), and therefore, not so bright. Given this possibility, I simply could not trust myself to make rational decisions on my own behalf. So I thought for a moment: What would awake me do right now?

The answer was clear: Seek out dream orgasms, of course!

Eric #31's voice chimed in: Excuse me, are you alright? You suddenly got quiet.

Me: No, I'm fine. Just fine. Hey listen, I would really like to have sex right now. Would you happen to be up for that?

Eric: Um, really? Seriously?

Me: Yes.

Eric: Um, sure, I guess.

Me: Sorry, that's not good enough. I only have sex with people who enthusiastically consent.

Eric: Oh, of course, yes. Yes, I will have sex with you. Enthusiastically! My place is just a couple of blocks away if you want to . . .

Me: Yes, that would be perfect!

The couple-block walk to Eric #31's place seemed to take an eternity, as I was concerned that I would wake up before we even got there. So I rubbed my hands together and did simple math problems in my head. This is what the internet says to do when you become lucid, in order to stay in the dream. And it seemed to be working, as I was still in the dream as we entered Eric's apartment. He showed me to his bedroom, and soon enough we were making out and taking off one another's clothes.

Unexpectedly, Eric exclaimed, "Fuck!"

Me: Yes, that is what we are going to do. We are going to fuck now.

Eric: No, I mean fuck, I ran out of condoms recently, and I just realized that I forgot to pick up more.

Me: No worries, I stopped by Lady Parts earlier on in the book, so I have some with me. Because apparently, I'm like that woman in the song "Little Red Corvette" who has a pocket full of condoms on her person. Except that I don't actually have any pockets because I wore a dress today. Also, unlike in that song, none of these condoms are used, nor are they Trojans, and even if they were, I wouldn't refer to them as "horses," because Trojans are not horses—they are simply the people who inhabited the ancient city of Troy. Nor would I refer to the men who donned said condoms as "jockeys," because like, what a weird-ass metaphor! Who would write such a thing?

Eric: Prince. I believe that Prince wrote such a thing. But hey, could we not parse lyrics right now? I need to concentrate.

Me: Oh, yeah, sure.

So then we engaged in penetration sex. And it was all fine and dandy. But sadly, there were no dream orgasms. At least not yet.

Me: Hey Eric, I don't think that I'm going to come this way. How about trying to stimulate me manually?

Eric: Okay. How's that?

Me: Yeah. Oh, yeah, that's much better.

Eric: May I ask, what are you doing with your hands?

Me: Rubbing them together. So that I don't wake up.

Eric: Wake up? But you are awake.

Me: No, I'm not awake per se. I am lucid. Because this is a lucid dream.

Eric: No, it's not. This is real.

Me: That's exactly what a dream extra would say. So I don't believe you. And, okay, I think I'm close. Faster please. Okay, here it . . . uuuuh, aaaaah, oh oh oh oh oh, oh no . . . fuck.

Eric: What just happened? Did you come?

Me: Yeah. But it was just a small baby orgasm. Not a big gargantuan dream orgasm.

Eric: Well, like I said, this isn't a dream. It's real. So it's no surprise that you didn't have a dream orgasm. Plus, all that hand-rubbing you were doing probably distracted you, preventing you from achieving a bigger orgasm.

Me: Yeah, you're probably right. That and the math problems.

Eric: Math problems?

Me: Yes, I was doing simple arithmetic in my head. In order to try to stay in the lucid dream.

Eric: Yeah, math and sex are mortal enemies. They never go together.

Me: Well, except for when people have math-sex.

Eric: Ugh, don't even get me started about math-sex!

Me: You know what? It just occurred to me that what just happened—me having awake sex with you when I thought it was dream sex—would make for a great comedy bit. I mean, it already has mistaken circumstances and punchy dialogue. All it needs now is a killer punchline.

Eric: How about: *It's like "Gift of the Magi," but only with shopping carts?*

Me: That doesn't really work because . . . wait a second, how do you know about that punchline? Unless you're not really you, but rather you're me. Which means that this is a dream after all!

Eric: Actually, you were whispering that phrase at one point while we were having sex. And I thought that it would make for a really clever punchline.

Me: Wow, I never realized that I unconsciously whisper potential punchlines during sex. Good thing too, because it would have been such a cop-out if I were to have ended this chapter with some "it was all just a dream" bullshit.

20. Content

Some readers may have been surprised last chapter when I mentioned going on a job interview. I can imagine some of you asking, "But Kat, I thought you made a living writing absurdist short stories and faux novels?"

To which I reply: "Ha!"

Nobody makes a living writing fiction. Well, unless you're the likes of J. K. Rowling, or George R. R. Martin, or a select few other novelists who disproportionately sport two initials in their names. And I don't even have one initial in my name, let alone two!

So while I technically "write for a living," what this means in reality is that I am financially dependent on other people paying me (not so handsomely, I might add) to write stuff on their behalf. And they don't just want any old thing that I write. No, they specifically want *content*. By which I mean internet content: the types of pieces that will pop up in people's web searches and social media feeds, and which will entice them to *click on the link!* Because the more click-throughs the piece generates, the more advertising revenue the media outlet makes. Which is how they can afford to pay me (albeit not so handsomely).

After a few years of freelancing, I decided to seek out more steady work. Through the grapevine, I heard about a new San Francisco-based tech-slash-media start-up called CliqueClick. Their website (which is another form of internet content) described them as: "Changing people's lives via a proprietary algorithm that optimizes social media sharing and trending content allocation."

And I had absolutely no idea what that meant. But their website also said that they were hiring writers, so I applied.

That was the interview I went to on the date of my date with Eric #31. And I ultimately landed the job.

I remember Brittany, the vice president of CliqueClick, taking me out to breakfast the morning of my first day of work. She shared with me the company's unflinching vision of "disrupting" the traditional news media model—you know, where news providers view themselves as "gatekeepers" who determine which stories and events are relevant and worth covering, and they expect audiences to passively "consume" this information. No, at CliqueClick, we recognize that individual users will inevitably differ in their tastes and interests, and that the news and information they receive should reflect these preferences. And we also understand that we cannot possibly know these individual users better than the people in their own lives: their family, friends, acquaintances, co-workers, etcetera. So what we do at CliqueClick—as News Facilitators™—is mine social media data in order to figure out how to tailor people's news and media feeds to best fit their families' and friends' preconceived notions of them.

Brittany also went on at great length about how she thinks that Brad, the head of the Algorithm Outreach Department, has a crush on her, but she fears that he's too introverted to ask her out, so she asked Monica from the Product Placement Integration Department to tell Clambake (yes that's his name—he's a programmer friend of Brad's) that Brittany would totally say yes if Brad were to ask her out.

Now at this point, you (dear readers) are likely dying to ask one of the following two questions:

1) Oh my god, your vice president acts like she is in high school. How old is she?

Well, um, twenty-three. Which is admittedly too old to be acting like a high schooler, but way too young to be the vice president of a company. But like I said, CliqueClick is dedicated to disrupting traditional business models. This includes the belief that company executives should have many years of prior experience under their belts.

2) I can't believe that your company even has a "vice" president—literally, a president in charge of wicked and immoral behaviors! Criminy!

I know, tell me about it! But all the tech companies have to compete against one another for employees, so they often do it via perks: They'll offer free food, do your laundry on site, provide a gym or an arcade room, and so on. So CliqueClick decided to top them all by offering to cater to employees' vices right there in the workplace. So when the algorithm outreach engineers need a break, they can go to the "vice room" and bet on sporting events, perform human sacrifices, and/or get massages that are really hand-jobs. From what I hear, they have an amazing selection of IPAs in the vice room. But I was never allowed in. Because I am merely a writer. And writers are not considered full employees, but rather "independent contractors" who just so happen to work forty hours a week "on campus" (which is what they call their workplace, even though it's not even a college).

This way, they are able to avoid covering benefits for workers whom they consider replaceable. Such as writers like me.

Anyway, after breakfast, Brittney introduced me to everyone in the Word Repurposing (aka, writing) Department. Our department was split into different teams. One team wrote brief summaries of each and every news story that day, so that we would always come up somewhere in online searches, no matter what the topic. Then we had another team that covered how people (whether they be politicians, celebrities, or random nobodies on social media) were reacting to these daily news stories. Yet another team covered other people's reactions to these reactions. And so on. Still other teams focused on churning out animated GIFs, exploiting the latest online memes, and scouring the internet for cute and/or humorous pictures and videos, primarily of animals and (to a lesser extent) human children.

Finally, I was part of the "slideshow and listicle" team, where our job was to invent lists that (if we have done our jobs correctly) people would feel compelled to click on. You know, things like, "Seven supermodels you won't believe are married to octogenarians," or "Eleven hip-hop artists you would never guess were originally from West Virginia," or "The seventeen most unrealistic uses of The Force in the latest *Star Wars* movie."

This seems like it would be easy and fun work, but it's actually far more grueling than you might imagine. For one thing, these sorts of listicles appear everywhere online, so it's really hard to come up with novel topics that haven't already been done to death. Second, according to the CliqueClick Style Guide, the list length can't be just any random amount, because our Consumerism Psychology Department has scientifically determined that prime numbers entice 11.2 percent more click-throughs than non-prime numbers. Which seems ridiculous to me. I mean, *what's so special about prime numbers?!*

Take, for instance, the number two. Sure, it's a prime number, but that doesn't make it indivisible or invincible by any means. Like, you can totally divide the number two by 1.6, and you get 1.25—both of which are perfectly fine numbers. But apparently, these numbers don't count when it comes to determining primes because they are not considered to be "integers." Which totally sucks for 1.6 and 1.25, but hey, at least they are "rational numbers," unlike numbers like the square root of two, which mathematicians call "irrational." Which sucks for the square root of two, but at least it's considered to be a "real number," unlike the square root of negative one, which my high school math teacher said was an "imaginary number," despite the fact that it often arises in real-life math problems. Don't ask me how that works.

In fact, the more I think about it, the more oppressive

mathematics seems to be. It's like this entire field of inquiry that is central to science and engineering—sure, I'll grant you that—but on the other hand, it seems utterly committed to reinforcing all these hierarchies: Real numbers are more valid than imaginary ones, irrational numbers are less worthy than rational ones, integers are superior to fractions, and prime numbers generate more click-throughs than non-primes.

I hate you math! Even though, earlier in this book, I proclaimed that I love math. It is a love-hate relationship. Between math and me.

Wait a minute, where was I? Oh yeah, my job at CliqueClick.

One day we had a company function, you know, to encourage all the employees to get to know one another. Even though some of us are considered to be "contractors" rather than actual employees—*don't get me started on hierarchies again!* Anyway, it was there that I was introduced to Eric #37. And I just had to date him, of course.

So after the shindig, I asked Brittany (our vice president) if she could ask Brad (who was now her boyfriend by this point) to drop word to his underlings in the Algorithm Outreach Department (where Eric worked) that I was potentially interested in Eric. That way, the word might spread to Eric, and he might ask me out.

Which he did. Which is how he came to be Eric #37.

We went out for drinks together after work. I offered to buy the first round of IPAs (which he also enjoys—in fact, he said it was his second favorite vice in the vice room). After I purchased our beverages, Eric #37 said to me: So was that a lottery ticket I saw in your wallet?

Me: Um, yeah.

Eric: You know, your chances of winning the lottery are literally zero.

Me: They're not literally zero. They are verbatim zero. By which I mean: almost, but not quite, zero.

Eric: I'm just saying that it's not rational to play the lottery. You're wasting your money.

Me: Are you calling me irrational then? Like the square root of two? Or π or e? And other such numbers?

Eric: I suppose.

Me: Look, I don't play the lottery because I think I have a good shot of winning. In fact, I'm pretty sure that nobody who plays the lottery thinks that their chances of winning are reasonable. Most of us play the lottery because we are financially struggling. I've been just barely making ends meet my entire adult life. And there's seemingly no end in sight. So every now and again, I will surrender one dollar for the opportunity to occasionally fantasize about what my life might be like if I didn't have to constantly worry about how I was going to pay bill X, or how I couldn't afford item Y.

Eric: But what if, instead of wasting that money on the lottery, you saved it?

Me: The interest rate on savings accounts these days is like 0.05% or less. So if I saved that dollar, it would accrue hundredths of a penny per year. It really doesn't seem worth it to me.

Eric: Oh well, at least you have all your CliqueClick stock options.

Me: What stock options? I don't even get basic health coverage here!

Eric: Oh.

Me: Look, the two of us are most likely numerous tax brackets apart, so it's probably best that we not talk about any money-related matters. Instead, why don't you tell me what you do.

Eric: I work as a programmer in the Algorithm Outreach Department here.

Me: I know that. But what do you do in your spare time?

Eric: What spare time? I'm here all the time. In fact, most nights, I sleep in the vice room. That's my number one favorite vice: sleep.

Me: Sleep isn't a vice. It's a necessary biological function.

Eric: Actually, I sleep much better here than I do when I go home. Because when I stay here, I don't have to deal with my ptosomaphobia.

Me: What a bizarre word. How do you pronounce it?

Eric: Ptosomaphobia.

Me: But what does that mean?

Eric: *How can you possibly not know what ptosomaphobia is?!*

Me: Um . . . I will now play my Young and Impressionable card. Which I have been saving ever since Chapter 15, "Easter Eggs." And which comes with +3 points for optimism, but -2 points for critical thinking.

Eric: Young and impressionable? You don't seem *that* young. I mean, I'm twenty-four and I'm pretty certain that you're older than me. Actually, come to think of it, how old are?

Me: I'm not allowed to say. My editor Mario insists that I not reveal that. Because so long as I remain somewhere vaguely in the mid-twenties to mid-forties range, my absurdist, sex-positive, yet highly confessional faux novel will appeal to the largest possible demographic. According to him. But anyway, what is ptosomaphobia?

Eric: It's the fear of falling bodies. See, whenever I am outdoors, I am constantly worried about things falling on top of me.

Me: What kinds of things?

Eric: You know: Meteors. Boulders. Airplanes. Helicopters. Gliders. Cranes . . .

Me: The birds?

Eric: No silly, the construction cranes. Although I occasionally worry about falling birds too. And helium balloons, once the helium runs out. Golf balls. Coins. Cufflinks. People . . .

Me: People? How could a person ever possibly fall from the sky and land on top of you?

Eric: Do you know anyone who is afraid of heights?

Me: Yeah, lots of people. Including me.

Eric: And why are you afraid of heights?

Me: Well, because I'm worried that I might possibly fall.

Eric: Precisely. And if being afraid of falling from a great height is a rational fear, then doesn't it follow that worrying about the possibility that one of these afraid-of-heights people might actually fall and land on top of you qualify as a rational fear as well?

Me: No. At least not according to my calculations.

Eric: Well, your calculator must be wrong.

Me: I don't use a calculator. I do it all in my head. Because I have a love-hate relationship with math.

Eric: Wow, you must really be a nerd!

Me: I'm not a nerd.

Eric: But I meant that in a good way. I'm a nerd too. Most of us here at CliqueClick are nerds!

Me: And that's precisely why I refuse to call myself a nerd. It used to be that "nerd" referred to someone who was socially ostracized because most people viewed their hobbies and interests as odd or esoteric. The average person back then didn't know or care much about computers, or science fiction and fantasy, or mathematics. So if you were into any of those things, you would be labeled with the pejorative "nerd." But nowadays, the world is very different: Many of us use computers daily, and *Games of Thrones* is the most talked about TV show, and everybody's dying to hear Nate Silver's latest statistical analysis of the upcoming election. In other words, all of these formerly "nerdy" things are popular now.

Yet despite this fact, many people—including powerful, wealthy, and/or prominent figures such as tech CEOs, comedians and television personalities, cable news anchors, sports writers, financial analysts, and acclaimed academics—still go around proudly calling themselves "nerds," as if they were some kind of oppressed minority. On top of that, some people seem to use the term "nerd" to insinuate that they are intellectually superior to the masses, or to insist that their interest in a particular video game or sci-fi universe is more authentic than those who take a more passing interest. It's all about reinforcing hierarchies. And it's all pretty gross, if you ask me.

Eric: Well, if you don't identify as a nerd, what do you identify as?

Me: I am a weirdo, I guess. Unlike "nerd," the word "weirdo" doesn't signal affiliation with any particular hobby, interest, or occupation. Nor does it imply that my interests are more authentic or superior than anyone else's. "Weirdo" simply means that I am someone who marches to the beat of my own drummer. I am someone who, for some inexplicable reason, simply needs to go to west Alameda. Even though nobody understands why. Does that make sense?

Eric: Sure. Everything except for the west Alameda part. But you do realize that someday, some people are going to appropriate the term "weirdo" in much the same way that they co-opted the word "nerd."

Me: If that happens, I suppose I will need to find something else to call myself instead. "Dorkball" perhaps?

Eric: This has been an interesting conversation and all, but it's probably time for me to play my Heading Home for the Evening card, which comes with +2 points for sleeping in my own bed for a change, but -5 points for grappling with my ptosomaphobia.

Me: Fair enough.

We both stepped out of the bar and onto the street. As we were saying our goodbyes, something fell from the sky and shattered on the sidewalk right beside us.

Eric: Holy crap, that was a close call! What the hell was that?!

Me: From the looks of it, I think it might have been a sand dollar.

Eric: A sand dollar? I've imagined lots of things falling from the sky, but never marine life! I thought I was relatively safe from aquatic organisms due to their propensity to be under water most of the time. But this incident brings all of that into question now!

Me: Actually, now that I think about it, I believe that Eric #13 lives in this neighborhood. He literally collects sand dollars. I remember him saying that, after collecting them on Ocean Beach, he would let them dry on his windowsill. Maybe one of them . . .

Before I could finish my sentence, an actual human being fell from the sky (or more precisely, from a second floor window) and landed on top of Eric #37. Once I caught a glimpse of this fallen stranger's face, my suspicions were confirmed: It was Eric #13. Both Erics screamed in agony, which I took as a good sign. Because, despite the likelihood of multiple broken bones, they were both literally alive and kicking.

So I like, called 911.

Twenty minutes later, as the paramedics were tending to both Erics' contusions and fractures, I contemplated the unlikelihood of this entire episode. I mean, what are the chances that 1) I would secure a full-time job, albeit one where I am deemed merely an "independent contractor," 2) one of my previous Erics would fall out of his apartment window while tending to his sand dollar collection while I just so happened to be in his neighborhood, and 3) he would land on top of yet another one of my Erics who I had only recently met at my new workplace, and who coincidentally— nay, ironically!—suffers from ptosomaphobia?

According to my calculations: zero. And not just zero verbatim. But like literally zero.

21. Punching vs. Sprucing

I am never quite sure whether I should "punch up" or "spruce up" the language.

So rather than putting the finishing touches on this piece and submitting it for publication, I've instead decided to pour myself a glass of wine, take the last remaining Percocet from my scar revision surgery two years ago, stare at the textured patterns in my stucco ceiling, and contemplate all the (if you ask me, quite significant) differing implications of "punching" versus "sprucing" up language as it applies to my forthcoming listicle about the thirteen most provocative dresses worn at this year's Academy Awards. Which will soon be heavily shared and/or linked to on a plethora of pop culture, and/or fashion, and/or entertainment, and/or Hollywood gossip, and/or serious news outlets desperate for advertising revenue, websites near you.

But not until I finish the damned thing.

22. Banana Slug of a Different Color

It was the worst possible time to be out on a date with Eric #41. Because earlier that day, I overheard someone at work mention that they went to college at UC Santa Cruz, and that their school mascot was the banana slug. And I thought to myself: How whimsical! What an unlikely creature to be a mascot! Are they even a real animal? If so, do they really look like bananas?

So while killing time on the internet just before said date with Eric #41, I searched for "banana slug." And one webpage led to another. And then another.

And now I am scarred for life.

It started out innocently enough. First, I learned that, like many animals, banana slugs are hermaphroditic, meaning they have both female and male reproductive systems. And it turns out that they also have these enormous corkscrew-shaped penises, which are often longer than the entire length of their body, and which emerge from a genital pore just near their heads. And then I read that when two banana slugs have sex, it typically involves simultaneous double penetration. But because their penises are so large, they often get stuck inside of their partner, and sometimes it can take up to several hours before they can disengage. Which is why banana slugs sometimes resort to *apophallation*—the scientific term for when one slug chews off their mate's penis after sex, thereby allowing them to finally separate. After which point, the aphallic (aka, penis-less) slug can still mate, but only as female rather than a doubly-genitaled hermaphrodite.

So now, here I am, sitting at a bar, sharing a drink with Eric #41. And I'm trying to make small talk, but honestly, the only thing that I can think about is what the world would be like if human beings mated like banana slugs.

For starters, it would mean that our genitals would be really close to our heads. This head-to-genital proximity would no doubt create dilemmas for the fashion industry. I mean, just imagine what hats might look like!

Second, it would mean that we could have double-penetration sex. Which sounds awesome at first—twice the fun, right? But surely it would be far more complicated than it sounds. I mean, we'd all have to be excellent multitaskers, as it must take oodles of concentration and coordination to competently perform these two sexual acts simultaneously.

Then once you've done the deed, you couldn't just say, "Sorry, I have to get up for work early tomorrow," and whisk off. No, the two of you would likely be stuck together for quite some time, as you both attempt to retract your large corkscrew-like penises out from inside one another. I'm sure it would be endlessly frustrating and exhausting. And you'd be so tempted to simply devour your lover's penis and be done with it. But you can't just do that. I mean, surely social etiquette would have developed regarding the proper amount of time one has to wait before apophallation would be warranted. Like, if it had only been five or ten minutes of attempted disengagement, then no way, no how—you'd have to give them more time than that. But after an hour, or two, or more, of not being able to separate, well then, at some point it seems like apophallation might be warranted.

But even then, you still might think twice before scarfing down your lover's penis. Because your penis is likely stuck inside of them as well. And as soon as you start chomping away at their bits, they will surely reciprocate. In other words, there would be this whole game theory aspect to having sex. It would be like the "prisoner's dilemma," but only with large corkscrew-like penises.

And eventually, you would have to come to terms with the fact that—if you continue to be a sexually-active banana-slug-like human being—at some point, your lover is going to eat your penis. There's no two ways about it. It's only a matter of time.

And after apophallation, you will be an aphallic banana-slug-like person for the rest of your life. And I'll bet you that some of the non-apophallized banana-slug-like people will likely start to look down on and make fun of you. Because you would now be a sexual minority. They might even invent horrible stories about aphallic people like yourself—for instance, claiming that you all blatantly disregard basic sexual etiquette and purposely chew off all of your lovers' penises, because now you have nothing left to lose. And while this is most definitely not true—it's merely a stereotype—others spread these rumors and hold this against you.

Come to think of it, you will likely spend years struggling with self-acceptance, having internalized many of these same horrible aphalliphobic attitudes yourself. But over time, you will eventually learn to overcome them, thanks in part to all the other aphallic banana-slug-like people that you have since met at the support groups and community gatherings. And naturally, you become active in the aphallic rights movement, and you show up to all the demonstrations, where you will proudly chant: "We're aphallic, we're here, get used to it!" Even though this does not rhyme. Not at all.

Eric #41: Hello, are you in there?

Me: What?

Eric: I said, "are you in there?" Because you seemed disengaged from the conversation.

Me: If only it were that easy to disengage . . . Oops, sorry. My mind was elsewhere.

Eric: Where was it?

Me: It was in a hypothetical alternate universe wherein human beings resembled banana slugs.

Eric: Ewww, gross. Now you've scarred me for life!

Me: I'm sorry.

Eric: Now I will never be able to shake the image of us all being that bright yellow color!

Me: Wait, what? What's so wrong with being bright yellow?

Eric: Yellow is the worst of all colors. THE WORST!

Me: Actually, I kind of like the color yellow. It's pretty. And soothing. Pretty soothing.

Eric: Are you kidding me? Yellow is an infamous boisterous thermonuclear burst of psychological awfulness.

Me: Are you sure we're talking about the same color?

Eric: Yes. Probably. I think.

Me: Because I remember as a child, lying in bed with insomnia, and obsessing over a philosophical problem that I incorrectly presumed that I was the first person to discover: What if we all perceive colors differently? And the color that I see and call "red" looks green to you? But because you were taught to associate this green-ish color with the English word "red," we both superficially seem to agree on what the color is, even though we experience it very differently.

And back when I was a kid, this seemed extremely troubling to me. But now, as an adult ex-linguist, it doesn't seem like such a big deal at all. I mean, while it remains a phenomenologically interesting question, pragmatically speaking it wouldn't make much of a difference. So long as we can agree that we are talking about the same thing (aka, a particular wavelength of light that we both call "red," or in the case of banana slugs "yellow"), we can engage in thoughtful and productive conversations about it, even if we experience it differently or have conflicting opinions about it.

Eric: Agreed! Thoughtful discussion is like the jagged yet ragged steam engine of lexicological necessity!

Me: The real problem, if you ask me, is when people use the same word to refer to very different things. Like, it would be impossible for the two of us to have a useful conversation about "sex" if for you the word exclusively refers to man-on-top, woman-on-bottom penetration sex, whereas for me it conjures up memories of being fisted by my girlfriend.

Eric: Or if the word "sex" leads you to obsess over banana slug apophallation, but causes me to thoughtfully ponder anglerfish mating practices.

Me: How do anglerfish mate?

Eric: Well, unlike the hermaphroditic banana slug, anglerfish have traditional male and female sexes. Except that the males are extremely small and almost completely useless. In fact, the only thing that male anglerfish are capable of doing is seeking out the much larger females of their species. And when they find one, they will bite into her. And the enzymes in the male's mouth will dissolve her tissue and cause both of their flesh and circulatory systems to permanently fuse. From that point forward, the vestigial male is merely a small sperm-providing protrusion that sticks out of the female.

Me: Great, now I'm scarred for life. Yet again. Twice in one day!

Eric: Scars are like the tiny dainty daily reminders of physiological reality!

Me: Why do you keep doing that?

Eric: Doing what?

Me: Saying those things.

Eric: Saying what things? Words? *You want me to stop using words?!*

Me: Not words per se. But those odd sayings you keep saying. You know, those shallow yet hollow collections of sesquipedalian senselessness—things like that.

Eric: Oh, you must be referring to my metaphorulations.

Me: What's a metaphorulation?

Eric: It's a neologism. That I created. To refer to my foreign foreboding forays of verboten verbosity.

Me: You may be weirder than me. It is a rare thing for me to say that.

Eric: Thanks, that means a lot to me.

Me: I guess my only question is: why? Why metaphorulations?

Eric: It is my distinguishing characteristic. The thing that makes me unique, that sets me apart from all other people. But this wasn't always my thing. Before metaphorulations, I was mostly known as the "baker's six-pack" guy.

Me: Baker's six-pack?

Eric: Yeah, you know how a baker's dozen is thirteen rather than twelve items? Well, whenever I would show up to a friend's party, I'd bring along seven beers and call it a "baker's six-pack." People found it hilarious! The first time, at least. On subsequent occasions, however, they would seem annoyed: They'd roll their eyes, make sarcastic remarks, and/or disinvite me from their party altogether. Over time, it became clear that I needed a new shtick. Hence the metaphorulations.

Me: Well okay then.

Eric: So what's your distinguishing characteristic? What makes you different from all other people?

Me: I don't know. There are lots of ways in which I am somewhat unusual—I primarily self-identify as an absurdist short fiction writer; I'm unduly concerned with the word patronizing being both a good and a bad thing; I am currently obsessed with the potential ramifications of banana-slug-like sex on human social interactions—but I very much doubt that I am the *only* person doing any of these things.

Eric: Then sorry, you must not be a unique person. You are merely another cookie-cutter person. Just like the rest of them.

Me: How about this: I'm probably the only person in the world who routinely and purposefully uses the word "verbatim" wrong.

Eric: To mean "approximately" rather than "word for word"?

Me: Exactly! How did you know?

Eric: Well, that's how my friend Eric uses it. Poor Eric. Still recovering from that bizarre accident involving a falling body that was an actual human body.

Me: But that's my Eric! Or one of my Erics. Specifically, #37. I work with him at CliqueClick. He learned to use "verbatim" like that from me.

Eric: You may have invented it. But now that it has started to catch on, you are no longer the only person doing that. Therefore, you are not unique.

Me: So let me get this straight: You're saying that, as soon as more than one person does something, that act is by definition no longer unique?

Eric. Precisely.

Me: Well then, check and mate! Because I now render you the founder albeit now floundering purveyor of pedantic shenanigans! Which is to say that, now that I've started using metaphorulations myself, you are no longer unique either.

Eric: Thanks a lot, you . . . jerk! You . . . useless parasitic male anglerfish! You . . . *YELLOW!!!*

23. For All Intents and Purposes

Honestly, my first reaction when Eric #41 called me "YELLOW" was to laugh. It just seemed like such a ridiculous attempt at insulting me! But then the more I thought about it, the more I questioned my response. To me, "yellow" is merely a pretty soothing color, so I took no offense to it. But then again, to him, few things are more awful than the color yellow. He meant it as this profound insult. So maybe I should have been offended? At least just a little?

And then I started thinking about what words I do get offended by or angry about. And I'm kind of all over the map with it. Like, if Eric #41 had called me a "bitch," I probably would have flipped out, because many times in the past, people have used that word to try to hurt or invalidate me. So for understandable reasons, I take offense to it. Even when my good friend Eric #3 says to me "Bitch, please!" in an obviously playful gay-guy sorta way, it will still bother me quite a bit, even though I know he's not trying to insult me.

But then again, there are still other potential slurs—like "dyke" or "slut"—that I've reclaimed and use in a positive way. If Matilda and I are holding hands walking down the street, and someone in a passing vehicle shouts "fucking dykes!" at us, I'll shout back "That's right, *we are fucking dykes!*" Or if some random dude-bro calls me a "slut," I will proudly say, "Yes, *I am a slut!* An ethical slut, whereas you are merely a confused slut!"

But the kicker is that other women will react completely differently: They will laugh off being called a bitch, but become offended if you call them a dyke or slut.

It's like, on the one hand, we are all speaking English, and we generally agree on the dictionary definitions of words. Yet at the same time, each of these words may evoke a completely different set of memories and meanings for us. Upon contemplating this, I realized that this book that I am now in the midst of writing (and that you are now in the midst of reading) is potentially full of thousands upon thousands of tiny little bombs that I don't know how to defuse! Because, while I may try my darndest to carefully and judiciously pick and choose my words, I can never know for sure whether some reader out there may find the words that I ultimately select (whether they be "verbatim," "Wonder Woman," "xylem," "yellow," or "Zyxxavxzy") to be objectionable or offensive.

This dilemma really hit home for me when I went out with Eric #43. We were sitting in a booth at Rudy's Can't Fail Cafe waiting for the waiter to serve us our brunch, when out of the blue Eric sniped: You know, I almost didn't go out with you.

Me: Okay . . . why not?

Eric: Because on your GoEros profile, you list yourself as bisexual.

Me: Yeah, a lot of people can't handle dating someone who doesn't limit their dating pool to a single gender.

Eric: No, it's not your sexual orientation that concerns me. It's the fact that you call yourself "bisexual." That word is really oppressive!

Me: What?

Eric: The word bisexual reinforces the gender binary—the notion that there are two, and only two, genders. Therefore it is oppressive to transgender people.

Me: But I know quite a few transgender people who call themselves bisexual, so they obviously don't think so. Plus, people have been identifying as bisexual for at least half a century now—you can't just one day decide that all these people have been asserting or implying that transgender people don't exist, when that has nothing to do with why any of us have chosen that label. On top of that, it's preposterous to take the prefix "bi" in bisexual so literally like that—it's akin to presuming that all gay men must be happy, or that all lesbians are from the island of Lesbos. Words don't work like that! They get their meanings through history and common usage.

Eric: I'm just saying that it is insensitive to others to call yourself bisexual. You should really use "pansexual" instead.

Me: Look, I have nothing against the word pansexual. But by your line of reasoning, I could argue that the word pansexual literally means being attracted to all people—every single one of them! Or it could mean being sexually aroused by certain types of cookware or cinematic maneuvers. Or perhaps it refers to attraction to people who are half-human half-goat, or to boys who won't grow up? Is that what you mean by pansexual? Because if so, that would be really fucked up!

Eric: No, not at all. Pansexual simply refers to people who don't limit their dating pool to a single gender.

Me: Which is precisely the same definition I used for bisexual several paragraphs ago. So rather than assume that either of these words are inherently objectionable or oppressive, we should consider the context in which they are used and the speaker's intent.

Just at that moment, the waiter arrived with our food. And as I took a bite of my Monster B.L.A.T., I thought about what I had just said. Particularly that last bit about the speaker's intent. It makes so much sense! I mean, in a world where we all react to words very differently, perhaps the best way to navigate this emotional Tower of Babel is for us to gauge the speaker's intent: We might take issue if they purposefully use a certain word disparagingly, but we might let the usage slide if their intentions do not seem malicious. And given this strategy, I could begin *99 Erics* with a disclaimer stating that nothing that I have written here is intended to hurt or demean anyone. That way readers will know not to be offended. It's ingenious!

Then Eric #43 chimed in: The other reason why I almost didn't go out with you is because of your profile photo. It is not very flattering, if you ask me.

Me: But I didn't ask you.

Eric: Have you ever considered wearing makeup?

Me: I do wear makeup sometimes. Like, for special occasions. But most days I don't.

Eric: Why not?

Me: Because of Sephora's box.

Eric: What's that?

Me: Well, wearing makeup everyday can be like opening Pandora's box, in that it can lead to unforeseen consequences. Specifically, once you start wearing makeup every day, then people begin to see that as your real face. And your real real face—the one underneath all the makeup—no longer looks like you, at least not in their eyes. So I'd rather have makeup me be my occasional special face, and sans-makeup me be the default face that people are used to seeing.

Eric: In other words, you'd rather be ugly most of the time.

Me: *Holy fuck, I cannot believe that you just called me ugly just then!*

Eric: I didn't mean any offense by it. That wasn't my intent.

Me: *Intent?!* It's the word "ugly"—everybody knows what it means! It has pretty clear negative connotations!

Eric: But I was simply using it in a neutral way. So calm yourself down, you salty dorkball.

Me: What did you just call me?

Eric: A dorkball. Of the salty variety, I believe.

Me: Why on earth would you call me that?

Eric: I have no idea. I mean, it wasn't really my decision to utter those words. Because I have no free will.

Me: @#$π%&*!

Eric: You can call me all the names you want, but I won't hold it against you. Because you have no free will either. Nobody does. We think we're so special because we have brains. But what's inside of our brains? Just a bunch of molecules, all following the basic laws of chemistry and physics. Electrical currents move through one nerve cell, causing neurotransmitters to be released, which leads to another electrical current in the adjacent cell, and so on. It's all just a matter of cause and effect, completely out of our control.

Me: That's silly, of course we have free will! I have freely chosen to believe in free will, whereas you freely choose to deny its existence.

Eric: You only think you've made a choice. But scientists analyzing brain scans have shown that, moments before we consciously make a decision or solve a puzzle, there is a big burst of brain activity—in other words, our neurons have already made the call before we are even aware of it! Ergo, we are not really in charge; our neurons are.

Me: But we *are* our neurons. All those cells and molecules are inside of *our* brains—they are part of Team Us. We have simply delegated all the decision-making to them. And when they make a choice, it's our choice, even if we are not fully conscious of the process and all the details. Frankly, I think that you are simply denying the existence of free will in order to avoid any responsibility for calling me ugly. And a dorkball.

Eric: Of the salty variety.

For all intents and purposes, that was pretty much the end of our date. Eric #43 was a jerkface. But his argument did lead me to do some research on the whole matter of free will. And I've come to the conclusion that the whole debate is pretty much comparing apples to oranges. Sure, on a micro-level, our brains may be mere chemical reactions and molecular interactions following the basic laws of physics. But on the macro-level—the one we consciously exist in—we clearly have free will. We make countless decisions every single day. We often vacillate between choices, or decide to change our minds later. So I'm not concerned about the whole lack-of-free-will thing. Although I am somewhat troubled by the fact that, statistically speaking, we are almost certainly not actual living and breathing human beings, but rather we merely exist within a giant computer simulation created by posthumans in order to test their theories about human society and history.

Or at least that's what the internet says.

Finally, there's the matter of different people having very different visceral reactions to language. For all intents and purposes, I don't think that there is anything that any of us can do about this. Language is a lot like politics in this regard: For every word, turn of phrase, or statement that you can think of, there will be some people out there who will accept or appreciate it, while others will no doubt dislike or detest it. And while it's true that, in the course of writing this book, I have at no point purposefully intended to upset or hurt anyone else, it would be naive for me to believe that nobody is going to take issue with, or object to, what I've written.

24. Shopping Carts, Part Two

People tend to envision the writing process as an act of pure creation or production: Writers conjure up all these words and sentences, and string them together to make paragraphs and chapters, ultimately building an entire book from scratch. And sure, that's one way of looking at it. But to me, writing feels more like *curating*. After all, the world is chock-full of all these wonderful and/or horrible ideas, objects, people, feelings, situations, and so forth. All of these things already exist out there, and I am simply picking and choosing which of these I wish to exhibit and/or place in juxtaposition to one another.

And a byproduct of curating a book like *99 Erics* is that countless aspects of the human experience—such as yodeling, or macramé, or the bubonic plague, or Lionel Richie songs, to name but a few—remain on the proverbial cutting room floor when all is said and done.

Writers are often asked about what we choose to *include* in our books (How did you settle on the name "Eric"? What's with all the math references?), but not what we exclude ("Why isn't there a chapter about yodeling?" "The bubonic plague killed roughly 200 million people, *how could you not even mention it?!?*"). Perhaps the bubonic plague and yodeling simply never sprung to my mind while I was writing *99 Erics*? (Although they probably would have had I been writing this book in fourteenth-century Eurasia, or nineteenth-century Central Alps, respectively.)

Alternatively, perhaps these things *did* occur to me at some point. Maybe one of the Erics was super-duper into macramé, and the two of us went out to karaoke where we performed a smashing duet of "Endless Love" together, but none of this made its way into the book. My potential reasons for omitting this information are numerous: Maybe I did write this chapter, but it was later cut due to length concerns or because it didn't mesh well with the rest of the book? Or maybe that specific Eric remains a character in the book, but I skipped the macramé and karaoke song details because they seemed irrelevant to the story I was telling.

Whatever the case, none of these expressions of the human condition are included in *99 Erics*. Other than me mentioning them here in passing. And maybe you are unconcerned by these omissions. But I'm sure that Hallo, Bin Ich Es Den Du Suchst? (Austria's premiere Lionel Richie yodeling tribute band) would beg to differ.

This whole notion of curation and omission has been on my mind a lot lately, ever since Eric #31 and I got together again—he's the one from the lucid dreaming chapter, remember him? He's been helping me with my burgeoning (or perhaps floundering is more accurate) stand-up comedy act. And I've been using my ex-slam-poet skillset to help him prepare some of his horror-slash-comedy bits for a local storytelling show.

It also turns out that we are both writing about our first date together for our prospective projects—you already read my retelling of that experience back in Chapter 19, "Shopping Carts, Part One." Eric is still working on his rendition, although he's a bit stuck at the moment.

Eric: So I wanted to ask you your thoughts about how I should handle the whole you-being-bisexual thing.

Me: Um, with safety goggles and cryogenic gloves.

Eric: No, seriously. I know that bisexual women are often stereotyped as being "easy" and attracted to "anything that moves." And I don't want to perpetuate that. But I'm worried that when I get to the part of the story where, out of the blue, you asked me if I would have sex with you, people will automatically assume that you did that because you're bisexual.

Me: What you need is a chapter called "Bomb," wherein you defuse all those stereotypes.

Eric: But I have seven minutes to tell my entire story. I don't have time for a whole defusing-bombs chapter.

Me: Then simply don't mention it.

Eric: But if I don't mention that you're bisexual, won't most people just assume that you're heterosexual? And won't that contribute to bisexual erasure?

Me: What you need is a whole 'nother chapter called "Patronizing," wherein you explain to your readers all of the perils of making unfounded assumptions about other people.

Eric: But I don't have readers—this will be a storytelling event. And like I said, I don't have that much time to work with.

Me: Look, I appreciate you asking me for my input here. But I'm afraid there is no right answer, at least as far as I can tell. If you mention that I am bisexual, then some people will pan you for not using the word pansexual. And still others will be offended because your character will seem like such an obvious bisexual stereotype. And if you make it overtly clear that I am a living breathing person rather than some bisexual caricature that you invented, then they will turn their hatred toward me for reinforcing stereotypes of bisexual people.

Eric: They won't hate you.

Me: Yes they will. I am a polarizing figure.

Eric: Well can I ask, in your book chapter about our first date, how did you handle the fact that I'm black?

Me: Um, I didn't mention it.

Eric: Seriously?

Me: Yeah, for a couple reasons. First off, I don't describe what anyone in the book looks like. Because I am not a very visual person. Second, it didn't seem pertinent to the story. So that detail ended up on the proverbial cutting room floor.

Eric: Me being black isn't simply some visual trait, like having male-patterned baldness or attached earlobes. The fact that I'm black means that, in most situations, people treat me differently—with less respect and more suspicion—than they would otherwise. It impacts how I navigate my way through the world. It is highly pertinent.

Me: As a queer person, I totally get that—the whole constantly having to react to other people's assumptions and stereotypes. To be clear, I wasn't saying that it's not pertinent to you as a person, just that it was not relevant information for that particular story.

Eric: But if you leave out that information, then your readers are simply going to assume that I'm white.

Me: Not all of them. Only the ones who live their lives in white-people-only bubbles—you know, like the type of people who live in the suburbs, name their children Connor, and watch the TV show *Friends* in syndication. But readers from more ethnically and racially diverse worlds won't likely jump to that conclusion. Much like how readers who actually know quite a few bisexual and pansexual people won't automatically assume that a character must be exclusively gay or straight simply because you've described them as being on a date with a woman or a man.

Eric: I think you're giving your readers far too much credit.

Me: Look, I could follow your advice and explicitly inform readers whenever a character that appears in my book is a minority of one stripe or another, even if it isn't necessary information. I could mention in passing that Eric #7 was Jewish, Eric #17 was bisexual, Eric #47 was transgender, Eric #61 was Latino, Eric #71 was Asian, and so on. But if I did that, it would likely come off as superficial tokenism. It might even seem performative, like I was announcing to the world, "Hey, look at me, aren't I such an open-minded person dating all these diverse people!" Not to mention the fact that, by mentioning the fact that Eric number fill-in-the-blank belongs to a certain minority group, I'd be insinuating that all the other Erics (for whom I did not mention this) must belong to the majority group by default. In other words, I would simply be reinforcing societal assumptions that white, heterosexual, cisgender, able-bodied, etcetera, people are the unmarked norm. And I'd rather not do that.

Eric: Then why don't you mention all of these aspects for every Eric in your book?

Me: But then every chapter would begin with a laundry list of qualities and identities for each Eric as I introduce them. Which isn't very elegant writing-wise. Plus, it doesn't leave much to the imagination. One of the great things about books—unlike TV and movies—is that they allow readers to fill in all the little unspoken details for themselves.

Eric: Such as making me white, because you didn't tell them otherwise.

Me: I'm starting to think that maybe I'm inclined to err on the don't-mention-their-identity side of this debate because I'm a bisexual person who seemingly reinforces all the negative stereotypes about bisexuals, whereas you're okay with me mentioning that you're black because you don't come across as especially stereotypical.

Eric: Or maybe I think you should explicitly state my identity because I move through the world as a visibly black man, but you feel more ambivalent about your identity because your sexual orientation is often invisible to other people.

Me: Perhaps. Or maybe this all boils down to you being the world's premiere omni-observational comedian who notices and comments on everything in your purview, whereas I am Kat Cataclysm, who is not a very visual person, and who is no good at describing . . . things.

Eric: Hmm, maybe . . . Oh, by the way, remember when

you said that you were searching for a story that would fit your *It's like "The Gift of the Magi," but only with shopping carts* punchline? Well, I think I've come up with one.

Me: Exciting! Do tell.

Eric: Two people who don't know one another go to the same grocery store. They're both planning to cook dinner for their dates that evening—one of the recipes calls for parsley, the other cilantro. But they both accidentally place these ingredients into each other's shopping carts. And since cilantro and parsley pretty much look alike, neither of them notices the mistake. And because these herbs taste so different, both of their dishes end up being ruined, and their dates break up with them as a result. So it's like "The Gift of the Magi," but only with shopping carts.

Me: Not bad. It definitely has the irony. And the shopping carts. But I don't think that's how O. Henry would have ended it. He would have had these two broken-hearted souls go to the same local bar to drown their sorrows, only to meet one another. They could each retell their stories, at which point they'd realize that they wound up with each other's missing ingredient! And they'd subsequently fall in love. The end.

Eric: But that's so contrived. And sappy.

Me: Have you ever read the original O. Henry?

Eric: No. Are there any people of color in it?

Me: I don't remember. Which probably means no. There probably weren't any bisexuals in it either. For all we know.

Eric: Hey, for the "shopping carts" version of "Gift of the Magi," what if one couple is seemingly lesbian and the other two gay men. So when these jilted lovers meet at the bar, readers will assume that their sexual orientations are incompatible. But then, when the story ends with their first kiss, readers will be surprised because they never expected them to both be bisexual!

Me: LOOK OUT, IT'S A BOMB! MUST DEFUSE IT!

25. Writing About Sex Is Like Praying About Agnosticism

Once I started my full-time writing job at CliqueClick, it really cut into my progress on my own book. As a result, the time I would set aside for my personal writing suddenly became super-duper precious to me. So when my good friend Kim asked me to write something for her anthology-in-progress, I was somewhat hesitant at first. But she was having a hard time finding potential contributors who could speak to the subject matter at hand. The working title for the anthology was *Best Atheist & Agnostic Bisexual Women's Erotica*, which is admittedly a tad overly specific, but Kim is an erotica writer who is fiercely committed to simultaneously challenging both the longstanding biphobia in queer literature and the sexism in the New Atheist movement. She reached out to me knowing that I'm an agnostic bisexual woman. And I agreed to help her out, even though I had no clue what I'd even write about.

Some of you may assume that I must have plenty of sexual adventures and escapades to draw upon for my piece. This assumption probably stems from the fact that I keep referring to myself as "sex-positive." Because, for some reason, as soon as you describe yourself as sex-positive, people will automatically assume that you've had tons of sex in almost every position and configuration imaginable, and/or that you are willing to freely discuss any and all of your sexual exploits at the drop of a hat, and/or that you probably facilitate sex-related workshops and maybe even have your own sex advice column, and/or that you must be one of those performance artists who work in the medium of female ejaculation, and/or that—*at a bare minimum*—you have a slam poem you occasionally perform about that time when you worked as a stripper for like two and a half weeks.

And I do none of these things. I call myself "sex-positive" simply because I'm against shaming people for their sexual desires and histories, not because I'm constantly having lots and lots of sex. Because I'm not, actually. As you've probably gathered by now, most of my dates with Erics have not panned out especially well. As for Matilda, well, we do have sex from time to time, but not nearly as often as we used to. I'm sure some people are immediately going to think "lesbian bed death" here, which is kind of fucked up—after all, I'm bisexual, not lesbian! But on top of that, nearly every single long-term couple experiences a sharp decline in the frequency of sex after their first year together. The phenomenon should simply be called "bed death"—so stop picking on lesbians!

Actually, even "bed death" is too harsh. Like, who decided that not having sex is tantamount to death? I'll bet it was probably some confused-slut dude-bro who was trying to guilt-trip his girlfriend into having sex with him when she wasn't interested. Which, suffice it to say, is the least sex-positive thing you could possibly do.

On top of not having had an especially large quantity of sexual experiences myself, I'm also really bad at writing about sex. Like, whenever I go to queer open mics or sex-positive spoken word events, I will hear all these amazing writers read hot and steamy stories about chance sexual encounters, or scenes at a play party, or perhaps some three-way they participated in. And for me, it will totally bring home the fact that I've had very few chance sexual encounters in my life. And while I've been to several play parties, I've mostly just hung out in the social area eating chips and guacamole, and chatting with the other not-so-exhibitionistic attendees.

And if I were to write about one of the few threesomes I've taken part in, rather than offer an erotic play-by-play of who sexually did what to whom, I would probably mostly write about all the hands. Because there are so many of them! (Although some of them admittedly belong to you.) And you can't even begin to keep tabs on all of them. And at some point, you'll just be there minding your own business, focusing on the giving and/or receiving that you are currently giving and/or receiving, when suddenly, out of the blue, someone's hand will unexpectedly touch you *there*, and you'll be like, "*Whoa, where did that hand come from?!*" While this anecdote accurately reflects my own personal experiences with three-ways, it probably wouldn't make for compelling erotica.

And the aforementioned queer and sex-positive writers are also way more adept at describing sex than I could ever hope to be. I mean, if I was going to describe a sex scene, I would be inclined to use very clinical words like breasts, nipples, penis, clitoris, labia, vagina, orgasm, etcetera. But these other writers somehow come up with all these wild euphemisms like "voluptuous mounds," and "turgid manhood," and "love button," and "gateway drug," and "flowery toolshed," and "tautological wand," and "macadamia nut," and "her Cascadia subduction zone ruptured," and shit like that. I honestly don't know how they do it!

So how could I ever possibly compete with all of these far more sexually experienced and well-versed writers who would also be contributing to *Best Atheist & Agnostic Bisexual Women's Erotica?*

Well, I couldn't possibly. But that does not mean that I'm doomed by any means. Because one thing that I've learned in my many years as a writer is that, rather than try to hammer your proverbial square self into a round hole, you should instead be true to yourself.

In this case, instead of attempting (and failing) at writing typical erotica fare, I decided to write a silly speculative short fiction piece that touched on the major themes of the anthology, while also

exploring my recent fascination with bizarre animal mating habits.
Here it is:

*Galactic anthropologists are pretty much in agreement: Of all the known species
to have ever populated the universe, none has had stranger mating practices
than the Zyxxavxzians. From the planet Zyxxavxzy. Because, rather than
being divided into two or more sexes which differ in their reproductive roles and
capacities, all Zyxxavxzians were pretty much anatomically identical. And
they had no reproductive systems to speak of, at least according to the standard
definitions set forth by the Galactic Consortium of Astrobiologists.*

*Given this, how were the Zyxxavxzians able to procreate and propagate?
Well, despite their physiological indistinctiveness, they tended to fall rather
neatly into two similarly sized populations based on their theological beliefs.
The first of these two groups—the devout monotheists—adhered to the
Ancient Zyxxavxzian Scriptures by worshipping the deity Skippy Bunbuns,
who was said to reside in a netherworld at the core of planet Zyxxavxzy.
There, He would tend The Great Bar, making mimosas, mojitos, and mint
juleps for all the pious recently deceased souls who strictly followed His Holy
Codes during their corporeal lives. In stark contrast, the second group—the
adamant atheists—vociferously denied Skippy Bunbuns' existence, and some
even outright mocked both His Holy Codes and His supposed legendary
bartending acumen.*

*Despite their incompatible religious beliefs, the devout monotheists and
adamant atheists just so happened to be (for lack of a better word) sexually
oriented toward one another. And during mating season each year, both groups
would congregate in the many Zyxxavxzian bars, clubs, and lounges—the
monotheists considered these Houses of Worship, whereas the atheists viewed
them as secular drinking establishments. There, the monotheists and atheists
would pair up with one another. Their mating rituals would always begin with
coy flirtation, move on to enchanting conversation, then climax with acrimonious
and arduous debates regarding morality, the origin of the universe, and the very
existence of Skippy Bunbuns.*

Somehow, the conflict that accompanied these heated theological debates would generate enough energy to produce little baby Zyxxavxzians (via a biological and/or spiritual process that remains unclear to this day).

Most Zyxxavxzian younglings would remain religiously unaffiliated during their early childhoods. Until puberty set in, of course, and a surge in hormones led them to inevitably adopt one of two diametrically opposed theological positions: Skippy Bunbuns is our One and Only Lord and Afterlife Bartender, or else he's a complete sham and his followers are all dupes incapable of critical thinking.

But then one day, Charlotte Pressnickles came along. Unlike her peers, who all held rigid self-righteous views on religious matters, Charlotte had a seemingly endless capacity for ambivalence. She understood that, while there was no tangible evidence to prove Skippy Bunbuns' existence, neither was there sufficient evidence to fully rule it out. And while she was open to the possibility that Skippy existed, she was fairly certain that His Holy Codes were written by ancient Zyxxavxzians rather than Him. After all, why would an omniscient and omnipotent being ever issue such trivial and arguably ethically suspect commandants as Code #117: "Thou shalt not covet thy neighbor's cocktail umbrella," or Code #223: "Failure to properly muddle the mint leaves when preparing a mojito is punishable by colonoscopy."

And while Charlotte would have liked to believe that there was some kind of afterlife—where she could be reunited and share a round of drinks with her long-lost Grandmonotheist and Grandatheist (who both passed away when she was a child)—she was highly dubious that such a place could possibly be located deep in the heart of planet Zyxxavxzy. After all, scientists have clearly demonstrated that the planetary core was comprised of molten ore that could reach temperatures as high as 10,000 Bradling units! Seriously, it's hard to imagine Skippy Bunbuns' famous Strawberry Daiquiris and Piña Coladas holding up at such extraordinary temperatures.

At first, Charlotte's failure to "choose a side" in the great Zyxxavxzian theological debate caused much consternation amongst the people. But over time, she began to accrue numerous followers who found what she had to say on the subject of religion ever so reasonable. And these disciples began spreading her word, often quoting Charlotte's Golden Rule ("The only thing that I know for sure is that I am not sure if I know anything for sure. Although I'm not 100 percent sure that I even know this for sure either"), and encouraging everyone to love their fellow Zyxxavxzians regardless of their religious views (or lack thereof).

Over time, most of the inhabitants of Zyxxavxzy converted to Charlotte's agnostic outlook, and they strived to love all members of their species regardless of their beliefs. Zyxxavxzy slowly evolved into a truly peaceful utopian planet.

Although without all that conflict and religious debate, the Zyxxavxzians were unable to reproduce. So they eventually went extinct.

THE END.

26. Ménage à Trois

Preliminary studies have shown that 15.2 percent of readers who peruse the Table of Contents for this book immediately skip ahead to this chapter because of its title. It's true! And if you are one of said readers, then you are likely not up to speed on the fact that, during the last chapter, I mentioned (in passing) that I've taken part in a handful of threesomes in the past. And given the popular misconceptions about threesomes and bisexual women, I fear that I now have yet another bomb on my hands that will require defusing.

Because I can't tell you how many times I've been on Ed's List, or Finder, or GoEros, or some other dating site, and some guy who lists his sexual orientation as "straight" will message me and chat me up. Which is totally fine—I have no qualms with dating heterosexual men. But then, at some point in the conversation, he will reveal his ulterior motive: "I see that you're bisexual. So is my girlfriend. I was wondering if you might want to have a three-way with us?"

And in that moment, it becomes crystal clear to me that this guy has not contacted me because he is queer-friendly and just so happens to like my online profile. Rather, he was likely perusing the bisexual section of this dating site with the express purpose of making a threesome happen—as if, in his mind, bisexual women like myself are simply some kind of special adaptor that they need to procure in order to complete a three-way circuit.

And, as many bisexual women know firsthand, if you come

out to your boyfriend as bisexual, or even mention in passing that you once made out with another girl, there is a decent chance that he will then try to pressure you into having a threesome, even if you're not actually interested. Having been on that side of the fence before, the last thing that I want is to get caught up in one of these scheming boyfriends' machinations. I mean, dude, if your girlfriend really does want to have a three-way with you and me, then *why isn't she the one messaging me?!*

Here's the source of the problem: Many straight guys misinterpret threesomes as some kind of hyper-heterosexual act, presumably because they get to have sex with two women rather than one. But this line of thinking is so misguided!

For instance, just last week, Matilda and I were kissing in public, and this confused-slut dude-bro came right up to us, all smiley and shit, and said, "Ladies, can I referee?" What a weird-ass thing to say! Because first off, referees don't even get to play in the game! On top of that, if Matilda and I were going to fuck that night (which we probably weren't, due to "bed death" that's not actually death), it would be really super-duper lesbo sex—like with lots of vibrators, and strap-ons, and latex gloves, and such. In other words, the proverbial game most definitely would *not* be played on Mr. Confused-Slut Dude-Bro's home court.

Many straight guys fantasize about three-ways being some kind of pinnacle act of heterosexual manhood. But in reality, three-ways are one of the queerest forms of sex imaginable. After all, they work most efficiently when all three participants share the same queer orientation—such as all lesbian, or all gay men, or all bisexual— that way, all three parties can sexually appreciate one another. In contrast, it's logistically impossible for three heterosexuals to engage in a proper threesome (unless of course, one or some of them are queering things up a bit). In fact, if an exclusively straight person does participate, the other two participants both need to be queer in order to achieve any kind of three-way reciprocation.

Thus, in conclusion, threesomes always involve queer sex, and (demographically speaking) they must be at least two-thirds queer. Heterosexual guys are free to participate in three-ways if they wish (provided that this doesn't involve scheming and/or pressuring women into joining them). All I ask is that you own the fact that you have just engaged in an act of queer sex. Hooray for you!!!

Just wanted to clear that up.

27. Gut Feelings

Whenever I meet a new Eric, I never know what to think of them. Sometimes they come off as charming and disarming, but then I'll worry that it might all be a facade designed to hide their true Machiavellian intentions. Other times, the Eric in question will come across as boring or mundane, and I'll want to write them off, but then it will strike me that perhaps there is a fascinating special person inside of them just waiting to shine, if I'd only give them half a chance.

And when I share these concerns with friends, they'll often ask me, "Well, what is your gut telling you about this Eric?" Or they will encourage me to "Do a gut check" or "Trust my gut instincts." But the thing is, I can't trust my gut. Not at all. Because I have irritable bowel syndrome.

And believe me, I've tried everything: I've taken digestive enzymes and myriad supplements, tinctures, bitters, and herbal teas (including rosebud tea, at Eric #17's suggestion). I've had food allergy panels, and tried food elimination, gluten free, Paleolithic, and FODMAP diets, all to no avail. It seemed likely that the root cause might be that my gut bacteria had gone awry, so I've consumed significant quantities of prebiotics and probiotics, and fermentable fibers and resistant starches galore, but none of it seemed to help.

Then one day, after reading an article about the use of fecal matter transplants to restore gut microflora, I began devising a plan to convince Matilda to lend me a stool sample of hers, so I could self-administer it DIY style. And as I was researching how to do this on the internet, it suddenly hit me: *"Oh my god, what the hell am I doing with my life?!"*

From that point on, I've been like, fuck it, this is just how I am. I am an irritable-bowel-syndromed person who will likely always have this condition. And if there were Pride parades for irritable bowel syndrome, I would totally march in them. I think. As far as I'm concerned, the only negative drawback of being an irritable-bowel-syndromed person (aside from the occasional cramping and diarrhea) is that I simply can't rely on my "gut feelings" or "gut reactions." So instead, I have to be completely cerebral. Like, 100 percent of the time. Which is really hard to do.

Take for instance my date with Eric #53. He insisted that we eat at his favorite pizza parlor, where they purportedly import tap water from Brooklyn to make supposedly authentic New York-style thin-crust pizza. I was intrigued, but then when it came to discussing toppings, Eric suggested pineapple and broccoli, but I outright vetoed the broccoli. Then I suggested sausage or pepperoni, but he vetoed that because he's vegetarian. So we settled on no toppings whatsoever.

After we ordered, Eric #53 got up to use the restroom. And left to my own devices, I found myself trying to ascertain (entirely cerebrally, without the help of any gut feelings) what I thought of him thus far. I mean, he seemed like a nice enough guy. But you have to admit that it's kind of weird to insist on authentic New York-style pizza, but then want to smother it in pineapple and broccoli—arguably the two least stereotypically New Yorker toppings known to humankind.

Then there's the fact that he's vegetarian. Not that there's anything wrong with that per se—there are many legitimate reasons why people decide to become vegetarian: a distaste for meat, health concerns, the horrible conditions agribusinesses inflict upon the animals they raise, and/or to reduce one's carbon footprint. (Although if this Eric is concerned about the last point, he should maybe reconsider eating pizza at establishments that ship containers of tap water all the way across North America.)

All of these reasons for being vegetarian are totally reasonable. But the cerebral part of my brain—which is flying solo right now, due to the lack of reliable gut feelings—began pondering: What if this Eric is one of those vegetarians who thinks that he is morally superior to people who are carnivorous, or that it is flat out unethical to eat animals? Because if he's one of those people, then we are bound to have a debate on our hands.

And the 100 percent cerebral side of me started plotting out the argument that I would make if this was the case. It went something like this: Fungi and microorganisms aside, the earth is inhabited by two types of creatures: plants and animals. Plants photosynthesize—they create their own energy from sunlight. In contrast, we animals selfishly refuse to photosynthesize; instead we get our energy from eating other living beings.

Plants are peaceful creatures who wouldn't hurt a fly (well, except for Venus flytraps, who literally eat flies), whereas animals are nothing more than homicidal freeloaders.

Therefore, when you eat a plant, you are slaughtering the innocent—it's as plain and simple as that. But if you consume an animal, it could be construed as comeuppance: They had it coming to them because of all the living beings they spent their lives eating!

Some people want to make this an issue about ethics, when arguably it is more about anthropomorphism than anything else. Animals have heads and bodies, eyes and mouths, and they move around, often on legs, just like we do. *We see ourselves in them.* But plants look nothing like us. They don't even move! They just sit there like rocks or stones, which I suppose are the same thing. And when you cut into a plant, they don't even bleed! Because they have no blood. They just have xylem and phloem, whatever the fuck that is. So when we see an ear of corn, or a stalk of asparagus, or a gaggle of potatoes, we don't identify with them. They are just *things* to us.

This explains why we are able to eat plants without remorse, and why we treat them in ways that we would never treat our fellow animals. For instance, even though I eat meat, I would never dream of eating an animal alive—that would seem unduly cruel to me. But every time we eat a raw vegetable, we are eating a currently living living being. When we walk through the produce section of the supermarket and see those automated misters, we like to think that they are simply preventing the veggies from wilting. But *wilting means dying!* Basically, those misters are nothing more than vegetable life support systems designed to keep those plants alive for us until we are ready to eat them!

Those of us who are carnivorous often draw the line at eating baby animals. Like, eating beef is okay, but eating veal (which are baby calves) might seem problematic. If it was on the menu, I might order duck, but I would never order duckling. But when I'm in the produce section, I will purchase bags of baby spinach or baby arugula without even thinking. Baby spring mix is basically a potpourri of leaves that were cut down well before their primes—they had their whole lives ahead of them! But I will eat them nevertheless.

Anyway, I am not trying to tell anyone how they should eat. I just think we should get over our anthropomorphism and recognize that plants are living beings too. They apparently have memories, communicate with one another, sense danger, and even release little chemical vegetable screams when they are sliced into—it's true, I read it in *The New Yorker* once.

Anyway, Eric #53 returned from the restroom. And because I had just developed this whole intricate argument in my mind while he was gone, I was half expecting him to begin interrogating me on my carnivorous ways. So I was surprised when he asked me a different question about my eating habits.

Eric: So why don't you eat broccoli?

Me: Because I am a supertaster.

Eric: What does that mean?

Me: Well see, there's this specific chemical in cruciferous vegetables such as broccoli, cauliflower, Brussels sprouts, and the like. And scientists have found that some people (such as myself, presumably) have a genetic variant in one of their taste receptors that causes them to experience this chemical as extremely bitter and unpalatable, whereas most people can't even taste it. This is why they call us supertasters. But it's a rather odd choice of terminology if you ask me, as it puts such an extremely positive spin on an otherwise negative thing. I mean, it's like calling someone a "superlistener" because they can't stand reggae music. Or calling someone "supersexual" because the very thought of having sex disgusts them.

Eric: Hmmm. Interesting.

That's right, that's what he actually said: "Hmmm. Interesting." What was I supposed to make of that?! Did Eric #53 really find my digression interesting? Or was it a sarcastic remark? Or just something he said to camouflage the fact that his mind had wandered off? Boy, I sure wish I had a functional gut to help me sort all these possibilities out.

Eric: So how has your week been going?

Me: Fine, I guess. I mostly worked this week. My listicle "29 Bizarre Animal Mating Practices That Will Scar You for Life" was heavily shared on social media, which I suppose is a good thing. I also just finished up a piece for an anthology my friend Kim is editing. So it's been a fairly productive week. Although one sucky thing did happen to me.

Eric: Really? What?

Me: Earlier this week I went to the dentist. And now I have no feeling on the tip of my tongue. Because of a novocaine injection gone awry. My dentist said that sometimes a nerve can become damaged if the needle hits it in precisely the wrong place. Which is apparently what happened to me.

And the first day after the incident, the numbness on my tongue felt a bit like how it feels when you accidentally burn your tongue by eating or drinking something that is way too hot. And admittedly, it's kind of strange that I am describing the lack of feeling in my tongue as "feeling like" something. But that's how it felt. Or didn't feel. Weird.

Anyway, it felt like a burnt tongue at first, until I realized that unlike a burnt tongue, I could still taste food just fine, because the damaged nerve is apparently only connected to touch receptors in my tongue, and not my supertasting taste receptors. But once I got over the idea that it felt like a burnt tongue, it started to feel more like a slightly novocained tongue—almost as if I had been at the dentist earlier that day, but now well into the afternoon, most of the novocaine had worn off except for the very tip of my tongue. Which is also weird: to have my tongue feel perpetually novocained, even though there are no longer any actual molecules of novocaine in there, because of damage inflicted by a novocaine needle.

So now, I am constantly reminded of being at the dentist. First, because my tongue feels numb, like I had just been to the dentist only earlier that day. And second, because that feeling (or lack thereof) ultimately reminds me that it was a real-life trip to the dentist that has temporarily or possibly permanently made me this way.

It is a very meta type of psychological trauma that I am dealing with here!
Eric: Hmmm. Interesting.

There it is—he said it again! If my gut was functioning normally, surely it would have something to say about this whole "Hmmm, interesting" thing! But sadly I'll never know . . .

Then our pizza arrived. And as we all know, pizza is often served piping hot. And while I was excited about tasting the tastiness of the pizza, I was also highly aware that my indefinitely numb tip of my tongue—which used to feel like it had been burnt by an especially hot food item—is now extraordinarily susceptible to being burnt by especially hot food items. So I carefully placed the tip of my finger onto the piece of pizza closest to me to gauge the temperature.

Eric: *What the fuck are you doing?!*

Me: Testing the temperature of the pizza. Before I stick it in my mouth. Because my tongue can no longer tell if it's too hot. Because of that whole novocaine story I just told you.

Eric: But now you've gotten your germs all over the pizza!

Me: Not all over the pizza. Just in that one small spot. On the piece I was going to eat anyway.

Eric: But now those germs are spreading all over, to all the other pieces!

Me: I really think you're overestimating how fast germs move. Bacteria can only move at a rate of about fifty microns per second.

Eric: What is a micron?

Me: I'm not sure, actually. But I think it's pretty darn small. I mean, it has the word "micro" built right into it.

Eric: Well it's too late. I'm sure your germs have traveled millions of microns by now.

Me: You're a germophobe, aren't you.

Eric: I suppose.

Me: That's hilarious!

Eric: There's nothing funny about me being germophobic.

Me: No, of course not. I have nothing against germophobes. Or vegetarians for that matter. What's hilarious is that I am your exact opposite. I'm not only carnivorous, but I'm also *germophilic*. Because of my irritable bowel syndrome, I have spent the last two years desperately trying to repopulate my gut with new beneficial bacteria. I've consumed god knows how many capsules of probiotics, and have eaten shit-tons of yogurt, kefir, sauerkraut, kimchi, and other naturally fermented products, in the hopes of adding new bacteria to my own dilapidated intestinal ecosystem. Hell, just last year I was even contemplating a DIY fecal matter transplant.

Eric: *Oh my god, that's the grossest thing ever!!!*

Me: Tell me about it. Hey, you know what they say?

Eric: What?

Me: Opposites attract. And if that's true, then we are probably a perfect match. And since I can't trust my gut instincts on this, I'm totally cerebrally going to make the call that I would be open to kissing you. Although I'm not sure how that would work. You know, due to all the germs in my mouth.

Eric: It's okay. I have a bottle of Listerine in my car. If you're open to that.

Me: Sure. Just so long as it's not cruciferous vegetable-flavored Listerine.

Eric: I don't think they even make that.

Me: Good. Because they shouldn't. They really shouldn't.

28. Law of Averages

Okay, so at the end of the last chapter, I said that "opposites attract." But the more I think about it, I'm not so sure about that. I mean, it could be true in certain cases. But other times, we are attracted to people who are similar to us in certain ways: because we share the same interests, tastes, temperament, background, or worldview. So why do we say "opposites attract," when we could just as easily make the case that "likes attract" as well?

It's also strange that, on the one hand, we frequently say "opposites attract"—which implies that attraction is relative, highly variable, and personally tailored to each individual. But then, at the same time, we as a society routinely describe certain people as being "attractive" and others as "unattractive"—which implies that these are intrinsic qualities that are set in stone, and which all people can readily recognize and agree upon. But both of these claims cannot possibly be simultaneously true! If they were both true, then all these attractive and unattractive people (being opposites in this regard) should naturally be attracted toward one another and form relationships together. Yet in practice, this doesn't seem to happen very often.

Here is yet another question: When we agree that a certain individual is "attractive," what do we even mean by that? What qualities do these individuals have that lead us to perceive them this way? Well, researchers have carried out experiments where they show subjects a series of photos of different human faces, and they ask these subjects to rate these faces based on attractiveness. It turns out that most subjects were not especially fond of distinctive features and faces. But when researchers created artificial composite faces (by averaging the sizes and shapes of all these various facial features), subjects tended to rate those faces as being most attractive.

In other words, the people who are generally considered to be "good-looking" are literally the most average-looking people imaginable. Imagine that!

This also means that when Eric #43 called me ugly a few chapters ago, what he was really saying was that he has bland tastes in women, and that I was too distinctive for him.

It has since occurred to me that, in addition to being attracted to average-looking faces, perhaps human beings are attracted to average everything? Here's what I mean: As we walk down the street or watch people on TV, each of us sees many of the same faces, so it's likely that we will all come up with similar mental images for what an "average" composite face should look like—this explains why people often agree about whether or not an individual is "good-looking" (aka, average-looking). But when it comes to the minutia of our everyday lives, well, those details can vary quite a lot. If you are a self-identified Christian "family man" who lives in the suburbs and enjoys boorish humor, and if you keep company with similar people, then your idea of an "average person" is going to be far different from that of an urban-dwelling agnostic bisexual polyamorous absurdist-short-fiction-writing lady who likes making math and linguistics jokes, and hangs out with similarly inclined weirdos (such as myself). If the two of us were to meet, we'd probably be way too distinctive for one another, and therefore unappealing. However, if we each met someone with more similar qualities—aka, a person who seemed *average to us*— then we'd probably find them far more fetching.

Wow, I think I may have just solved the mystery of human attraction! If only I had a convenience sample of college students, and a better grasp of P-hacking, I'm pretty sure that I could get my "Law of Averages" Attraction Hypothesis published in a major sexology journal!

29. By Her Bootstraps

One of my favorite places to write is this brewery-slash-pub with an outdoor patio not too far from my apartment. One day, after finishing up some writing there, I packed up my stuff and headed downstairs to use their restroom. As I opened the door to the ladies' room, I was shocked by what I saw.

Me: Oh my god, you look just like me! What are you, my clone or something?

Their response: No, of course not, that would be ridiculous. Kat, I am you. Literally you. But from the future.

Me: No way, get out! How trippy! But why did you come back in time to visit me?

Future me: Aren't you going to ask me to prove that I'm future you first? For instance, by telling you something that only you would know?

Me: No. I totally trust you.

Future me: But I already picked out the perfect nugget from our past to use as proof. Which was way more challenging than you might imagine. Because I couldn't choose a really significant moment from our life, because then other people would likely also be aware of it. So it has to be unimportant enough that we wouldn't have bothered telling anyone else about it, but not so trivial that we wouldn't have committed it to memory in the first place.

Me: So what did you come up with?

Future me: Remember that day we couldn't find our tube of lidocaine in its usual desk drawer? Well, a few weeks later, while cleaning the apartment, we found it underneath the bed.

Me: Yes, that did happen. Although I assured readers that tube would not be making a reappearance. So you have basically made a liar out of me.

Future me: Sorry. But now that I've convinced you that I am future you, I have to pass along some crucial information.

Me: Okay. What is it?

Future me: This may sound strange, but you need to begin writing a book. You will call it *99 Erics*. And it will be all about your misadventures dating ninety-nine different people named Eric.

Me: Um, I've already started working on it. In fact, I'm probably more than halfway finished by this point.

Future me: But that's not possible! I mean, why on earth would you—after randomly meeting some emo guitarist named Eric as part of your self-imposed experimental overcoming-conflict-avoidance therapy—suddenly decide to commit yourself to dating ninety-eight additional people named Eric, and then fashioning those tales together into a faux novel? It doesn't make any sense! Who would ever come up with such a bizarre premise? Unless, of course, your future self (aka, me) came to you and compelled you to write *99 Erics*, thereby establishing a temporal causality loop, one that skirts the need for any explanation for how the book was originally conceived. *99 Erics* simply always was, and always will be.

Me: But I vividly remember coming up with the idea myself! It was a Monday, and I was drinking my morning coffee and checking my email, when I saw a message from Eric Number One. In it, he shared the news that he was writing a song about me. So I decided that I should write a short story about him. Then I thought: What if it's more than one short story? What if it's a whole book about absurd dating experiences? And what if all the dates just so happened to also be named Eric? And the idea tickled me pink. That's how the idea originated.

Future me: No, no, no. That's all wrong. You had completely moved on from Eric Number One. And then one day (aka, today) you encountered your future self (aka, me) who planted the seed in your head to write the book.

Me: Well, if that's how it was supposed to happen, then you must have traveled to the wrong place in the timeline, as I'm already well into writing it.

Future me: No, I'm pretty sure that this is the exact time and place that I originally met the previous future me.

Me: But if that's true, then where are they? Shouldn't they be here right now? Along with the previous previous future me? And so on.

Future me: That's not how this works. This is not an infinite regress with an interminable number of Kats. There is only one of us. We just so happen to be caught up in a neat and tidy reverse causality loop wherein an event from the future causes an effect in the past.

Me: Well, perhaps I broke the causality loop by spontaneously deciding to write the book myself before your arrival?

Future me: Possibly.

Me: Or maybe I'm Kat #1 from the original unadulterated virgin timeline—the one who first wrote *99 Erics* and who (at some point in my future) goes back in time to tell my former self about the book, thereby creating the causality loop.

Future me: Wait, I'm confused: Would this mean that you're my former self? Or that I'm your former self?

Me: The former former self. I think. Or maybe the latter.

Future me: But wait a second, this can't possibly be the original unadulterated virgin timeline, because how could I even be here then?

Me: Hmmm, good point. Maybe instead of being a straightforward time loop, it's more like a Möbius strip. And during the first pass I spontaneously come up with the idea for *99 Erics*, but then you arrive and alert me to the fact that (in your rendition of the timeline) you got the idea for the book from me. So then

I feel compelled to go back in time—to the second pass of the Möbius strip—to tell you to write the book. And you naturally presume that it's a closed causality loop that requires you to go back in time to give me the idea for the book, even though you end up arriving in the first pass of the Möbius strip—the one in which I spontaneously start writing the book. So I'm your future me, and you're my future me. Does that make sense?

Future me: I suppose. But now my head hurts.

Me: You and me both.

Future me: Well, either way, since you're already writing the book, I guess my work here is done. I should probably return to my time then. But before I go, one bit of advice: Whatever you do, don't go out with Eric #73.

Me: Why?

Future me: I don't want to talk about it. Because not talking about it is my coping mechanism. Just trust me when I say that Eric #73 is the WORST ERIC EVER!

Me: But as you must know, I am assigning Erics numbers based upon chronological order. So there has to be an Eric #73. Otherwise I will never get all the way to ninety-nine.

Future me: Well, don't say I didn't warn you.

Me: I have one more question, if you don't mind. How were you able to arrive precisely here, at this exact location? Because you can't just travel back in time to some specific spot on Earth without somehow adjusting for the fact that our planet is constantly rotating, plus it's whirling around the sun at a speed of 66,000 miles per hour. Not to mention the fact that our entire solar system is also orbiting the Milky Way Galaxy, plus the universe itself is expanding. Given all this, how is it possible for you to pinpoint the precise location in both time and space to return to?

Future me: Time Gate. The answer to your question is a Time Gate. It just sort of appeared, out of nowhere. Don't ask me how it works.

30. Origin Story

Eric #61 seemed pretty laid back for a businessman. Or at least that's what I presumed he was, because at one point early on in our conversation, he mentioned that he owned his own business—Shotgun Enterprises—which he assured me had nothing to do with making or selling actual shotguns. He took me to one of those restaurants right on the bay at Fisherman's Wharf—which is this supposedly quintessentially "San Francisco" part of San Francisco that is always teeming with tourists, yet rarely ever frequented by actual residents of San Francisco.

This particular restaurant is known for their seafood, so I ordered the Dungeness crab cakes. And since they didn't have that great of a beer selection, I ordered a glass of Zinfandel.

Eric: So you're going to have red wine with seafood? How interesting. Most wine enthusiasts would insist on pairing your dish with a white wine. Perhaps a Chardonnay or Sauvignon Blanc might have been a more appropriate choice?

Me: I don't believe in food rules. And besides, if my wine pairing tendencies seem unusual to you, it probably has to do with the fact that I was raised Catholic. Because during communion at mass each Sunday, we would have to consume the body and blood of Christ. And the body would be represented by a white communion wafer, which seems to imply that Jesus—if you were to actually eat him—would be considered by nutritionists to be "white meat," much like chicken or fish. But the blood of Christ was always represented by a red wine. Although the priests never let us drink it. Nor did they explain why. Perhaps they were concerned about potential bloodborne pathogens?

Eric: I'd imagine it was because they didn't want young children drinking the wine. Because they might get drunk.

Me: As if young children aren't already drunk! Anyway, that's probably why I gravitate toward atypical wine pairings. Because I was raised Catholic. Hey, while we're on the subject, have you ever read the phrase "for Christ's sake" on the written page?

Eric: I'm not sure that I have.

Me: Because whenever I see the word "sake" spelled out, I immediately think of Japanese rice wine, rather than the English noun meaning "purpose" or "benefit." So "Christ's sake" could potentially be yet another non-traditional wine pairing for communion wafers.

Eric: Wow, I'm a bit taken aback by how sacrilegious you are!

Me: I'm not being sacrilegious. This is merely innocent wordplay. Plus some harmless poking fun at wine snobbery.

Eric: Still, it's surprising to hear all this coming from you, given how religious you are.

Me: What? I'm not religious. I mean, I was raised Catholic. But I'm not anymore. I am a recovering Catholic. As well as a recovering slam poet. There are many things that I'm recovering from. Anyway, what made you think I was religious?

Eric: For starters, you said you worked for CliqueClick. Aren't they a conservative Catholic news and social media site?

Me: No! Not at all. They are neither conservative nor Catholic. For Christ's sake, they have a vice room right there on the premises! With occasional human sacrifices! Although I believe there may have been occasional human sacrifices in the Old Testament . . .

Eric: That's strange, because every time I've been on CliqueClick, it's full of all these religious articles.

Me: That's because they are tailoring your newsfeed based on your family and friends' expectations of you.

Eric: Oh, that would explain it, as my family is very Catholic. Anyway, I also assumed you were religious because your last name is Catechism.

Me: No, it's Cataclysm. Like a cataclysmic event.

Eric: Oh, wow. How'd you get that name?

Me: What do you mean, "How did I get it?" You wouldn't have asked me that if my last name was Smith. Or Murphy. Or Jackson. Or Cohen. Or Garcia.

Eric: Well, that's because they're all common names.

Me: You claim it's because they are common, but in actuality it's because you view these names as belonging to the "unmarked" category—the ones you take for granted and view as the default. So when you are introduced to someone who has one of these unmarked names, you don't think twice about it, nor do you question their legitimacy. But as linguists have shown, by necessity, this process creates a second category of names—those that are "marked": the ones that seem exotic, strange, or unexpected to you. In your mind, these marked names seem to stand out—even though they are just names, no better or worse than any other—and seemingly require an explanation. So you start barraging people who have such names with all sorts of comments and questions—like, "What an unusual name! How do you pronounce it? Where does that name come from? What's your heritage?"—that you would never ask of people whose names remain unmarked in your eyes.

Eric: But I was just . . .

Me: It's like how, when people seem normal to us—aka, unmarked—we don't feel compelled to ask them all sorts of questions about where they came from, or how they came to be. We are perfectly content *not knowing* whether they grew up in rural Michigan, or the suburbs of St. Louis, or smack dab in the heart of New York City. Nor do we compulsively ask them about their parentage, their childhoods, or any potentially transformative moments that led to them becoming the person they are today. In contrast, the moment that a person does something that takes us by surprise—for instance, if they were to exhibit some sort of supernatural power—then we will immediately mark them as a "witch," or "monster," or "superhero," or what have you. And we will demand an explanation, and desperately desire to know their so-called origin story: Where was Superman born? How did Wonder Woman get her special powers? What series of events led Bruce Wayne to become Batman?

I guess what I'm saying is: *Why can't you just accept the fact that my name is Kat Cataclysm and leave it at that?!*

Eric: How did you figure out that I have supernatural powers?

Me: Excuse me?

Eric: My superpower—you must have known. Otherwise you wouldn't have brought it up just then.

Me: Honestly, I didn't know. Until now! So what's your superpower?

Eric: Wow, what a hypocrite! Look who's suddenly the one bombarding the marked person with all sorts of questions now!

Me: Sorry. You're right. My bad. I'll let it go.

Eric: It's okay actually. I don't mind talking about it. My superpower is that, whenever I am in a vehicle, I never hit any red lights. Ever.

Me: That's a fairly esoteric superpower to have.

Eric: Tell me about it! And for most of my life, I had no idea, because (as you also seemingly surmised) I grew up smack dab in the heart of New York City. Washington Heights, to be precise. So we didn't own a car; we walked and took the subway everywhere. Sometimes I'd ride the bus, but it wasn't like I was paying any attention to red lights along the way.

But then I moved out here to the Bay Area, where more people have cars. And whenever friends would give me a lift, they would always comment about what great time they were making and how they weren't hitting any red lights. And then it occurred to me: Have I ever been stuck at a red light? Apparently, the answer is no. At least not since I started paying attention four years ago.

Me: Wow. What a story. I guess it's a good thing that I'm not religious after all.

Eric: Why is that?

Me: Well, if I did believe in the kind of god who is purportedly omnipotent and has some grand master plan, then I'd probably be devastated right now. Like, why would that god, rather than eliminating all the violence and poverty and injustice in the world, instead use their divine intervention to make this one single person impervious to red lights? If my god did that, I would lose all faith in them.

Eric: Actually, many people who are religious believe that god is intervening in their lives in countless highly specific and arguably trivial ways all the time. Some people believe he helps them win football games or find parking spots. So in their minds, my having the power to elude red lights would likely seem par for the course.

Me: I suppose. So how are you using your superpowers?

Eric: What do you mean?

Me: Well, in every superhero origin story, they ultimately decide to use their supernatural powers, not for selfish ends, but to benefit all of humanity. So I'm asking you how you are using your superpower for the greater good.

Eric: Um, I'm not, really. It's not the sort of superpower that is well suited for saving lives or fighting evil. So instead, I started my business—Shotgun Enterprises—where I rent myself out to rich people, primarily tech CEOs, so that they can get to wherever they are going much faster.

Me: Wow, that's really depressing.

Eric: It's not so bad really. At least not for me. I just hang out in their limousines all day, mostly reading books. I'm currently reading a wonderful YA novel called *Smells Like Teen Dystopia*. Have you read it?

Me: No. Although I did write an absurdist short story with the exact same title a couple years ago. See, this is precisely why I stopped internet-searching my story titles!

Eric: So now that I told you my origin story, what's yours? Where did the name "Kat Catclysm" come from?

Me: Well, shortly after I moved out here, my friend Gabriella really wanted to start a punk band, and she enlisted me as her lead singer. So I chose the name "Kat" as a tribute to my favorite frontwoman, Kat Bjelland. And I picked "Cataclysm" because I thought it sounded kinda badass. We only played about three or four shows, but I decided to keep the name anyway.

Eric: Wow, what a really anticlimactic origin story.

Me: I know, tell me about it!

In addition to having origin stories, the other thing we often expect of superheroes is that they will have some kind of secret identity: They will spend most of their time pretending to be seemingly normal people—Clark Kent, Diana Prince, Bruce Wayne, and so on—rather than living full-time in their superhero personas. This always confused me as a young child. I mean, if you happen to be Wonder Woman, why not *just be Wonder Woman all the time?!*

But as I got older, I began to understand. The problem is (forgive me for saying it again) the fucking laypeople—the people who don't possess any superpowers, and who view the lack of supernatural abilities to be the unmarked norm. And while these laypeople might appreciate the occasional miracle (such as god granting them a parking spot, or being saved by a superhero), they are fearful of anyone who seems fundamentally different from them. Anyone who seems like a weirdo. And they will invariably dismiss these weirdos as dangerous, deviant, demonic, disturbing, disgusting, delusional, despicable, and/or other pejorative adjectives that probably also begin with a "d."

I do not have any superpowers to speak of. But I do know a thing or two about being a weirdo. And the secret to surviving and thriving as a weirdo is to not let the laypeople pressure you into being mild mannered, or force you to hide your true identity.

If you just so happen to be a weirdo, then simply roll with it. Embrace it! Be an unabashed unapologetic weirdo 24/7. (Which, if you do the math, turns out to be 3.428571428571428571 repeating indefinitely. Which might not seem like a lot at first. Until you start counting the number of decimal places.)

This is why, after spending the first twenty-some years of my life trying to accommodate other people's expectations of me, I decided to completely ditch my birth name and permanently go by the name Kat Cataclysm. It is a reminder to myself to be myself, all of the time. Laypeople be damned.

Anyway, there's a reason why I'm telling you all this. When I got home after my date with Eric #61, I found a note from Matilda. It was a Dear John letter. Except that it was addressed to me.

I mentioned early on that Matilda is also a weirdo. This is something that we had in common—it was the source of countless inside jokes and rituals that only we understood. But unlike me, Matilda also has this whole mild-mannered persona as a Democratic operative. And her co-workers all like to think of themselves as progressive and open-minded, when in reality they are all extremely concerned with keeping up appearances. Matilda's co-workers accepted her as a lesbian, but only *after* it became fashionable to do so; twenty years ago, these same people probably wouldn't have wanted anything to do with her. And despite their current tolerance with regards to Matilda's sexual orientation, they would no doubt view other aspects of her sexuality—such as her kinkiness and ethical non-monogamy—to be scandalous and unacceptable.

One of Matilda's Democratic operative co-workers recently stumbled upon my *99 Erics* blog, and found it populated with stories about me dating a panoply of Erics. They jumped to the conclusion that I must be cheating on Matilda. So they told her about it. And rather than cop to the polyamorous nature of our relationship, Matilda pretended to be upset about my supposed "cheating" on her. In order to keep up appearances.

In other words, she basically broke up with me in order to maintain her secret identity.

Although that's not how Matilda sees it. In her mind, I was the one at fault, for being reckless with sensitive information. She feels like I betrayed her, even though I didn't. Our agreement was that I wouldn't write about our relationship together; there was no mention of me not being able to write about my own sexual interests and experiences with other people. And she didn't mind my *99 Erics* project when it seemed like a lark—a literary endeavor that most likely wouldn't see the light of day outside of our own queer, poly, and sex-positive circles. Neither of us imagined that one of her co-workers would randomly find my blog and blab about it.

Which is yet another reason why the internet is like the worst thing ever.

Anyway, I am writing this several months later. And while I still have *all the feelings* about Matilda choosing her job over me, I'm not really mad at her. The cerebral part of me (which still to this day cannot rely on any gut feelings) now views our breakup as somewhat inevitable, because on one important level we were incompatible: She wanted to be picture perfect Diana Prince expertly navigating the world of normalcy, whereas I wanted to be outspoken badass Wonder Woman 24/7.

And while I have a lot of anger about this whole affair, none of it is directed at Matilda. After all, if her co-workers weren't such close-minded busybodies determined to police other people's behaviors, then Matilda wouldn't have had to make the choice between her career and me. So fuck them!

And frankly, I'm also kind of pissed off about how much the gay rights movement really fucked everything up. Sexuality is this super-duper diverse and complicated aspect of humanity. Yet for some reason, they decided to focus on making this one single thing—aka, same-sex relationships—palatable to the straight mainstream, rather than challenging sex-negativity more generally. And now, here we are, living in a brave new world where many of my friends feel comfortable being out as gay, yet they still often feel lots of pressure to hide the fact that they are bisexual, or they wouldn't dare tell their families that they are ethically non-monogamous, or they constantly worry about losing their jobs if their employers were to discover they are kinky, or they fear winding up in jail if they are ever caught engaging in sex work.

I don't want to live in a world where it's merely safe for people to be gay. I want to live in a world where it's okay for people to be unabashed unapologetic weirdos.

31. Good Grief

So then you just lie in bed for a seemingly endless stretch of time. Because you are devastated. You feel like a Mack truck just hit you. And the moment you think that, you realize that that's probably unfair to people who have actually been hit by trucks. Because they probably suffer god knows how many fractures, concussions, lacerations, and quite possibly far worse.

In comparison, you are not doing so bad. You, my friend, are just really really really sad. Your eyes are watery, your head congested, the skin around your nose and mouth raw from tissues. Your brain is racing all over the place. Your chest is so heavy that it feels like you are being crushed alive. You can barely breathe. It occurs to you that this heavy-chested feeling is the very reason why they call it a "broken heart." Even though your actual coronary system is probably functioning just fine. Unlike the rest of you.

And even though you've spent most of the last few days lying on this bed, you still have not gotten used to the emptiness that now fills this room: the missing furniture, clothing, photographs, knick-knacks and bric-a-bracs, and so forth, that Matilda took with her when she left.

A few concerned friends will occasionally show up to console you. They will try their best to cheer you up, even though you know it's a lost cause. They will invite you to some party, or suggest the two of you go out to see the latest superhero movie together. But you'll reply that you're just not feeling up to it. And they will tell you that everything is going to be okay, that time heals all wounds. But you will remind them that some wounds actually require sutures. Plus antibiotics. Perhaps even an overnight hospital stay.

Let's face it: Time isn't all it's cracked up to be.

In moments like this, people will reflexively talk about how your grief will ultimately come to pass. This is the "wave metaphor" for grief: It comes out of nowhere, sweeps you off your feet, temporarily engulfing you, but it eventually moves on, and you will (at some point in the not so distant future) land on your feet, thereby returning to normalcy.

But you know in your recently broken heart-of-hearts that this wave metaphor is complete bullshit.

No. You are 100 percent sure that this grief-stricken version of you—the one who has been non-stop lying in this bed, repeatedly analyzing every last word of Matilda's Dear John letter, mentally replaying that final excruciating argument the two of you had as she was moving her things out—that version of you is permanently wrecked. And she is never returning back to her old self.

But what *is* going to happen is that, with each passing day, you will physiologically change. The internet says that about 50 billion human cells die in the average person per day. And they are constantly being replaced by brand new ones: cells that never even met Matilda, and never lived through that horrible break up.

And as I discussed back in Chapter 13, "Socially Constructed Ice Cream," our brains can't possibly remember everything. All those moments from last week that you now vividly recall—unexpectedly bumping into a friend on your way to work, that random shopping errand in San Leandro, that tasty sandwich you ate for lunch—almost all of these memories will be culled in order to make room for more immediate sensations and information. Similarly, your life with Matilda will largely disappear from your recollection too. And the few shards of memory that do remain—a handful of extra-special and sometimes completely random moments the two of you shared over the last several years—they will increasingly seem distant, reduced to mere fragments and fractured images.

And eventually, you will weave a narrative out of these shattered and scattered memories, and it will go something like this: Matilda and I had a lot of wonderful times together, but ultimately we wanted different things out of life.

So knowing all this, grief-stricken you must come to terms with the fact that she is destined to lie on this bed for god knows how many weeks or months, until she eventually becomes an entirely different person. Physiologically speaking.

And when you finally do become this new different version of you, your main challenge will not be overcoming grief. It will be overcoming inertia. And the physiologically new you (who has somehow regained the ability to laugh) chuckles at the fact that "inertia" is a lot like the word "patronizing": It can be both a good and a bad thing. And right now, you are chock-full of bad inertia—the kind that compels you to remain a lump on the bed. But what you really need is the other type of inertia: the good inertia, which pushes you at a constant speed toward where you want to go. But in order to get from bad inertia to good inertia, you are going to need a little push.

Then the phone rings. It's your editor Mario. He reminds you about your looming manuscript deadline. Holy crap, there are still many more Erics to date and chapters to write!

That's when you finally get out of bed. You are wobbly at first. But then you put one foot in front of the other—just like that Winter Warlock guy from that stop-motion animated Christmas special from the '70s. You proverbially brush your teeth, jump in the shower, dry yourself off, and throw on some clothes. And then you go walking out the proverbial door.

Once you get over the initial drama and trauma of a big break up, it suddenly hits you that you are single. Yet again. And while there are definite advantages to being single, these seem to pale in comparison to the one really depressing realization that you cannot overcome: By definition, being "single" means that every relationship that you've ever had in your life has ultimately failed. Even the relationships that you fondly reminisce about—the ones that were happy, healthy, stable, and special, at least for a while—they failed on your watch too.

And when you are younger, this track record of failure is still fairly short, so you can easily convince yourself that you are not to blame. You just haven't met the right person yet.

But the older you get, when you look back on your life, there is a trail of dead relationships that stretches as far as the eye can see. And at some point, you are going to have to start taking all those dead bodies seriously.

So after Matilda and I broke up, I started thinking back to all my past relationships, trying to figure out why they all failed. And I noticed a pattern: Each and every one of them involved *two people*. And if you think about it, two people are not always going to want all the same things. In fact, they may even want *different* things. And the more that I considered it, the more it seemed clear that this whole "two person" thing was the primary factor that derailed all my past relationships.

Then it occurred to me: What if I tried having a relationship with only one person in it?

So I asked myself out.

And I was kind of surprised when it happened, because I had never really thought of myself in a romantic or sexual way before. But I seemed nice enough, so I said sure, why not.

I suggested a nearby restaurant. We both laughed about the fact that we ordered the exact same entree. As the conversation continued, we learned that we are both absurdist short fiction writers, avid lucid dreamers, and we both love movies that involve temporal paradoxes. It was uncanny how much we had in common!

We're even both Libras, which is super-important, because scientists have shown that up to 91.7 percent of relationship failures may be attributed to mismatched astrological pairings. (And I'll bet you the rest of the failures are due to the whole "two person" thing.)

Anyway, we were really hitting it off, so I took a chance and said: "No pressure or anything, but would you like to go back to my place afterwards?" And I enthusiastically consented!

We took it slow at first: holding hands on the way home, light kissing and cuddling on the sofa, which eventually led to heavy petting in the bedroom. It was super-fucking hot—as if we both knew exactly where and how to touch one another.

Then I whispered, "Are you kinky at all?" And I eagerly replied, "Yes." I could feel the sexual tension building until I heard the words, "But just so you know, I am strictly a bottom."

"Fuck, me too."

So now we're just friends. But really really close friends. Like, we're practically inseparable.

And nowadays, I'm no longer into the whole one-person relationship thing. Instead, I am dating the square root of negative one person. And it's fantastic. Unimaginable, even.

32. Book Cover

Eric #67 surprised me by showing up to our date wearing a white turtleneck shirt with white corduroy slacks and white sandals. I tried really hard not to make any snap judgments about his fashion sense (or lack thereof), because as the saying goes: You can't judge a book by its cover. Which is a cliché to be sure, but it also happens to be totally true.

Like that one time, when I was at my local bookstore perusing all the books, and this really provocative cover jumped out at me: It was this old-timey photo of a woman wearing a corset. And it compelled me to pick up the book and take a closer look. So I started reading the first few pages until it became clear that this was a dreadfully boring academic treatise on macroeconomics during the Victorian era. And I suddenly found myself shouting out, "WHAT THE FUCK, BOOK COVER?" while standing right there in the middle of the bookstore's Victorian Era Macroeconomics section.

Anyway, this whole not-judging-a-book-by-its-cover aphorism has been on my mind a lot lately, ever since I got that call from Mario last chapter. He invited me to his office to show me the galleys for the *99 Erics* book cover. Admittedly, it's a bit of a mind-fuck to be shown the cover of a book that you are still very much in the process of writing. But I guess the publisher needs to have this prepared ahead of time, so that once I finally do submit my finished manuscript, they can immediately move ahead with printing and promoting the book.

I showed up at Mario's office, and he showed me the cover. It was basically a photo of a naked male torso. But not just any old naked male torso. This guy was ripped—like you could see the contours of every single abdominal muscle he had. And the title "99 Erics" was scrawled in red lipstick across this guy's chest. Then Mario showed me the back cover copy, and it read: "What happens when a polyamorous bisexual woman takes it upon herself to sleep with every guy in the San Francisco Bay Area named Eric? In this sexy and steamy faux novel full of trysts and turns, Kat Cataclysm leaves nothing to the imagination."

Seriously.

So naturally, I expressed my concerns about how this cover totally misrepresents the book's subject matter. For starters, I've only seen like five or so of the Erics shirtless, and not a single one of them has high-definition abs! Plus, people who pick up the book will be expecting to be regaled with tales of my sexual exploits, when the truth is that I am really really bad at writing about sex, and the only play-by-play account of sex that I explicitly recount in the book (at least up to this point) was that one time when I thought that I was lucid dreaming during the whole thing. Unless of course, you also count my descriptions of banana slug, anglerfish, and Zyxxavxzian sex—the last of which doesn't even meet the standard definition of "sex" as ordained by the Galactic Consortium of Astrobiologists!

Let's face it: If the book cover were to accurately depict my actual sex life of late, it should simply be a picture of my favorite vibrator. Full stop.

So I told Mario he should scrap the whole thing and come up with a completely different cover. But then he suggested that I take a close look at my book contract, wherein I would find that I have absolutely no rights or authority to veto the book cover. Because apparently publishers do not consider the book cover, the back cover copy, nor even the title, to be part of the book's "content."

Rather, they view all these items as mere promotional material.

Which pretty much explains why you can't judge a book by its cover. So there you go.

Anyway, there I am, out on a date with Eric #67, and he is dressed in white from head to toe. So I asked: If you don't mind me asking, what's up with all the white?

Eric: I'm trying to cultivate a unique image.

Me: But why?

Eric: Because my goal in life is to become famous. Like, outrageously famous. For the usual reason.

Me: Because, like many of us, you were raised in a dysfunctional family that never made you feel loved, and now as an adult you constantly crave attention and adoration?

Eric: No, the other usual reason.

Me: Which is?

Eric: Well, because I'm really attached to all my things. You know, my material possessions: my car, furniture, appliances, linens, toiletries, all my shoes, my *Donnie Darko* action figure collection, the stuffed tardigrade that I've had ever since I was a child, and so on. I suppose this makes me sound materialistic.

Me: That's okay, I'm a materialist myself sometimes. Especially when it comes to ice cream.

Eric: The thing is, I don't have any family to speak of, and don't plan on having any children. So my material possessions are basically all I have. It's almost like they *are my children*. And god forbid, if one day I am hit by a Mack truck and unexpectedly die, there would be no one to take care of all my possessions. In fact, they'd probably all be separated from one another, and auctioned off to other less materialistic people who wouldn't care for them nearly as much as I do. In contemplating this horrific hypothetical scenario, it occurred to me that if I were to become famous—like *super-duper famous*—then when I pass away, my fans would probably build a museum to celebrate my life. And this museum would likely include all of my worldly possessions—thus, they would be well taken care of by professional curators and archivists for all eternity.

Me: Wow, that's something.

Eric: You probably think that I'm strange.

Me: Well, "strange" might be a bit much. Let's just call you "distinctive." Anyway, I suppose that I can somewhat relate, as I do have a tendency to anthropomorphize inanimate objects myself sometimes. Just the other day, I noticed a dress in my closet that I've only ever worn once before. And I found myself feeling really bad for that dress. Because way back when it was hanging on the rack in the store, it probably imagined being purchased by some high-femme lady who would wear it out all the time. But much to its chagrin, it was bought by someone like me, who only wears dresses occasionally, like for job interviews and shit. That dress must be heartbroken.

So I guess I understand your tendency to anthropomorphize your material possessions. But what I don't get is the part where you want to be famous.

Eric: Why not? Lots of people want to be famous!

Me: And for the life of me, I can't understand why. Because people treat celebrities like shit! They really do. Like, when you're famous, other people feel entitled to constantly comment on your dress and appearance, and to dissect and critique your every move. They'll stare at you, or holler at you as you are walking down the street. And even if you're just minding your own business at some bar or club, people will think nothing of coming right up to you and engaging you in conversation. Actually, now that I think about it, people treat celebrities pretty much the same way that they treat young women. There is a feminist analysis in here somewhere—I'm pretty sure of it.

Eric: I appreciate your concern, but my heart is set on becoming famous.

Me: So may I ask how you plan to become famous?

Eric: Very good question. I researched the subject extensively, trying to find the most efficient way to achieve fame. I began with a sample size of 9,803 famous people: I analyzed all their biographies, and created spreadsheets detailing every variable imaginable. And after crunching all the numbers, I noticed a clear pattern. It turns out that there is a correlation between fame and having some kind of talent. You know, like being an elite athlete, or a standout singer, performer, actor, director, writer, and so forth. The problem is, I am somewhat bereft of talent. Given this (or my lack of this), I think my best game plan is to become one of those people who is famous simply for being famous. You know, perhaps I'll be on some reality TV show where I will completely shine as "the guy who only wears white." Then the tabloids will start following me around. And I'll get invited to do all the talk shows. Occasionally, I'll do something relatively harmless yet controversial that will keep my name in the news. You know, the usual stuff.

Me: And what if that doesn't pan out? Do you have a back up plan?

Eric: Well, I majored in business in college, so I suppose that I could always go back to school and get my PhD in the burgeoning field of Victorian era macroeconomics, and make a name for myself that way.

Me: Awesome, good luck with that!

33. The One & Only Writing Tip You Will Ever Need

Back in "the good ol' days"—which, by most accounts, were actually quite horrific for large swaths of the population—there were just a few basic holidays: the big religious ones like Christmas and Easter (which conveniently happen to fall right around previously existing pagan celebrations) and the big national holidays such as Thanksgiving, 4th of July, and such. Over time, additional days were set aside to memorialize various people and movements: Presidents Day, Veterans Day, Labor Day, Martin Luther King Jr. Day, and so on. But in recent years, things have got completely out of hand. Now there is Talk Like a Pirate Day; Wear a Bracelet to Work Week; National Tinned Anchovies Month; you name it!

Within writer's circles, November has increasingly become known as National Novel Writing Month (or "NaNoWriMo"), in which amateur and professional writers alike attempt to churn out a first draft of their new novel in a mere thirty days, whilst simultaneously chronicling their experiences online. With November approaching, Grant (head of CliqueClick's Word Repurposing Department) encouraged me to write a listicle to coincide with this not-so-momentous occasion. You know, something along the lines of "19 Ways to Overcome Writer's Block," or "29 Mistakes Novelists Should Avoid Making," or "41 Writing Tips from Famous Authors."

But if I were to write a listicle along this line, I'd be inclined to call it: "The One and Only Writing Tip You Will Ever Need!" Sadly,

Grant immediately vetoed this idea, primarily on the basis that the number 1 is not considered to be a prime number, so we'd lose all those extra click-throughs. But this makes absolutely no sense to me. After all, the number 1 is only divisible by 1 and itself—which is the defining definition of prime numbers! That, along with being a positive integer, which the number 1 most certainly is. But Grant just babbled on and on about how "being greater than 1" is yet another criterion for prime numbers. Which seems like such an arbitrary rule to me. I mean, clearly that rule exists for the sole purpose of singling out the number 1 for exclusion!

This is yet another example of mathematics being oppressive and not treating all numbers equally.

I'm sure that my mathematically inclined readers are totally with me on this. But those of you who are more on the verbal side of the spectrum (if it even is a spectrum—for all I know, it could be some kind of multi-dimensional coordinate system) probably don't give a rat's ass about prime numbers. Instead, you might be more curious about what my "One and Only Writing Tip You Will Ever Need!" would be.

Well, here it is: *Don't listen to anyone else's writing tips!*

See, writing is a lot like politics or attraction, in that people are going to fall all over the map with regards to what they like or dislike. Some readers will enjoy the dense academic prose of a Victorian Era Macroeconomics treatise. Others may prefer the light reading and chaste romance of a YA dystopian novel, or the graphic sex scenes and theological questioning of a *Best Atheist & Agnostic Bisexual Women's Erotica* anthology. On top of that, some readers will inevitably be annoyed by your use of the word "whilst," or they may find the word "yellow" offensive, or feel like you're butchering the English language if you use words like "like" and "verbatim" in unconventional ways.

As the saying goes: You can fool some of the people some of the time, but you can't please them all.

Or something like that.

The purpose of writing is to communicate ideas with other human beings. So long as whatever you write reaches and resonates with *some* people, then you are doing your job right. Or well enough, at least. But some writers fail to appreciate this. And in providing writing tips, they will go far beyond offering suggestions about how to communicate effectively, and veer into the territory of cut-and-dried, hard-and-fast writing rules.

For example, many famous authors have encouraged other writers to "kill" adverbs, or have described adverbs as "plagues," "mortal sins," and the "road to hell." Seriously, are we supposed to entirely eradicate one of the eight parts of speech? While we're at it, why not get rid of prepositions? Or conjunctions? Or adjectives? Speaking of the latter, adverb-haters who abhor words like "suddenly" or "slowly" usually won't take issue if you use adjectives like "sudden" or "slow." In fact, most adverbs are basically just adjectives with the suffix "–ly" tacked onto the end! And I don't think that it's a coincidence that adding vowels (often Ys) to the ends of masculine or neutral words has the effect of turning them into feminine or diminutive ones. In other words, this hatred of adverbs (especially of the "–ly" variety) seems largely driven by implicit sexism and ageism! Which means that language—much like math—is also oppressive and promoting inequalities!

Here is another example of an arbitrary and over the top writing rule: Kurt Vonnegut urged writers not to use semicolons under any circumstances, because he believed that they were "transvestite hermaphrodites representing absolutely nothing." For starters, I'm pretty sure "transvestite hermaphrodites" are not an actual thing. Unless of course, there are some non-apophallized banana slugs out there who have a penchant for wearing clothing associated with aphallic banana slugs. Second, even if there were such a thing as "transvestite hermaphrodites," they would by necessity represent *something.* At the very least, they would represent crossdressing banana slugs. Or (if Vonnegut's assertion is correct) they might represent semicolons. This is basic linguistics people—the signifier and the signified—get with the program Vonnegut!

Thirdly (which, despite being an actual English word employed correctly here, some writers will surely chide me for using, along with my use of the words "correctly" and "surely" just then), semicolons themselves also represent something—namely, a pause or break in a sentence that is more pronounced than that provided by a comma.

I have no qualms with Vonnegut disliking or detesting semicolons (and everything that they may or may not stand for), and he has every right to profess that as his personal preference. But where does he get off telling other writers what they should or shouldn't be doing? For fuck's sake, Vonnegut inserted a picture of his asshole into the text of his novel *Breakfast of Champions.* And it wasn't even a halfway decent picture of his asshole either! It pretty much just looked like an asterisk.

As the saying goes: People who live in glass houses made out of poorly drawn assholes should not throw stones at punctuation marks that may or may not represent crossdressed banana slugs.

Or something like that.

34. Textbook Answers

So I'm at the laundromat and this guy randomly comes up to me. He says: Hey.

Me: Hey.

Guy: So what brings you here?

Me: Um, I suppose that I am waiting for my wash to wash. Or my dry to dry.

Guy: And what's with all the textbooks? (He gestures at the stack of textbooks sitting just to my right.)

Me: I don't know, I haven't figured that part out yet.

Guy: What do you mean?

Me: Well see, I have writer's block right now. Which is rare for me—I almost always have something to say. But at the moment, I am plum out of ideas.

Guy: I think the word you are looking for is "plumb," not "plum."

Me: What are you, my editor?

Guy: Sorry. But I still don't get what writer's block has to do with that stack of textbooks.

Me: It's a writing prompt. Whenever I'm at a loss for what to write about, I play *Clue* with myself—you know, like the board game: Colonel Mustard in the Conservatory with the Rope, or Miss Scarlet in the Billiard Room with the Candlestick. So I picked a place and an object off the top of my head: I put Kat Cataclysm in the Laundromat with a Stack of Textbooks. And now I'm just supposed to start writing. But nothing is coming, I'm afraid.

Guy: I came, didn't I?

Me: I suppose. But right now you're just a generic guy.

Guy: No I'm not! I am a character with great depth. And width. Depth and/or width.

Me: Oh yeah? Tell me something about yourself then.

Guy: Well, I enjoy listening to music. And working out. Taking long walks on the beach . . .

Me: See, like I said, you're completely generic. Do you even have a name?

Guy: Why, of course I do. It's . . . Eric. Eric Guygen.

Me: Eric Guygen is the worst anagram of "generic guy" imaginable. You didn't even bother to mix up the letters, for Christ's sake!

Eric: But I had you at Eric, didn't I?

Me: Hmmm. Well, what do you do for a living?

Eric: I'm a consultant.

Me: What does that even mean?

Eric: Well, if someone needs some kind of expert advice, they will hire me as a consultant. Then I assess the situation and make my recommendations. You know, consulting.

Me: God, this isn't going anywhere.

Eric: Would it help if I did something completely out of the blue. Like tap dance? Or yodel?

Me: I promised readers a few chapters ago that there would be no yodeling in this book. And I already reneged on one promise so far.

Eric: You mean that tube of lidocaine?

Me: Stop mentioning it—it wasn't supposed to make a reappearance! Anyway, I think we need something way more interesting than tap dancing or yodeling to save this chapter.

Eric: Oh my god, there's a tornado right behind you!

Me: I don't believe you. Besides, that's way too over the top.

Eric: Well, what if we turned our attention back to the

textbooks. What subjects do they cover?

Me: I can't decide. On account of my writer's block.

Eric: Perhaps one of the textbooks could be called "19 Ways to Overcome Writer's Block"?

Me: That doesn't really sound like a textbook title, it sounds more like a listicle. In fact, it's the very same listicle that I ended up writing last chapter, just after Grant vetoed my "The One and Only Writing Tip You Will Ever Need" idea. Plus, how-to-cure-writer's-block advice is always so trite: go for a walk; change your surroundings; eliminate all distractions; read a book for inspiration; and so on. These suggestions are all fine and dandy if you're just slightly stuck—like when you need to turn bad inertia into good inertia. But they don't do a damned bit of good when your writer's block is caused by absolute existential despair.

Eric: Why are you experiencing absolute existential despair?

Me: Well, my longtime partner broke up with me a few chapters ago. And just as I was recovering from that, my country elected a reality TV show celebrity to be its president.

Eric: Oh dear!

Me: The funny thing is, I kinda sorta predicted this might happen a few years back. It just made too much sense. Exhibit A: For the life of me, I can't understand why so many people like reality TV. Exhibit B: For the life of me, I can't understand why so many people vote against their own interests. Ergo, some day the American people were bound to elect a reality TV celebrity for president against their own interests. Q.E.D.

Eric: Wow, have you ever considered competing on the TV show *America's Top Syllogists?*

Me: That's not even a real reality show. Anyway, if you would have asked me back then which reality TV star would most likely become president, I probably would have guessed one of those *Jersey Shore* people, you know, the ones with the nicknames like "Pooki" and "The Predicament"? Or maybe a Kardashian, or one of the myriad *Real Housewives*. But instead, it ended up being the narcissistic blustering billionaire who ran on a platform of racism, xenophobia, misogyny, and general hatred of the constitutive Other. And I was already a depressive progressive to begin with, mostly because I couldn't fathom how our political system could ever escape the clutches of the corporate oligarchy. But that whole time, it never occurred to me that we might potentially plummet into outright fascism. Which depresses me even more so.

Eric: Hey, what's that sound? Is that people laughing?

Me: Yeah. This place is a comedy venue in the front and a laundromat in the back. I think tonight is their open mic night.

Eric: But that doesn't explain all the people laughing.

Me: Good one! Perhaps you should be a comedian yourself?

Eric: Nah, I'm too generic of a person. I'd probably tell boring and banal jokes like, "Why do they call it a restroom—it's not like you can take a nap in there!" Or, "Guys, have you ever noticed how women all go to the restroom at the same time?"

Me: Why are all of your jokes about restrooms? And the second joke isn't even true. Like, I've been a woman my entire life, and I have never once purposefully timed my restroom usage to coordinate with other women. Most women go to the restroom by themselves. When they need to go. I'm pretty sure of it.

Eric: Well, if you're such the comedy expert, why don't you take a shot at it? You mentioned a few chapters ago that you were working on a comedy routine.

Me: Yeah, but it's not ready yet.

Eric: Too bad, I already signed you up to perform.

Me: When did you do that? You've been right here talking to me this whole entire time.

Eric: Remember when you got up from your computer five or so minutes ago?

Me: Yeah, I took a writing break to use the restroom.

Eric: Ah-ha, that would explain why you subconsciously came

up with all that restroom dialogue for me! Anyway, while you were in the loo, I went into the other room and signed you up for the open mic. Hark, I think I hear something.

(Faintly, from the other room): Next on the list is an open-mic-night virgin. Let's hear it for Kat Cataclysm.

Me: Holy crap . . .

I reluctantly walked up to the stage, lugging all the textbooks with me. As I placed them down on the stage just to my left, I noticed that the one on top was a Physics textbook. So I took that as a prompt for my comedy routine.

Hey folks, how are you doing tonight? I'm actually not doing so well myself, because I recently found out that I have become quantum entangled with another person named Ellis. This basically means that, although we are separated by a great distance, actions performed on Ellis have an effect on me. Last week, while I was driving, Ellis decided to go on a drinking binge, and I ended up crashing my car into a telephone pole. I wasn't hurt, but the next day I had to take my car to the quantum mechanic.

Nobody was laughing, so I tossed the Physics textbook aside. Now the book on top was on Sex Education.

How many folks out there are sterile? A show of hands . . . anyone? Anyone? Okay, just me I guess. So I'd imagine that some of you out there will eventually choose to bear children. Although I'm not sure why. I mean, WHY WOULD YOU EVER TURN YOUR CHILD INTO A BEAR?!

That routine wasn't working either. So I took a look at the next textbook—it was on History.

They say that history repeats itself. But I don't think that's really true. Take the War of 1812, for instance. I don't think we are ever going to have one of those again.

Still nothing. So it was onto the next textbook: Economics.

They always say, "Be the change that you want to see in the world." Which is why I decided to become thirty-seven cents. Speaking of change, I hate it when people talk about "loose change" or making a "fast buck." Seriously people, STOP SLUT-SHAMING MONEY!

Absolute crickets. So I reluctantly grabbed the final textbook. It sported the unlikely title: *19 Ways to Overcome Writer's Block*. I opened it up to the first chapter, which was simply called "Go for a Walk."

So that's what I decided to do.

35. Freudian Slip

Sometimes when I am typing the word "make," I'll look up at my computer screen to find the word "male" instead. At first, I dismissed this as a plain old typo—after all, the letter "k" lies right next to the letter "l" on the keyboard. Albeit on the left. But I've since caught myself making this same mistake on numerous occasions, so I started questioning whether there might be something more to this than a mere mistake. Perhaps it was a Freudian slip: While typing the word "make," I subconsciously think about "making it" with someone, and since I am attracted to men, I accidentally type "male" as a result?

This seemed like a reasonable hypothesis. But then one day, while I was actually trying to type "male," a brand new typo rushed forth from my fingertips: "msle." And I had no idea what it meant. But if I was going to be honest with myself, I had to entertain the possibility that this too was a Freudian slip. And therefore, I must be subconsciously attracted to "msle"s. Whatever they are.

So of course I searched the internet for "msle" and found that it seemingly stands for one of two possible things: Multisensory Structured Language Education or Modified Soil Loss Equation. This left me in a pickle, because how was I to know for sure whether I was subconsciously attracted to holistic approaches toward increasing literacy, or methods of estimating soil erosion?

But then a few subsequent internet searches led me to the webpage for Eric Kishotenketsu, a professor in UC Berkeley's Environmental Sciences Department, whose lab has published a few research papers utilizing the Modified Soil Loss Equation. And right then and there, I came out to myself as sexually oriented toward methods of estimating soil erosion. And/or the people who study such things.

Or at the very least, I was questioning.

Since this guy is a professor at a prestigious university, I'm sure he's super-busy supervising the grad students who teach his Biogeochemistry 101 course for him while he is out in the field collecting soil samples, writing up his latest results for publication, prodding his peers to submit their research articles to an upcoming special issue of the research journal *Land Degradation & Development* that he is guest editing, preparing a presentation that he will soon give at some other prestigious university, all while spending many a late night revising revisions of his latest grant application. Plus, for all I know, he could be married or otherwise monogamously coupled, and therefore have little to no interest in going out on a date with some absurdist short fiction writer whom he doesn't even know, and whom (unbeknownst to him) is primarily interested in the fact that his name is Eric. And to a lesser extent, because she now identifies as soil-erosion questioning.

So I decided to contact Dr. Kishotenketsu (or Eric #71, as I will call him henceforth) under somewhat false pretenses. In my introductory email, I told him that I was a writer for the internet news outlet CliqueClick, and that I was interested in interviewing him for an article that I was planning to write about the ten most pressing questions facing environmental scientists today. (Although the piece would later turn out to be a listicle about how to tell whether or not you are sexually oriented toward specific fields of scientific inquiry. And it would be seven rather than ten items, because Grant is such a stickler about prime numbers.)

The following morning, Eric #71 replied to say yes, he'd be delighted to be interviewed for the piece, especially by a reporter from CliqueClick, given the relentless work we are doing to educate the masses about science. (I didn't have the heart to tell him that we do no such thing, it's just our algorithm giving him that impression.)

We settled on meeting at this pizza-slash-pub place right near campus, where all of the food items are named after planets or else ancient Greek and Roman gods. Which I suppose were pretty much the same things in the eyes of the ancient Greeks and Romans. After our initial hellos and ordering of food, Eric #71 started asking me about the article I was supposedly planning to write.

Eric: So what sorts of personal details will you need about me? The story about how I first became interested in science as a child? Anecdotes that demonstrate how I am constantly obsessed with questions about how water, wind, and unsustainable agricultural practices lead to soil erosion?

Me: Why would I need any of that stuff?

Eric: You are writing a pop-science article, correct?

Me: Um, yeah.

Eric: Well, pop-science articles are a lot like Olympics coverage: both presume that audiences will be far more interested in human interest stories than the actual subject at hand. So I figured that you'd probably want to center your story around me personally: portraying me as an engaging yet eccentric character who is on some kind of grand quest, augmented with behind-the-scenes photos of me and my students working with expensive-looking lab equipment, and perhaps even interviews with people whose lives have been saved or improved thanks to the efforts of soil scientists.

Me: Oh. Okay, good point. Let me ask you a few personal questions then. Who were the scientists that first inspired you to become a scientist yourself?

Eric: Hmmm. Well, if you are talking about the entire history of science, obviously Aristotle was really important.

Me: Aristotle? Are you kidding me?

Eric: Well sure, he helped to invent the scientific method.

Me: Yeah, but almost all of his theories were wrong. Like, seriously wrong! For starters, he thought the sun and all the planets revolved around the earth. And that heavy objects fall faster than lighter ones. Whereas I've known these things aren't true since elementary school!

Eric: But . . .

Me: Plus, Aristotle was super-duper sexist. He believed that women were inferior to men because we don't produce semen, which he believed to be some kind of "life force." He also claimed that men have warmer blood and more teeth than women.

Eric: Really? But everyone has thirty-two teeth. All he had to do was count them.

Me: Exactly, but he didn't even bother to because he was so blinded by sexism. Just like most famous scientists. Take Sigmund Freud for instance. He believed that all young girls suffer from penis envy, which is ludicrous—most girls' initial reactions to learning about penises are amusement or indifference. Freud also infamously claimed that vaginal orgasms are mature and clitoral orgasms immature. But how could he possibly know this? I mean, I'm pretty sure that you would need to actually have those body parts in order to assess any such differences. And what on earth is a "mature" orgasm anyway? Is it when, instead of screaming: [in orgasm voice] "ugh, ugh, fuck me harder, oh god, oh god, yes, yes!" you instead exclaim: "ugh, ugh, I am a responsible person who is considerate of others, ugh, I'm non-judgmental and well organized, yes, yes!"

Eric: Is this where I'm supposed to interject, "I'll have what she's having"?

Me: Or how about Charles Darwin, who may have been right about evolution in a general sense, but whose sexism led to claim that males are "eager" and promiscuous when it comes to sex, but that females are "coy" and need to be courted.

Eric: Well, that does make sense, doesn't it? After all, men have a seemingly endless supply of sperm, and aren't burdened with the costs of bearing children . . .

Me: *WHY WOULD YOU EVER TURN YOUR CHILD INTO A BEAR?!*

Eric: Excuse me? What did you just say?

Me: Sorry. It was a joke. A joke that nobody ever laughs at. Not even in simulated comedy clubs that exist entirely within the confines of my own mind.

Eric: As I was saying, unlike men, women have a limited number of eggs, and have to carry their own offspring to term. So of course they will be pickier about who they mate with, and favor fit and successful males who are capable of providing resources for her and her offspring.

Me: On the surface, that might sound like a plausible theory. But in reality, it's not true at all. Take me for instance: Most of the men who I've had sex with were not especially fit, nor successful, nor capable of providing any resources for offspring. Plus, I'm bisexual, so I also often have sex with women, the majority of whom do not make any sperm whatsoever. Basically, my sex life has nothing to do with picking and choosing the best partner to fertilize my eggs. Because that's not even going to happen. Because I'm sterile.

Eric: You're sterile? As in germ-free?

Me: No, I actually love germs—I take probiotics all the time on account of my irritable bowel syndrome. But I am germ cell-free, by which I mean free of fucking Fabergé eggs. So it seems clear to me that Darwin's claim—that men are "eager" and women are "coy"—is not only incorrect, but is merely a thinly veiled way for confused-slut dude-bros to justify their desire to have lots of sex, while shaming women who also seek out lots of sex.

Eric: What is a confused slut?

Me: It's complicated. When my book comes out, check out Chapter 17, "Ethical Slut vs. Confused Slut"—I explain it all there. My point is that women and men do not strictly adhere to specific sets of mating practices. We all vary greatly. As with politics, the interpretation of words, and literary preferences, human beings fall all over the map when it comes to sexuality. As a species, we are polymorphously perverse.

Eric: Isn't that a Freudian term?

Me: Yes it is. But Freud used it to describe children during the developmental stage from infancy until about five years old. Although if you ask me, categorizing children according to their supposed sexual impulses seems somewhat . . . perverse.

Eric: So far you've only asked me one interview question. Do you have any others for me?

Me: Um, sure. Let me think . . . In your mind, what's the most important scientific invention of all time?

Eric: Wow, that's a tough one. The computer? Penicillin? The steam engine?

Me: Wrong! It was the cup.

Eric: The cup?

Me: Yes, the cup. Isn't it obvious? I mean, just look around us—there are cups everywhere!

Eric: I mean, sure, cups are useful, but . . .

Me: Useful?! They seem pretty vital to me! Just think about it: When other animals want to quench their thirst, they have to aimlessly wander around until they stumble upon a puddle, or pond, or stream. But thanks to the inventor of the cup, we can now carry beverages around with us wherever we go. I mean, just think of how different dating would be were it not for the cup. The standard "would you like to go out for drinks sometime?" would involve both parties getting all dolled up, then meeting up at a nearby body of water. I'd imagine the conversation would go something like this:

Person 1: So, what do you do? [laps liquid]

Person 2: I'm an English literature professor. [laps liquid] The focus of my work is on homosociality in Dickensian literature. And you?

Person 1: Well, I fancy myself as a bit of an inventor of sorts. [laps liquid]

Person 2: Oh, what sorts of things do you invent? [laps liquid]

Person 1: Well, my latest project is something I am calling "the straw." It's still a work in progress, but if it pans out, it would allow us to drink from puddles and ponds without having to use our tongues. [laps liquid]

Person 2: Wow, that's fantastic! Be sure to patent that!

Eric: You have an unusual perspective on things. I find it quite charming. Actually, since you brought up the subject of dating, would you be interested in going out on a date with me sometime?

Me: Sure. Although I should tell you up front that I'm not 100 percent sexually oriented toward methods of estimating soil erosion and/or the people who study them, such as yourself. I'm really just questioning at this point.

Eric: I didn't even know that that was a thing.

Me: Neither did I. I only just found out in the beginning of this chapter. So I guess what I'm saying is that I'm willing to give it a try, but when all is said and done, it may turn out that you are simply not my typo.

Eric: I think you meant "not my type."

Me: That's what I said.

Eric: No it isn't. I distinctly heard you say "typo" rather than "type."

Me: Oh, never mind that—that was just a typo.

Eric: How do you know that it wasn't some kind of Freudian slip?

36. Worst Eric Ever

I fucking hate Eric #73! He initially came across as sweet and charming and trustworthy. But it was all a sham—one that I could not see coming due to my lack of gut feelings. He played me like a fool. And now I fucking hate that fucking asshole. And I will never trust another person named Eric #73 ever again.

37. Emotionally Labored

One of the best perks of being a writer (or perhaps the only perk, given that I don't get actual benefits like healthcare, retirement, etcetera) is that I don't have to do any emotional labor as part of my job. Granted, I do have to appeal to and appease readers when writing my listicles and absurdist short stories. But at least I don't ever have to physically smile at them, or ask them how their day has been, or act genuinely concerned when they complain about how they didn't want cheese on their cheeseburger (even though they very clearly ordered a "cheeseburger," which just so happens to have the word "cheese" built right into it).

I have nothing against the exchange of basic pleasantries: the "hellos" and "how are you doings" and the like. But increasingly, employers seem to be ratcheting up the amount of emotional labor that they expect out of their employees. It's no longer sufficient that workers simply be affable. Nowadays, they need to be downright enthusiastic and effusive. And as a result, whenever I go to my bank to deposit a check, I am barraged by all these personal questions: "So what have you been doing with your day so far?" or "What are your plans for the weekend?"

And now I'm expected to do counter-emotional labor in response to their emotional labor!

And believe me, I in no way enjoy plastering a fake smile on my face while replying, "Before coming here to deposit this check, I basically spent the entire day lying like a lump in my bed waiting for my body to physiologically change in the wake of Matilda leaving me." Or receiving confused stares from the clerk after telling them, "My plan for this weekend is to date two different people named Eric for my ongoing book project. But frankly, my heart is no longer in it ever since Eric #73's shenanigans."

I'm not sure who it is behind the scenes that unilaterally decided that customers and clients must want service workers to pretend to be our best friends. But whoever these deciders are, I'm pretty fucking sure that they're not queer. Nor weirdos, for that matter. Because if you just so happen to be queer and/or a weirdo (like me), then these seemingly well-intended questions will often feel like an onslaught of little bombs to you.

Here's an example: Last year (before the whole novocaine debacle), I was at the dentist having my teeth cleaned, and the hygienist kept trying to enthusiastically engage me in conversation. Which is difficult enough considering that she was poking around inside of my mouth at the same time. But right off the bat, one of her first questions was, "Are you in a relationship with anyone?" So I said yes. And she asked, "What's his name?" So I replied, "Matilda" (because we were still together back then). And she was like, "Oh dear, sorry."

And I could tell that she was suddenly overcome with all this heterosexual guilt, because she tried to rectify things by telling me the story about how her fourteen-year-old nephew had just come out as gay, and how her family were all so very proud of him. And honestly, I couldn't care less about this woman's nephew—nothing against him personally, it's just that (as a general rule) I am not a big fan of fourteen-year-olds, because they remind me of how viciously mean my classmates were to me when I was fourteen. Not to mention the fact that fourteen year olds are still pretty much drunk! And not to mention the fact that whenever we say "not to mention the fact," we always subsequently mention the fact! Which makes absolutely no sense, if you think about it.

Then my hygienist pivoted to one of the oldest questions in the book: "So what is it that you do?" When people ask this, they are never expecting you to say, "I enjoy watching baseball games," or "I often take walks around Lake Merritt." No, when they say "what do you do?" they are very specifically asking you about your occupation. And for so many years back when I didn't have a job, or a steady job, or a job that I cared much for, this was always such an awkward question for me, because I knew that they would likely judge me based on my answer (or lack thereof). But given my current employment situation, I was able to respond: I'm a writer at CliqueClick. And when she asked me what I write, I replied: listicles. Suddenly the conversation stalls, because she is not particularly internet savvy, and she tells me that she has no idea what CliqueClick or listicles even are.

So now I'm the one who feels bad about alienating her with my esoteric occupation. So in order to bring her back into the fold, I reflexively mention that I am also currently working on a novel. And her face lights up, because of course she knows what a novel is! She then asks, "What is your novel about?" Then it hits me that I have completely fallen into a trap. A trap made entirely out of my own emotional labor. Not to mention hers. Because now there are only two possible courses of action for me: honestly describe the premise of my book (which will likely shatter her misconceptions of me as a nice monogamous lesbian lady, and lead her to presume that I must be some kind of "slut," which in her mind is never paired with the crucial modifying adjective "ethical"), or else flat out lie about what my book is about. Sure, I could try to say something vague, like that my book is about "men" or "dating." But in my experience, such vague responses almost always lead to further follow up questions (such as "what kinds of men?" or "is it a lesbian dating book?") that will once again coerce me into either lying or honestly replying.

Let's face it: It's a lose-lose situation for me. And it's all because of emotional labor.

38. Bad Actor

Once upon a time, in the not so distant past, personal ads were quite stigmatized. The ads themselves were hidden in the back pages of newspapers, and the people who relied on them were openly derided as "pathetic" and "desperate." But then the internet happened. And along with it came Ed's List, where you could look for a new apartment, a used car, and/or someone to have no-strings-attached sex with, all in one convenient location. Soon enough, mainstream online dating sites like Catch.com and eMelody popped up, along with more niche offerings like Ashley Hamilton and PetLife. And nowadays, there are mobile apps like Finder and Gaydr, where you can swipe through people's profiles whenever you feel horny and/or bored.

As a result of living in this brave new world of online dating, we have all learned important new life skills. For instance, many men seem to have mastered the art of photographing their naked torso in a bathroom mirror. And many women have acquired the vital life skill of not responding to men who post shirtless bathroom mirror selfies on their profiles.

Another online-dating-related skill that most of us have developed is the art of casually purveying a crowded cafe, bar, or restaurant, in the hopes of recognizing your date, despite not knowing exactly what they look like, because all you have to go by is their profile picture, which (let's face it) may not be very representative. When doing this, you have to strike the right balance between making a visual connection with your prospective date when they arrive, while simultaneously avoiding prolonged eye contact with all the other random people in the establishment, as this will likely creep them out. If you are a woman, the degree of difficulty for this task is increased, as you will also need to ensure that your glancing around the room will not be misinterpreted by men as you signaling your availability or interest in them. This is especially true when you are a woman sitting alone in a bar. And it is especially especially true when that bar is located in a hotel (such as this one, on the second floor of the Oakland Marriott) that is chock-full of traveling businessmen who have nothing better to do than to try to hook up with someone tonight. And this is especially especially especially true if you continue to nonchalantly peruse the bar crowd for over twenty minutes straight, because your date just so happens to be late.

Thankfully, before any strange men hit on me, Eric #79 arrives. He's average looking (by which I mean very conventionally attractive) and dressed business casual.

Eric: My apologies for being late. I forgot to take the time change from traveling into account. Your 8 p.m. is my 10 p.m., which is normally when I sleep.

Me: You go to bed each night at precisely 10 p.m.?

Eric: Yes, but for only twenty minutes. See, I'm on an Uberman sleep schedule, where I take six twenty-minute naps spread evenly throughout the day: at 2 a.m., 6 a.m., 10 a.m., 2 p.m., 6 p.m., and 10 p.m.

Me: Oh.

Eric: I take it that you're monophasic then.

Me: Monophasic? Are you referring to birth control pills? Because I don't take those.

Eric: No silly, I meant sleep. I assume you're a monophasic sleeper—that is, someone who sleeps once a day for a whopping eight hours.

Me: Oh. Yes, I am one of those sleepers. Although it's more

like six or seven hours on most days. By the way, feel free to order yourself a drink—I already got myself an IPA while I was waiting here. Also, I believe this place has food if you're hungry, although it's mostly bar food and sandwiches.

Eric: No thanks, I'm an intermittent faster, and today is one of my fasting days. Plus, even if I were eating today, it wouldn't be a sandwich, as I am on a strict Paleolithic diet.

Me: Oh really? I myself am on a Proterozoic diet.

Eric: What's that?

Me: I only eat organisms that existed prior to the Cambrian explosion.

Eric: There was an explosion in Cambria?

Me: Sorry. It was just a joke. A not very good joke apparently.

Eric: So tell me Kat, what do you do?

Me: Do you mean for a living? Because that can be a loaded question.

Eric: For a living, in your spare time, while you're sleeping a whopping six or seven hours a day—however you want to answer it.

Me: I'm a writer. Which is what I do for my day job, and also in my spare time. Plus, I often dream about missing writing deadlines when I sleep.

Eric: Wow, it sounds like you lead a very sedentary lifestyle.

Me: Seriously?! Instead of asking me about my writing, you critique my sedentariness? If that's even a word?

Eric: Sorry, I wasn't sure that you would want to talk about your writing. I mean, for all I know, you could be someone who writes about unsavory or taboo subjects. Or maybe you compose those inane little lists that literally litter the internet. In those cases, I'd imagine that you'd rather avoid the topic of writing all together. You know, out of embarrassment.

Me: Fair point. But also, I am not completely sedentary! I do move around. Somewhat. My fingers are always typing. And I am constantly using my brain. And brain activity counts as activity. I'm pretty sure of it.

Eric: If you're going to be sitting all day, I highly recommend applying ice packs to your belly and the back of your neck—this will help turn white fat cells into brown fat cells, thereby boosting your metabolism!

Me: What are you, some kind of fitness guru? Although I'm not sure why they're always called "gurus." It's a really strange word pairing: "fitness guru." It's almost as weird as "Democratic operative."

Eric: No, I'm not a fitness guru. But I am a life hacker.

Me: Oh, so you're like a genetic engineer then? My boyfriend from college, Eric #2, went to grad school for that. He was always talking about recombinant DNA.

Eric: Your college boyfriend's last name was Number Two?

Me: It's a long story.

Eric: Well, sorry to disappoint, but I do not hack anybody's genetic codes.

Me: Then is the life hacking you do more physiological in nature? Such as eating foods that you know you're allergic to? Or taking melatonin in the morning rather than evening to mess up your circadian rhythms?

Eric: You seem to be under the misconception that hacking is an inherently bad thing. Like something that only bad actors engage in.

Me: By bad actors, do you mean like William Shatner or Keanu Reeves? Seriously, individuals who hack into people's computers and steal their personal information are bad, but not that bad!

Eric: Hacking simply refers to finding a clever way to solve a problem. So a computer hacker might create an ingenious shortcut solution using computer code. Whereas I—being a life hacker—create ingenious shortcut solutions to make everyday life more efficient.

Me: So what you're saying is that "hacking" can be both a good and a bad thing? Like "patronizing" or "inertia"?

Eric: Pretty much.

Me: Okay. But I still don't understand why you call these things "life hacks." Why not just call them being efficient? It seems really inefficient to make up a whole new word to describe being efficient.

Eric: Well basically, it's branding. It's way easier to get people to visit my website when it's called MostAmazingestLifeHacks.com than if I had named it BeingEfficient.com.

Me: What is MostAmazingestLifeHacks.com?

Eric: It started out as a blog about life hacks, but it has since blossomed into a burgeoning business empire. I've written three books: *Most Amazingest Life Hacks, More Most Amazingest Life Hacks,* and *Most Amazingest Life Hacks for Dummies.* I'm constantly invited to do interviews on the daytime talk show circuit, and my Most Amazingest Life Hacks infomercials run late at night on cable TV. In fact, that's why I'm here at this hotel, for the Association of Life Hackers Annual Conference.

Me: Wow. I didn't know that any of this was even a thing.

Eric: You betcha it's a thing. A big thing! Which is why I'm on the Uberman sleep schedule, so that I have enough time to work out and take care of my body, while also spending sixteen hours a day running my life-hacking business empire.

Me: Wow, you must really trust future you.

Eric: Come again?

Me: I said, you must really trust your future self. Because you seem to be constantly working like a dog, and living this extremely ascetic and sleepless lifestyle, in order to obtain future success and wealth. But what's to stop future you from taking all the money that you've been making, and spending it wildly on food and booze and recreational drugs and misadventures? If that were to happen, future you would have all of this fun and gratification at the expense of present you.

Eric: But I would never do that to myself!

Me: It's not about doing it to yourself. Future you will be a completely different person than present you. Physiologically speaking. Sure, you both will share many of the same formative experiences. But future you will be neurologically shaped by new experiences that present you has never had—at least not yet. On top of that, over the course of each year, 98 percent of our atoms become swapped out for other atoms. In other words, future you will be an entirely different person on the molecular level. So I'm not sure why you would trust them with your life-hacking business empire.

Eric: Wow, I never thought about it like that before. You're right—I should live for today. Fuck future me! I think I'm going to order myself a rib-eye steak and an expensive bottle of wine! Perhaps I'll even sleep in tomorrow!

Me: That's the spirit!

Eric: And afterward, would you be interested in doing heroin with me?

Me: What?!

Eric: I said, do you want to do heroin with me later tonight? I've heard that it's a really intense and incomparable high.

Me: Um, no.

Eric: Why not?

Me: Because, while I don't want to live my life solely for the benefit of future me, I also don't want future me to become a heroin addict.

Eric: Well then, how about we steal a car together?

Me: No!

Eric: Why not?

Me: Because I don't want future me to go to jail either.

Eric: But just imagine the adrenaline rush that present you will feel speeding down the street at eighty miles an hour in a stolen vehicle!

Me: Holy shit. I think I just life-hacked you.

Eric: No you haven't. I am not any more efficient than I used to be.

Me: No, I mean I life-hacked you in a bad way, in that I've reprogrammed you toward nefarious ends. Which I suppose makes me a bad actor!

Eric: Indeed, I've found your performance in this chapter to be emotionally flat and wooden.

39. Days of Future Passed

What I just said to Eric #79 also applies to me: I wouldn't trust future me any farther than I could throw her. Which isn't very far. Because I've met her before, in the restroom of my favorite pub after the Time Gate appeared, and she's pretty much my same size.

I have nothing against future me, mind you. I'm sure that she is a lovely person, and we obviously have a lot in common. But at the same time, I'm also aware that I'm the "future me" to all sorts of past iterations of me, and I know for sure that they would have been extremely surprised and/or disappointed by how I turned out. Elementary-school me always imagined that when she grew up to be an adult, she would stack her kitchen cabinets full of Oreo cookies, and that she would eat them whenever she pleased. Little did she suspect that her "future me" (aka, present me) would have completely lost her sweet tooth, and would instead prefer savory foods, such as anchovies and blue cheese.

Or how about teenaged me, who was very briefly yet stridently into Ayn Rand. That teenaged version of me was convinced that she was politically aware and righteous, and she'd be shocked to learn that her "future me" would be horribly embarrassed by her political naivety, not to mention taste in literature.

Frankly, every major thing that has happened to me—whether it be dating Eric #2 in college, or coming out as a baby dyke in San Francisco, or having skin cancer, or the two years that I wasted on poetry slam—has set me off on a different life path, one that I could not have imagined previously.

When I first started this book project, I was a completely different iteration of me. I was the Kat Cataclysm who was in a happy long-term relationship with Matilda. And when I first started dating all these Erics, I was primarily looking for writing fodder rather than a new relationship, as I always had Matilda to go home to when all was said and done. But that iteration of me ended when Matilda left me. And during that interim period of grieving, as I was waiting for my body to physiologically change, I had absolutely no desire for sex or human companionship.

To most people, the notion of completely losing your sex drive might sound a bit scary or tragic on the surface. After all, sex is this amazing life-affirming act, and suddenly you no longer have the capacity to desire or appreciate it. But the funny thing is, in real life, when you actually *do* lose your sex drive, you don't really miss it. Not at all. Because how can you miss something that you don't even want in the first place?

But now it is twenty Erics later. (Plus, some additional time passed while I was lying in bed like a lump.) And I finally just experienced the first hint that my sex drive may be starting to come back—specifically, last chapter, during the moment when I first met Eric #79. While I was a bit annoyed by how late he was, I found him quite attractive, and I could hear a little voice in the back of my head say: "I would totally have sex with this guy." But unfortunately, we had no chemistry whatsoever. And chemistry is such a vital part of attraction and desire. Like, if you happen to be Beryllium, you can try dating all the Lithiums, Borons, and Argons you like, but you're not going to form a covalent bond with any of them.

And when it comes to chemistry, I now have to keep in mind that I am a new (albeit not necessarily improved) version of me. And that can be like gaining or losing a proton or electron, and now suddenly you have all these different needs. Like, maybe now you are looking to pair up with atoms that can offer you two electrons rather than one. Or perhaps you used to be Platinum your whole life, but then one day you wake up to realize that you've lost a proton, so you're Iridium now. And you don't know a single thing about being Iridium!

In addition to questioning what I want out of a relationship right now, this new version of me is also questioning my creative endeavors. After all, here I am, still working toward finishing this *99 Erics* project—which for you, dear reader, maybe doesn't seem like such a long time, because you only started reading this book a few days or weeks ago. But for me, it's been a year and a half in the making so far—after all, it's hard to find the time to date Erics and write up chapters, especially when you have a full-time job, and your life is falling apart left and right.

And in the time that has passed, some of my fellow writers have gone on to new projects and to achieve new successes. Eric #31's one-person horror-slash-comedy show just opened up at The Marsh last month, and it's generating a lot of buzz. And shortly after our date, Eric #3 (due to his writing acumen and experience working at Lady Parts) got a job in Hollywood as a writer on the new hit HBO series *Toy Store*. (If you've seen it, then you know that it's a super-vanilla-straight-mainstream depiction of a sex toy store cooperative, but it's up for all these awards, and now Eric #3 is working on his own pilot, probably about gay men who hate hipsters, even though they are really hipsters themselves.) And his friend, Eric #19 (remember him: the filmmaker who I killed off in the county-fair-themed restaurant many chapters ago, although he didn't actually die in real life), well, his zombie film has already been released, and it's garnered all these great reviews. (Even though the absurdist-short-story-writer character that was not based upon me was super-duper two-dimensional, if you ask me.)

While Eric #3, #19, and #31 have all moved onto their next projects, here I am still writing *99 Erics*—which frankly, wasn't even my idea originally. This whole thing started out as past me's personal pet book project. But now, a year and a half later, it's present me (aka, me!) who is stuck with the task of completing her book for her. And while I dutifully continue to date and write up all the remaining Erics, I will occasionally come up with my own exciting new ideas ("wouldn't it be fun to create a *Kat Cataclysm's Absurdist Short Fiction Hour* podcast?" or "what if I wrote a graphic novel about the lives of barnacles?"), but I don't have any spare time to commit to them right now.

Of course, once *99 Erics* is released, plenty of time and energy will become available to follow up on these new potential creative projects. But sadly, when that happens, I won't be the person who gets to develop them. Because that task will fall squarely on future me.

I'll bet she'll resent that. Knowing her.

40. Great Expectations

All readers have expectations. Whenever we pick up a novel, we will expect it to take place in some kind of setting that is populated with characters. We will also expect that one (or perhaps a few) of these characters will be our protagonist(s), who we will root for as they endure a series of predicaments that will ultimately build up to some kind of climax and eventual resolution. Depending on the genre, we may expect that our protagonist will come of age, find romance, solve murders, explore new worlds, battle monsters, have hot and steamy sex, learn a valuable life lesson, and/or possibly even save the world.

If you wish to write fiction, then you must be cognizant of all these reader expectations, and you must strike a delicate balance between appeasing and defying them. Because your audience really wants their expectations to be met—they want the story to unfold in a logical manner, with the mystery being solved, the protagonist being triumphant, and everybody living happily ever after. However, if you satisfy *all* their expectations, they will likely find your story to be unbearably boring and banal. So it is incumbent on you to surprise readers by defying some of their expectations with regards to plot, character, setting, style, genre, and/or other facets. If you do this well, your novel will seem . . . novel! Your readers will find it to be a breath of fresh air, perhaps even groundbreaking.

But therein lies the rub: We all harbor different expectations. And just because something strikes you as novel or surprising, it doesn't mean that your readers will feel the same way. You may think that giving your villain some sort of physical defect or deformity will make them more ominous or fascinating, but it will likely strike many of us as horribly cliché and ableist. You may think that revealing a character to be queer mid-story makes for a surprising plot twist, but folks like me will see that time bomb coming from a mile away. And you may believe that readers will be shocked by the murder scene you have in store for them, but those of us who have read all those how-to-write-a-novel books will have noticed you planting that Chekhov's gun in an earlier chapter, and we've been impatiently waiting for it to be fired ever since.

Anyway, I've been thinking a lot about expectations lately, ever since my date with Eric #83. We agreed to meet at that cafe near Oakland City Hall, the one that got rid of WiFi because they wanted their establishment to be this place where folks come to meet and engage in conversation with other people, rather than sit alone on their laptops doing work. But ever since they implemented that change, I now often go there by myself to work on my *99 Erics* manuscript, because the lack of WiFi removes the temptation of internet distractions. Anyway, I told Eric #83 that I would arrive early to get some writing done, and that they would recognize me by the "All Fallacies Are Pathetic" sticker on my computer.

I was totally immersed in writing up an earlier date with an Eric—the one who, much to my surprise, turned out to be vocalist Braggy E. from the 1990s-era rap-metal band Inane Potty Mouth (I didn't recognize him without his face paint)—when I heard a woman's voice tentatively say, "Excuse me, are you Kat? I'm Eric, your date."

I have to admit that I was caught off guard. I was expecting this Eric to be a man, as all the previous Erics had been. Upon hearing this person's voice, my first thought was that maybe this Eric is a butch dyke or genderqueer person who chose the name Eric to reflect their masculine identity. But when I looked up from my computer, Eric #83 struck me as a conventionally feminine woman, except for the ill-fitting masculine clothing they were wearing. Despite their manner of dress, they didn't really set off my gaydar, or transdar, or queerdar, or whatever you wanna call it. But then it occurred to me that the very notion of gay/trans/queer-dar is pretty fucked up! After all, it is based entirely on our own personal expectations about how gay/trans/queer people should (or shouldn't) look and act.

Fucking expectations.

All of those thoughts took a half-second for me to process. And regrettably, I probably looked a little startled for that half-second. My bad. But I tried to quickly recover and move forward sans expectations regarding this latest Eric.

Me: Nice to meet you Eric, please have a seat. How are you doing?

Eric: I'm afraid I'm not feeling like myself today.

Me: Sorry to hear that. I'm actually just getting over a cold myself.

Eric: No, I mean I'm *literally* not feeling like myself today. Because this *isn't* my body.

Me: Um . . . okay. Whose body is it then?

Eric: I'm not quite sure—I'm still trying to figure that part out. All I know is that this morning, I woke up with a woman's body.

Me: Oh, I see, so you're male-identified then?

Eric: I'm not sure what you mean by that. I've been a man my whole life, but today I woke up as a woman.

Me: But do you still identify as a man? Do you prefer he/him/his pronouns?

Eric: Just look at me, I'm obviously a lady now!

Me: Oh, oh, okay, now I get it. You're not a real person.

Eric: What?!

Me: Real people don't magically change genders overnight. So you must be fictional—you know, like a character in someone else's story. Let's see . . . if you don't mind me asking, is there anyone out there who has a grudge against you? You know, someone who might want to turn you into a woman as a means of embarrassing or punishing you?

Eric: Not that I know of.

Me: Good, because the last thing I would want is to be non-consensually roped into somebody else's forced-feminization storyline. Plus, can I just say that there's nothing horrible or embarrassing about being a woman, other than the fact that some men presume that women are so inferior to them that it would be a horrible or embarrassing fate to be turned into one.

Eric: I don't feel horrible or embarrassed. Mostly I just feel confused.

Me: Hmmm, I see. And you mentioned that you don't recognize the body that you have now. So it doesn't belong to a lover, or friend, or family member, or co-worker of yours, correct?

Eric: That is correct.

Me: Then that rules out a *Freaky Friday* swapping-bodies-with-someone-else scenario. That pretty much narrows it down to an individual magical transformation of some kind. And it probably all began with a mad scientist? Or an evil curse? Or a lightning storm? Or magic amulet?

Eric: Oh, yeah, I forgot to mention that an exotic-looking stranger gave me a magic amulet yesterday. I wore it around my neck before falling asleep last night. Do you think there might be some sort of connection?

Me: Exotic-looking stranger, heh? Let me guess—were they albino? Or a dwarf? Did they have a scar across their face? Or . . .

Eric: Actually, they were an albino dwarf with a scar on their face. How did you know?

Me: Good god, who the fuck is writing you?! Actually, I don't even have to ask. From what I can gather, your author is an able-bodied cisgender hack writer who thought that it would be clever to write a story about someone who had to live as the other gender for a period of time. Even though this premise has been done to death. And instead of interviewing transgender people who have actually experienced living in the world as both women and men at different points in their lives, and who could have told them this premise had been done to death, your author instead decided to invent a story out of thin air based entirely upon every gender stereotype they could think of.

Eric: How could you possibly know all this?! If you're so smart, then tell me what has happened in my story so far.

Me: Well, the first chapter established your character as a gender-normative man, most likely one with a flimsy backstory. Then the second chapter opened with you waking up and stumbling to the bathroom, too groggy to notice what has happened to you—even though it's impossible that you would not have noticed such a drastic change to your body right away. Of course, it's only just as you're about to urinate that you notice something's "missing." So you look in the mirror and see for the first time that your body is female—even though you could have just looked down at your body to ascertain this. Predictably, you screamed in horror. Your neighbor probably overheard the scream and knocked on your door to make sure everything was okay, leading to an awkward conversation where you had to make up an explanation for who you are. You probably told him you are . . . Erica—Eric's sister visiting from out of town—even though it's improbable that anyone would name their two children Eric and Erica.

Then once the neighbor leaves, you have a moment to explore your new body. And this probably involved you squeezing your breasts and moaning "oh wow" or "holy cow," as if it's this extremely pleasurable experience for you—even though it wouldn't be, because squeezing your own breasts is an entirely different sensation from fondling another person's breasts, or having a lover fondle yours. Anyway, then you remembered that you had a date scheduled with me for later that day. Which likely makes this your Chapter 3.

Eric: You're right, everything you just said happened to me. Almost to a T.

Me: And can I just add how unrealistic it is that you would even keep your date with me? If I had just undergone a magical gender transformation, I would immediately cancel all my week's appointments so that I could gather myself and assess the situation. Especially if the appointment in question was merely a personal ad date with someone I hadn't even met yet.

Eric: That makes perfect sense. So why do you suppose my author compelled me to meet you today?

Me: I'll tell you why: Your author is trying to put you into conflict.

Eric: Conflict?

Me: Yes, conflict. It's what all the how-to-write-a-novel books tell authors to do. Basically, your author is going to make your life a living hell, by placing you into awkward and/or precarious predicaments in each and every chapter.

Eric: Oh no! What kinds of predicaments?

Me: Many of these will be situations where other characters will expect you to know "womanly" things that you are oblivious to.

Eric: Fucking expectations.

Me: Or your author may depict you fumbling with simple everyday tasks—such as putting on a bra, or walking in heels—even though being a woman isn't *that* complicated. It's not rocket science.

Eric: *Why would my author do all these mean things to me?!*

Me: Because your author has an extremely heteronormative view of gender—you know, men-are-from-Mars-and-women-are-from-Venus-type bullshit. And they are merely using you as a rhetorical device to promote that agenda.

Eric: That jerk!

Me: But hey, you don't have to allow yourself to be exploited by your author in this way. For instance, rather than trying (and failing) to live up to all these gender expectations, you can just dress and act however you want. And instead of learning the lesson that your author has laid out for you—"wow, being a woman is this completely foreign world that I could have never understood, nor related to, were it not for my magical transformation"—maybe instead you come away realizing that being a woman is really not all that much different from being a man—we're all people, after all. But the one major difference that you experienced is that now that people see you as a woman, you have to deal with systemic sexism: men talking over you, or down to you, or sexually harassing you, and so on. Perhaps these experiences even inspire you to become an outspoken feminist?

Eric: Wow, that never would have occurred to me. Thanks so much for the tip! By the way, I know that we only just met, but would you be open to being my "in the know" friend—you know, the one person in my story who knows about my magical transformation, and in whom I can confide?

Me: Sorry, it turns out that I'm actually the protagonist of my own story, and I need to get back to it.

Eric: Oh really? What is your story called?

Me: *99 Erics.*

Eric: What's it about?

Me: It's about me writing a book called *99 Erics.*

Eric. Oh. I wasn't expecting that.

41. Technologically Sound

Eric #89 had just moved to Oakland from New York City, and he was hoping that I could show him around a bit. He suggested first meeting up at Musket and Sextant, one of those trendy bars in Uptown. Normally, I wouldn't go to this sort of place of my own volition, but he said it was close to his work. Eric ordered one of their many fancy cocktails—a "Debris Slide"—and it had like eight different ingredients in it: obscure liqueurs, various bitters; I think it even had elderberries in it. I ordered my standard IPA. The bartender looked disappointed in me as he served it. It was only after we settled in at our table that I noticed that the bar had a croquet court in the back. I didn't even know that was a thing.

Eric: Can I ask, are you okay? You seem rather quiet.

Me: Sorry, I was just distracted by the croquet court. And also by a song that's been stuck in my head all day. This morning, I heard "Puff the Magic Dragon" for the first time in a long while. I had forgotten how sad that song is. So sad. I mean, can you even imagine growing up with the name Jackie Paper?

Eric: Well, I've had a different song running through my mind ever since we planned this date.

Me: Oh yeah, what song?

Eric: It's one of my all time favorites, although you probably haven't heard of it, because it's by this obscure indie rock band that I first heard on my old local college radio station. It popped into my head because it has your name in it. The chorus goes:

[singing in the key of E minor] "And her name was Kat. She's like a cataclysmic event . . ."

Me: I know that song. It was literally written about me. Also, the band who sings it—The Orange Dolphin Puppet Revival—they're an emo band, not an indie band. Which is apparently a completely different thing.

Eric: When you say it was literally written about you, do you mean "literally" in the strict sense of the word? Or were you using "literally" in an imprecise playful manner similar to how many people use the word "verbatim" these days.

Me: I meant literally literally, not verbatim literally. Also, for the record, I am the person who started the trend of using the word "verbatim" creatively.

Eric: Wow, that's incredible! So, tell me Kat, what do you do?

Me: Do you mean for a living? Because that can be a loaded question. Especially now, given that I recently lost my day job.

Eric: Oh no. What happened?

Me: Well, I used to work in the Word Repurposing Department at CliqueClick, on the slideshow and listicle team. That is, until I wrote a listicle called "11 Things That May Surprise You About the Common Cold." And it went viral.

Eric: That's a good thing, right?

Me: Normally, yes. But in this case, it went literally viral, in that everyone who read the piece came down with a cold. It was a mess. The Centers for Disease Control and Prevention had to step in, and U.S. Surgeon General Anthony Reddick even made a speech about it, wherein he famously dubbed it the "uncommon cold." To this day, nobody understands how that particular influenza virus could be transmitted via computer screens and mobile devices. Nevertheless, epidemiologists confirmed that my listicle was the root cause of the epidemic. It was a real PR mess for CliqueClick, so they pretty much had to fire me.

Eric: That was you? Holy crap! I never would have imagined

that I would be on a date with the person responsible for the notorious uncommon cold! In fact, I'm sharing libations with the mastermind behind malignant rhinovirus machinations, verbatim misusage, and the muse of college radio tunage!!!

Me: Um, was that an attempt at a metaphorulation?

Eric: It certainly was! Don't tell me you invented those too?

Me: Well, I didn't invent them. But I kinda sorta stole the idea from someone else. And I suppose that I helped popularize them via my listicle, "41 Cheeky Metaphorulations Chock-Full of Random Rhyming and Annoying Alliteration."

Eric: Amazing! You must be quite famous!

Me: Actually, I've managed to accomplish all of these achievements without garnering any acclaim or accolades whatsoever. In fact, one of them even cost me my job.

Eric: I'm really sorry to hear that.

Me: It's okay, I suppose. I wasn't really content writing internet content. So what do you do? For work or otherwise.

Eric: Well, I moved out here because I was recently hired to be a lead designer for Goober.

Me: The tech giant? The ones who just built that monstrosity of a building where the old J.C. Penney used to be?

Eric: Yep. That's where I work—it's Goober's new headquarters.

Me: So what are you the lead designer of? Their search engines? Their social media platform? Their online retail store? Their mobile devices? Their self-driving cars?

Eric: No. I'm overseeing Goober's Internet of Things Division.

Me: The internet of things?

Eric: You know how all of our computers, phones, and tablets are connected to one another by way of the internet? Well, this new technology will extend those connections to everyday appliances.

Me: That sounds pretty creepy to me. Like, will my refrigerator or television be able to send me harassing emails and leave nasty comments on my latest blog post?

Eric: No, no. Nothing of the sort. All of your appliances will remain completely subservient, I promise. In fact, you will be able to simultaneously control them all via our soon-to-be-released Goober Circumlocution. It's a home assistant. All you have to do is give it a command like, "turn on the lights," or "play some Beatles music," or "add an event to my schedule." And then it will do those tasks for you.

Me: So it will listen in on everything that I say? But what if hackers—the bad kind, not the good kind—listen in on my private conversations? Or what if the government uses it to spy on me?

Eric: No worries, the Goober Circumlocution does not listen to or record anything that you say. Unless, of course, you say its name. Then, and only then, will it respond to your commands.

Me: Oh. What's its name?

Eric: Kat.

Me: Kat?!?!

Eric: Yes, Kat. I named it after that Orange Dolphin Puppet Revival song that I enjoy so much.

Me: But that song was named after me!

Eric: I didn't know that at the time.

Me: But what if *I* bought the Goober Circumlocution and set it up in my home? Whenever someone visits me and calls me by name, your device would start listening in on us!

Eric: Um . . .

Me: And what if someone in my home said to me, "Kat, please order us a pizza." And so I ordered them a pizza. But home assistant Kat would also order them a pizza. Now we're stuck with two pizzas! Who is going to pay for that extra pizza?!

Eric: Well . . .

Me: And what if we then decided to watch cute cat videos on GooberTube. And while doing so, we made remarks like, "Look at that cat fall off the table!" or "Watch this cat play the piano!" But your device would hear us giving it commands: "Kat, fall off the table"; "Kat, play the piano." That's bound to confuse the poor thing!

Eric: Oh, I hadn't considered that cat video scenario before . . .

Me: Well, you should have. And it's not just you. It's all the tech companies. Everyone's so busy trying to disrupt the established way of doing things, and to corner all these new markets, that no one ever considers the potential negative ramifications. Take my ex-employer CliqueClick: They set out to be pioneers in tailoring people's news and media feeds to match their families' preconceived notions about them. But CliqueClick never considered the possibility that some of these family members might be racist conspiracy theorists—this oversight led to a deluge of right-wing fake news on their platform that helped to elect a fascistic reality TV celebrity to be president. And just today, I read an article about how Goober's self-driving cars are already out on the streets of Oakland, transporting passengers to and fro. Have these cars been adequately tested? Does anyone know if they're even safe?

Eric: Well, that's not my department. But I'm sure they've been tested. Having said that, there is always some risk whenever a new technology is introduced. Hell, there's still a risk with manual-driving cars for Christ's sake! That doesn't mean that we should abandon that technology entirely. We shouldn't let these small but acceptable risks stop us from moving technologically forward. Anyway, not to change the subject . . .

Me: But you just have.

Eric: Excuse me?

Me: Why do we always say, "Not to change the subject," when that's exactly what we intend to do? It's like when we say, "Not to mention the fact," and then go on to mention the fact!

Eric: Er, good point. So, to change the subject: You said that you'd show me around Oakland. Any suggestions?

Me: Well, we could head toward Downtown Oakland, which is where I live. There's a bar there called The Hatch that I like—it's a hole in the wall, but they have reasonably priced pints and cheap food. They even sell pitchers, which practically no other place around here does. At least not anymore.

Eric: Okay, I'm game. Should I call us a Goober Ride?

Me: No way, no how. I'm not letting an inadequately tested computer-driven car drive me anywhere. Plus, Downtown is only a few blocks away from here.

Eric: Really?

Me: Yes. Downtown plus Uptown Oakland combined is only about twenty-some blocks long.

Eric: Wow. I guess I'm not in New York City anymore.

We walked south on Telegraph, then turned left onto one of the numbered streets, and meandered though my neighborhood. I pointed out my favorite Cantonese restaurant—the one with the house-special squid dish that's so delicious, and for the longest time it only cost $6.50, but last year, out of the blue, they raised the price to $13.95, presumably due to rent increases. And the place just around the corner that had happy hour sushi each weekday— I'd always drag Matilda there whenever she was feeling down, and we'd get a rock'n roll, a 49ers roll, and two green teas, and it would always raise her spirits. But real estate developers bought the building last year and didn't renew their lease, as they wanted to cater to more upscale clients. Then there's that small diner where I would grab a cheap eggs-bacon-toast breakfast and some coffee, and write in my journal for a bit, before heading off to whatever crappy job I had at the time. But that diner has since been replaced by the gourmet pizzeria known for their "duck bacon" and "venison meatball" pizzas.

Eric: What's that?

Me: I'm not sure. I can't tell whether it's an art gallery or boutique clothing store. I suppose it's possibly both.

Eric: Is it me, or do you sound a little bit resentful?

Me: Look, I have nothing against any of these new places that have opened up. I just hate how fast my neighborhood has changed—like, in just the last few years or so! It's like gentrification on hyper-overdrive. Just last week, a friend who lives a few blocks away from me got a letter from her landlord tripling her rent. Triple! I could never afford that. Luckily, I live in an older building that is protected by rent control. So I'm relatively safe, just so long as my landlord doesn't invoke owner move-in or the Ellis Act.

Eric: Ellis Act?

Me: Yeah, it's a California law that allows landlords to evict everyone on the property in the event that they take the building off the market, or turn it into condos. That recently happened to another friend of mine who . . . *WHAT THE FUCK!!!*

We had just reached our destination when I saw the headlights moving toward us. Upon hearing me scream, Eric #89 turned to look at what I was pointing at, but to his eyes, it was merely a car driving at an average speed down the road. (In contrast, having lived in this neighborhood for years, I instantly recognized that it was going the wrong way down a one-way street.) As Eric #89 turned back toward me to say, "What's the big deal?" the vehicle started to swerve, then mounted the sidewalk. I dived inside The Hatch. But Eric wasn't so lucky. After I heard the crash, I ran outside to find Eric lying on the ground unconscious.

I called 911 to have them send an ambulance. The dispatcher asked me to describe the car. It was a block a way, smashed into the art-gallery-slash-boutique-clothing-store window display. I walked in that direction to get a closer look. As I did, I could make out the words "Goober Ride" on the side of the vehicle. Unsurprisingly (at least to me), there was no driver.

Eventually, the ambulance came, and I gave them my description of events. I would later learn that Eric #89 sustained serious, albeit not critical, injuries. The following day, officials at Goober issued a press release claiming that the incident was an "Act of God," as it was apparently caused by a coronal mass ejection—a solar eruption releasing particles and electromagnetic radiation that interfered with Goober's satellite network. If you ask me, they really should have had a contingency plan in place for that. Not to mention the fact that it's hypocritical to call yourself a science-and-technology company, but then blame god whenever something bad happens.

As you can imagine, I was pretty shaken up by the whole incident. I walked the couple blocks back to my apartment, entered my building, and checked my mailbox. There, I found an official looking letter. It was from my landlord. I opened it.

The letter said that I was being Ellis Acted from my apartment.

42. Trombone Lessons

I vividly remember the day when I decided that I would make San Francisco (and later, neighboring Oakland) my permanent home. It was during my first week here, back when I was crashing at Gabriella's place. I was on a MUNI bus for whatever reason—maybe I was job hunting, or simply exploring the city—and this older woman (probably in her sixties or seventies) climbed aboard. She sported dyed-orange hair. Not the kind of orange that is trying to pass for natural redhead, but a bright almost fluorescent orange. And she was carrying a trombone case.

I was enthralled. In the sleepy Northeastern towns that I grew up in, there were no elderly women with dyed-orange hair who played the trombone. Or at least, none that I was aware of. What was even more amazing to me was that, as she walked down the bus aisle and took her seat, nobody gave her a second glance. The other riders did not find her presence to be surprising or noteworthy. This woman's idiosyncrasies were apparently par for the course in San Francisco.

Right then and there, I made two life decisions: First, I promised myself that, on my sixty-fifth birthday, I was going to dye my hair a fluorescent orange and start taking trombone lessons. Second, during the interim, I was going to make the San Francisco Bay Area my home. I had finally found a place where I could be an unabashed weirdo and not be scrutinized for it.

Back then, people who wanted to make lots of money moved to New York. And people who wanted to become famous moved to Los Angeles. But if you didn't have any grand ambitions—if you just wanted to be a freak, yet live in peace—you moved to San Francisco. That's why the beats came here. And the hippies. And the queers. And throughout the years, most of the people who lived and migrated here, by and large, appreciated the Bay Area's diversity and countless eccentricities.

Star Trek. Godzilla. Invasion of the Body Snatchers. X-Men. Superman. Pacific Rim. Monsters vs. Aliens. Terminator. Towering Inferno. Planet of the Apes. San Andreas. Mega Shark Versus Giant Octopus. These are but a few of the movies and film franchises that have destroyed parts or all of San Francisco at one point or another. I have long believed that these filmmakers were likely driven (at least unconsciously) by a Sodom-and-Gomorrah-type mentality: of course the North American city most closely associated with homosexuality and other flagrancies would be destined to be annihilated by a natural disaster or some powerful unearthly force.

Given this, it's ironic that the thing that actually destroyed San Francisco was something far more mundane: money.

When I first moved to the Bay Area, most of the tech companies were clustered down in Silicon Valley, in and around San José. But over time, they metastasized their way up the peninsula, settling in San Francisco, and eventually making their way across the bay to Oakland. I have nothing against tech per se—I wrote this faux novel on a computer, and I obviously worked for CliqueClick for a stretch. The problem is that all these tech companies have turned the Bay Area into a giant magnet for people who want to make tons of money. And by and large, this latest round of entrepreneurial newcomers couldn't care less about all the weirdos and diverse peoples who thrived here previously, and who are increasingly being priced out of their own cities.

I just want to make it clear that this isn't some kind of "Death of San Francisco" novel. I'm sure that novel has already been written. Probably multiple times by now. The Death of the San Francisco Bay Area isn't the plot of this faux novel. Nor its theme. It's merely the setting.

The setting is the backdrop to a story. And what's at the forefront is me: the protagonist. So we should focus our attention not on the San Francisco Bay Area being gobbled up by an unrelenting series of tech and housing bubbles, but rather on how these developments will impact our protagonist's story arc.

After receiving the Ellis Act letter from my landlord, my first reaction was to search Ed's List—not for new Erics to date this time, but rather for apartments. Much to my chagrin, everything was way more expensive than I remember it being not all that long ago, when Matilda and I first moved into my current place. Having recently lost my job at CliqueClick, and not being eligible for unemployment benefits (because they hired me as an independent contractor rather than an employee), there was no way that I could afford any of these apartments on my own. Not even the studios. So I began putting feelers out to fellow writers in the local literary scene, and friends from weekly queer karaoke, and people I knew from monthly poly happy hour, and so on, to see if anyone in an existing rent-controlled apartment was looking for a roommate. Everyone said they would let me know if they heard of anything.

Being out of a job, I had more free time than usual. So I took a "me day" to gallivant around San Francisco. I took the MUNI N-Judah to the end of the line, hung out at Ocean Beach for a bit, then wandered through Golden Gate Park and Upper Haight, then made a right on Divisadero and walked down to the Castro. From there, I took 18th Street to the Mission District, and ended up at my favorite restaurant—one of the few still remaining from my first days living here. Despite having just taken a monster of a walk, I did not come across a single orange-haired trombone lady.

But what I did find, at the restaurant table next to mine, were two men who both had BOOMING MAN VOICES, much like my ex Eric #2. Since they were so loud that I couldn't even hear myself think, I was forced to listen in on their conversation. And they were talking about this app that they were building, the purpose of which was to flip houses, but they were putting an "eco-friendly" low-carbon-footprint spin on it. And as they spouted business buzzwords like "cross-platform" and "market share," it really drove home the point that San Francisco is no longer the same place that I originally fell in love with. It used to be a city of artists, misfits, and minorities of all stripes. Now it has become an industry town.

Then the song "Puff the Magic Dragon" popped back into my head. And I suddenly realized that the song isn't really about how horrible it would be to be named Jackie Paper. It's actually a metaphor for my relationship with the Bay Area. I am Puff the Magic Dragon—a weirdo who had all these amazing adventures with a city named Jackie Paper. But one day, Jackie Paper grew up to become a computer whiz kid who'd rather spend all their time hanging out with venture capitalists, thus leaving me behind, sad and alone.

Or maybe I'm Jackie Paper, and San Francisco is Puff the Magic Dragon, and it's time for me to grow up and leave it behind.

I suppose the metaphor could work either way.

Since this is an Ellis Act eviction, I have a few months before I will need to move out of my apartment. That gives me just enough time to meet my looming manuscript deadline, plus deal with all the book editing and such, before having to pack and ponder what my next move will be.

43. Home Base

For decades on end, confused-slut dude-bros have championed a baseball metaphor for sex, where kissing is getting to "first base," feeling breasts is "second base," touching genitals is "third base," and penile-vaginal penetration sex is "scoring" or reaching "home base." According to this metaphor, intercourse (and presumably male orgasm) is the only thing that counts—all other aspects of sex are either not accounted for, or dismissed as mere foreplay.

As a sexually experienced adult woman and baseball connoisseur to boot, allow me to submit for your approval the following new and improved baseball-metaphor-for-sex: Penetration sex is akin to catching a baseball, in that it's an important, albeit far from the only, skill that one can develop.

When you first start playing baseball, catching the ball can be quite challenging and requires substantial practice to master. This is why, on teams full of novices (e.g., in little leagues), the best defenders are often positioned at first base, since the ball is thrown to first on the majority of plays, and you need somebody there who can reliably catch it. However, once you reach more advanced levels (e.g., professional baseball), typically the worst defenders are placed at first base. Because by this point, every single player is well versed in catching baseballs. And the best defenders have mastered additional (and far more difficult) skills, such as chasing down fly balls in center field, or making spectacular off-balanced throws across the diamond from shortstop, or calling the game and pitch framing as catchers.

In other words, most of us are capable of becoming quite proficient at straightforward vanilla penetration sex. But it's another thing entirely to master more esoteric or intricate sexual skills.

I bring this up because of Eric #97. He just so happens to be a writer at my favorite sabermetrically-oriented baseball blog *GameTheory*. Every so often, *GameTheory* has informal meet-and-greets with fans in various cities across the country. As I was entering the homestretch of writing *99 Erics*, I learned that they were hosting their next meet-and-greet at a brewery near the ballpark in San Francisco, and that Eric Aptronym would be one of the writers attending. While it seemed unlikely that I'd be able to snag a date out of it, I figured it couldn't hurt to try. Obviously it panned out, since I've already referred to him as Eric #97. In other words, I have given away the ending yet again, as I am wont to do. Even though I didn't want to wont to do it.

Never having been to one of these events before, I had no idea what to expect. I knew that *GameTheory*'s writers and readers tend to be more amiable and introspective than the stereotypical hyper-competitive and chauvinistic sports fan. But at the same time, this *was* a sport-themed gathering, so it was inevitable that at least one or two bulletheads might be in attendance. As soon as I arrived and scanned the thirty or so people in the room, I could tell that the guy wearing the Dave Matthews Band concert t-shirt was going to be a problem. He was boisterously spouting his opinions and talking over everyone else. I was quiet at first, but he was becoming increasingly annoying, so as soon I saw an opening (as he was bragging about his favorite pitcher having twenty-one wins last year), I interjected: "But everybody here knows that 'wins' is not an especially informative statistic when evaluating a pitcher."

Dave Matthews t-shirt guy appeared visibly startled—he had that look of contempt on his face that I've seen before in men who feel appalled or disrespected by the fact that a lowly woman would have the gall to question them. He snorted: "Well, little lady, why don't you make the case for *your* favorite pitcher then." His condescension was so blatant that a couple people in the room audibly gasped, and I noticed Eric #97 (who was standing at the front of the room) step forward, as if he was about to intervene. But he didn't need to—I totally had this.

I batted my eyelashes, twirled a lock of my hair, and in the most cutesy-ish girly-girl voice I could muster, I said: "My favorite pitcher is R. A. Dickey, because he throws an uncleball, even though he was born without an NaCl ligament."

Sorry if that joke is a little too inside baseball for most of you. The point is that it had its intended effect: Eric #97 and the other attendees busted out laughing, and Dave Matthews subsequently shut his trap. After that, the conversation was cordial and interesting, as we discussed myriad baseball and non-baseball-related topics. As it got closer to 8 p.m. (when the meet-and-greet was scheduled to end), people started to wander off, and I finally got the opportunity to chat one-on-one with Eric #97.

Eric: Sorry about that situation earlier. That guy was a real jerk.

Me: Yeah, he was. I also wasn't a big fan of the guy who kept insisting that the Giants should move Buster Posey to first base.

Eric: I know. Why on earth would you even consider that given how much defensive value he has as a catcher.

Me: Yeah, but on top of the poor point he was trying to make, that guy struck me as odd.

Eric: Odd in what way?

Me: I don't know exactly. He just seemed a bit uneven to me.

Eric: But those mean the same thing. Odd literally means uneven.

Me: Oh. Good point.

Eric: So what do you do when you're not making jokes about knuckleball pitchers born without UCL ligaments?

Me: I'm a writer.

Eric: Oh, do you write about baseball?

Me: Not really. Except for this one absurdist short story I wrote a few years back about how, in response to plummeting TV ratings, Major League Baseball's commissioner decided to change the format of the game. Instead of the usual offense versus defense, it would now be offense versus nonsense. Rather than pitch the ball to the batter, the team on "nonsense" would do an interpretive dance, or write experimental poetry, or paint abstract impressionist art, and the like. Then the team on "offense" would have to become offended by the artistic endeavor in question, and pen scathing critical reviews in response. Does that make sense?

Eric: It makes perfect nonsense. Anyway, if you ever become interested in writing about baseball, shoot me an email—we're always looking for new writers.

Me: I'm flattered by the offer. But I'd imagine that you are looking for writers who are willing to immerse themselves in all sorts of statistical analyses and number crunching. And while I deeply respect that work as a reader, I'm not sure that it would be my cup of tea as a writer, given that I have a love-hate relationship with math. On account of math being oppressive.

Eric: What do you mean by that?

Me: Well, math is chock-full of all these hierarchies, where some numbers are deemed more "valuable" than others. Like, take integers for example: What's so special about them? Why is the number 10 more important than 7.6? It's probably only because human beings have ten fingers on our hands. But if we had been born with 7.6 fingers instead, then we'd probably have a completely different numerical system based on fractions rather than integers!

Eric: Actually, if we had 0.6 of a finger, we would probably just count it as a whole finger. After all, we count the pinky as a whole finger, even though it's probably only worth a fraction of an index or middle finger.

Me: Hmmm. Okay then, here's another example: prime numbers. What's the big deal about them? Why are they so special?

Eric: Actually, computer encryption often relies on prime numbers—extremely large prime numbers. In fact, some of these extraordinarily large prime numbers are so vital to computer encryption that it's illegal to share them with other people.

Me: Are you telling me that there are actual illegal numbers?

Eric: Yes.

Me: Wow, mathematics is even more oppressive than I thought.

Eric: In addition to computer encryption, another practical application of prime numbers is math-sex.

Me: Math-sex? What do you know about math-sex? I've only heard second-hand stories about it.

Eric: Well, the premise of math-sex is quite simple really: Mathematics plays a central role in physics, chemistry, and biology, and therefore governs all of our molecules, cells, and even our entire bodies. So if you are able to tap into the power of mathematics during sex, then you can greatly enhance the experience. For instance, if, while having sex, you were to kiss or touch or stimulate your partner once, then twice, then three times, five times, seven times, eleven times, thirteen times, and so on, their brain will unconsciously recognize this primordial pattern of prime numbers, and begin to release dopamine, oxytocin, and other hormones and neurotransmitters that facilitate sexual pleasure. The end result is incredibly intense and long-sustained orgasms.

Me: No way! Are they as big as gargantuan dream orgasms?

Eric: Even bigger. I've tried math-sex with a number of numerical sequences: primes, triangular and square numbers, the Lazy Caterer's Sequence, binomial coefficients, and even counting out the decimal places of numbers like π or e. But in my experience, math-sex works best when you use the Fibonacci sequence, probably because it appears all the time in biology.

Me: Wow, I just have to try it!

Eric: Well, it takes a long time to master, because you first need to memorize all the numbers in these sequences to the point where they are second nature to you, and then you need to deploy them during sexual encounters.

Me: I've done simple math in my head during sex—you know, in order to stay lucid in my lucid dreams—but never anything as complex as the numerical sequences you just described.

Eric: Well, as long as one person knows the sequence, the other person can simply lay back and enjoy it.

There was a brief pause in our conversation, as I pondered all this new information. While doing so, I took a sip of my IPA. Eric #97 took a corresponding sip of his gose, although I'm not sure how he could even drink that beer given how sour it was. Sorry, but I have completely soured on all things sour. Anyway, our sipping of beer gave me a few seconds to formulate a game plan.

Me: Hey, Eric. I know we just met, and this may seem super-duper forward of me. But I haven't had a big gargantuan dream orgasm since I stopped lucid dreaming, on account of me deciding that it's probably best that I not constantly question my waking reality. So I was wondering if you would be open to me buying you a drink, and us getting to know one another a bit better. Then, after said drink, if you are open to it—nay, *enthusiastic* about it—perhaps maybe we could have math-sex together?

Eric: Sure, I'm game. But you should know that I'm sharing a hotel room with my *GameTheory* co-workers. So if we do decide to get mathematical later on, it would have to be at your place.

Me: Sure, I'd be happy to host you in my humble abode.

Eric: You live in an adobe?

Me: No. I live in a plain old one-bedroom apartment. That's my home—my abode, if you will.

Eric: Oh, sorry about that. I'm a little bit dyslexic, is all.

Me: No worries.

There have been a handful of times in my life that, upon meeting an absolute stranger, I felt almost as if we had known each other for years. It happened with Gabriella when we first met in college. It happened with the sweet bookstore guy I met as a baby dyke— the one who helped me realize that I was really bisexual, and who encouraged me to become an absurdist short fiction writer. It happened with Matilda, when we first met on the outdoor patio of El Rio during a Trans March benefit show and were immediately finishing one another's sentences.

And now it was kinda sorta happening with Eric #97. We had baseball in common, to be sure, but there were also other things: He likes some of those weird seventies prog rock bands that I grew up listening to; we both adore movies that have fractured timelines; we both recently developed a fascination with barnacles. We even have similar senses of humor—in fact, Eric #97 was the first person to ever laugh at my "a paraprosdokian walks into a bar and no one gets the joke" joke!

So of course I took him home with me.

If I was a hack writer, this next section would probably begin with: "The following morning, I woke up in Eric #97's arms." Not only is that cliché, but it's entirely unrealistic. Sure, you might initially fall asleep in your lover's arms, but at some point, you are going to roll over in search of a more comfortable position. Plus, even if you were perfectly content sleeping on a lumpy human being rather than a fluffy pillow, eventually the weight of your body is going to make your lover's arm fall asleep. And upon waking up, they will immediately start flapping their arm wildly in a pathetic attempt to shake away the pins and needles.

And that doesn't sound very romantic, does it?

Besides, Eric #97 and I didn't sleep much. After he showed me the practical application of the Fibonacci series, we spent the rest of the night drifting in and out of sleep, with intermittent making out, cracking jokes, and random conversation.

At one point in the morning, Eric said: Hey, I noticed the

DVD case for *Kill Bill: Volume 1* on your nightstand. That's one of my favorite movies! Did you just watch it?

Me: Yeah, although I didn't quite finish it yet. On account of the *GameTheory* meet up last night.

Eric: How far did you get?

Me: I had to stop at the part where the Crazy 88 are all lying in a dodge of blood.

Eric: Dodge of blood? What's that?

Me: Oh, "dodge" is my term of venery for blood. You know, like a pride of lions, or a gander of geese. A dodge of blood.

Eric: Actually it's a gaggle of geese. Gander refers to male geese. On top of that, blood is its own plural.

Me: I know, I know. I just like using words creatively is all.

Eric: What made you decide to watch it?

Me: I got a freelancing gig writing for *Fence Sitters*. They wanted me to write a listicle for them about notable female film protagonists from the aughts. It doesn't pay especially well, but at least they're not forcing me to stick to prime numbers.

Eric: Oh, *Fence Sitters*, the bisexual women's online magazine?

Me: Yes. You know of it?

Eric: Yeah, my ex was a bisexual activist and she used to read *Fence Sitters* all the time.

Me: Are you bi yourself? Or queer in some other way? If you don't mind me asking.

Eric: No, I'm basically heterosexual.

Me: Although you are into math-sex. Which probably makes you at least a little bit sexual-minority-ish.

Eric: Maybe. But math-sex practitioners haven't been historically oppressed in the way that gay people have been.

Me: True. But that's likely due to most people not being aware that math-sex even exists. I'll bet you that, if the religious right were to find out about math-sex, they would immediately condemn it as immoral, and try to pass legislation criminalizing the practice.

Eric: Perhaps.

Me: Also, historical oppression doesn't always align with our current circumstances. Nowadays, many straight people openly accept gay people, yet they may nevertheless remain skeptical of, or squicked by, bisexuality, polyamory, or people who are kinky.

Eric: Hmmm. Speaking of, I don't know if math-sex counts as "kinky," but it's only 8 a.m., and my flight doesn't leave until later this afternoon. So I was wondering if maybe you'd be up for . . .

Me: Yes! Enthusiastically!

So then we started to have math-sex again. While the Fibonacci numbers the previous night were extraordinary (which is a very different thing from being merely extra ordinary), Eric suggested that we give the Catalan numbers a go this time around. It was amazing: Even though I consciously have no fucking clue as to what Catalan numbers even are, I could feel my entire body resonating with and reverberating to this particular numerical series.

And just as Eric reached 742,900, I heard a knock at my apartment door. I chose to ignore it. A few seconds later, I distinctly heard my lock unlock, my doorknob turn, and my apartment door open.

Then I screamed.

But not because of the intruder. I screamed because I was in the throes of math-sex.

All abodes are different. (As a testament to this, some abodes are in fact adobes.) While it is commonplace for bedrooms to be tucked away upstairs, or toward the back of most homes, my apartment does not fit this mold. Rather, my front door opens up to a tiny foyer, from which guests (or intruders, as the case may be) have a clear view into both my living room (to the left) and bedroom (to the right).

So as I was screaming amidst my gargantuan math-sex orgasm, Eric #97 turned and spotted two ominous human silhouettes entering my apartment. Reflexively, he grabbed the *Kill Bill: Volume 1* DVD case off my nightstand, and hurled it at them. The DVD case spun end-over-end—much like a dagger or throwing star in a Quentin Tarantino movie—until it struck one of the shadowy figures in the elbow.

"Owww!" shouted a familiar voice.

It was my landlord. He had just barged into my apartment. As if he owned the place!

Me: *What the fuck are you doing here?!*

Landlord: My contractor wanted to get some measurements, so we can plan all the necessary renovations to convert your apartment into a condominium.

Me: But you need to give me twenty-four hour notice before entering my apartment—you know that's the law! This is my home base after all.

Landlord: Do you mean "home base" as some kind of a sexual metaphor?

Me: No. It's a tag metaphor. This is my home base, where I'm supposed to be safe.

Landlord: Well, the two of you are both naked and obviously fooling around, so I just assumed that you were referring to sex.

Me: Even if I was, the sex that we're into isn't the type that involves a hierarchy of "bases" that represent successive levels of conquest. Nor is it the type of sex that pits lovers against one another—offense versus defense—as though we are on competing teams. Eric and I are on the same team. Team math-sex!

Landlord: Math-sex? What in Christ's name is that? Is it some kind of Satanic sexual ritual? Does it involve the number 666?

Eric: I can assure you that 666 is neither a Catalan number, nor a Fibonacci number, nor a prime. Although it is a triangular number.

Landlord: Criminy, I had no idea that you were into defiling numbers! I mean, I always figured that you and Matilda were into lesbian sex—but hey, whatever the two of you choose to do in the privacy of your own bedroom . . .

Me: Which isn't private right now. Because you just illegally entered it.

Landlord: . . . but now that you've turned straight, you're apparently taking part in demonic arithmetic sexually-deviant orgies!

Me: This isn't an orgy—there are only the two of us. Plus I'm not straight. I'm bisexual! It's a very basic word, with a very simple definition.

Landlord: You black magic woman! With your evil ways!

Me: Don't you dare stereotype me as the antagonist in a Santana song. Look, I'm picking up my phone right now. And if you don't leave my abode within the next five seconds, I'm calling the Oakland Tenants Rights Association on you . . . Okay then: [while pressing digits on the dial-pad] One. Five, one, zero . . .

Landlord: Okay, fine, we're leaving.

As soon as they shut the door behind them, Eric #97 and I collapsed on the bed. Then we started giggling about how ridiculous that whole scenario had been.

Eric: Wow, you were right about how people would react if they knew about math-sex. Your landlord went completely apeshit— did you see how scared he was?

Me: See, this is why I think that it's such a misnomer to call them "landlords." Because they are not godlike in any way, shape, or form. Like, if he was really a "lord," he wouldn't have been so afraid of us dabbling in the practical applications of numerical sequences.

Eric: Yep. Plus on top of that, "lord" is a pretty boring name for a deity. You'd think that, if he was actually an omnipotent being, he'd be able to come up with a more snazzy name for himself than "landlord."

Me: Exactly.

Eric: Hey, if you were a deity, what title would you go by?

Me: Oh, that one's easy: God Empress of the Known Universe.

Eric: I like it. It's confident, yet modest.

Me: Hey, you've been pleasuring me all this time. How can I reciprocate?

Eric: Do you know any numerical sequences?

Me: Well, thanks to my old listicle job at CliqueClick, I've committed the first twenty-five prime numbers to memory.

Eric: That should suffice!

44. And the Rest

When I finally turned in my manuscript to my editor Mario, he seemed a tad concerned about the overall length.

Or as he put it: *It's fucking over 500,000 words long!*

Me: I know, isn't it awesome?!

Mario: No. No it isn't. It's way too long. It's *Infinite Jest* length.

Me: And that became a bestseller!

Mario: Yes it did, but in spite of its length, not because of it.

Me: You know, all the writing guides say that it's better to use "despite" rather than "in spite of."

Mario: Of course I know that—I am an editor after all! Nevertheless, I continue to use "in spite of" rather than "despite."

Me: Are you doing this out of spite?

Mario: None of your beeswax! Anyway, you are going to have to trim it down to about 80,000 words if you want your manuscript to be published.

And that, dear readers, is why I wasn't able to include a chapter for every Eric. But just to prove that there actually were ninety-nine Erics who participated in the making of this book, here is a brief synopsis for each Eric who has been edited out:

4. The Eric who didn't know who Orson Welles was.

6. The Eric who went on at great length about the differences between jelly, jam, preserves, and marmalade.

8. The Eric who took off his shirt in the middle of our date to show me his new nipple piercings.

9. The Eric who suddenly broke into song.

10. The Eric who kept referring to himself as "the goldfish whisperer."

12. The Eric who said that he was having déjà vu, so I immediately started flailing my arms while screaming, "Was I doing this in it?" and he replied "Oh my god, yes you were, how creepy!!!"

14. The Eric who fondly reminisced about his days as a bike messenger.

15. The Eric who was into macramé, and with whom I performed an "Endless Love" karaoke duet.

16. The Eric who composed avant-garde music exclusively in the Locrian mode.

18. The Eric who endlessly complained about how eyes and teeth were not covered under his health insurance plan.

20. The Eric who couldn't be bothered with small talk.

21. The Eric who kept bragging about his visit to the Rock and Roll Hall of Fame.

22. The Eric who objectified my Baker's cyst.

24. The Eric who became a film critic in order to overcome his fear of films.

25. The Eric who inexplicably kept humming the Keris song "Milkshake."

26. The Eric who tried to convince me that I should turn *99 Erics* into a choose your own adventure book.

27. The Eric who was into breatharianism.

28. The Eric who was a "Jar Jar Binks is a secret Sith Lord" truther.

30. The Eric who tried to date rape me.

32. the eric who wrote in all lowercase and without punctuation just like e e cummings

33. The Eric who claimed that he grew a beard so that one day he could shave it off and no one would be able to recognize him.

34. The Eric who kept referring to our date as "clandestine."

35. The Eric whose last name was actually Lehnsherr, although he exhibited no ability to manipulate metal or generate magnetic fields.

36. The Eric who was pretty sure we had met once before in a haberdashery.

38. The Eric who wouldn't let his fingers go anywhere near garbage disposals.

39. The Eric whose second person preferred pronouns were thou, thy, thine.

40. The Eric who showed up early for our date because he follows metric time rather than the standard sexagesimal system.

42. The Eric who was attempting to reclaim the word "troglodyte."

44. The Eric whose meralgia paraesthetica was acting up.

45. The Eric who claimed to have graduated summa cum laude from the Electoral College.

46. The Eric who wouldn't shut up about the *Games of Thrones* fan theory: $K + E = A$.

48. The Eric who was writing a rock opera about behavioral economics.

49. The Eric who apologized for sweating like a pig, but then I informed him that pigs don't sweat, because they have no sweat glands, which is why they roll around in the mud all the time, as it's the only way they can cool down.

50. The Eric who trademarked the term Minglecize™.

51. The Eric who had a loveseat in his apartment, although he swore that he never used it for love.

52. The Eric who was born and raised in the United States, yet pronounced "privacy" like a British person.

54. The Eric who always dreamed of becoming the world's leading left-handed dentist.

55. The Eric who thought that stepladders were related to regular ladders through marriage.

56. The Eric who gave lip balm a bad name.

57. The Eric who could never remember the difference between "ontology" and "epistemology."

58. The Eric who tried to neg me, but I didn't fall for it.

60. The Eric who thought that I was being selfish because I refused to share my entree with him.

62. The Eric who believed in an elaborate conspiracy theory involving the Illuminati, Nazis, the Apocalypse, and Denver International Airport.

63. The Eric who tried to pay for our dinner in bitcoin, but the restaurant refused to accept it.

64. The Eric who begged me not to write about him.

65. The Eric who insisted that he was a free speech absolutist. So I replied, "No you aren't." And he said, "Yes, I am." And then I said, "I'm going to tell everyone far and wide that you don't even believe in free speech," and he screamed, *"It's not true, you can't say that!"* So then I teased him about trying to restrict my free speech.

66. The Eric who had egg on his face.

68. The Eric who was letting his fingernails grow out for the *Guinness Book of World Records.*

69. The Eric who claimed that Pannotia was a far superior supercontinent to Pangaea or Rodinia.

70. The Eric who accused me of wearing "plot armor" because I am the only character in this book guaranteed to survive through the end of the story.

72. The Eric who made a point of pronouncing silent consonants.

74. The Eric who first introduced me to the fascinating world of barnacles.

75. The Eric who would freeze all of his toiletries before going to the airport so that they would be solids as he passed through security.

76. The Eric who was overly concerned about orphans and

widows.

77. The Eric who never returned from the restroom.

78. The Eric who (much to my surprise) turned out to be vocalist Braggy E. from the 1990s-era rap-metal band Inane Potty Mouth.

80. The Eric who could have benefited from hindsight.

81. The Eric who asked me about the scar on my face, so I told him the entire story about how I had the worst type of the best type of skin cancer you could possibly have.

82. The Eric who said that he really enjoyed my listicle about how to tell whether or not you are sexually oriented towards specific fields of scientific inquiry.

84. The Eric whose initials were EKG.

85. The Eric who was working on a screenplay for a buddy cop movie with the working title: *Mortar and Pestle*.

86. The Eric who wouldn't be caught dead without his tape measurer.

87. The Eric who slyly dropped the word "gallimaufry" into our conversation.

88. The Eric who desperately wanted me to be the Juliana Hatfield to his Evan Dando.

90. The Eric who made a living writing that creepy ambient background music that you often hear on podcasts.

91. The Eric who asked me my favorite joke, so I recited "No Soap, Radio!" to him. But then he showed me the *Wikipedia* page that claims that this is not an actual joke, but rather a prank, and that only dupes are supposed to laugh at the punch-line.

92. The Eric who thought the game whack-a-mole constituted cruelty toward animals.

93. The Eric who literally let his hair down in the middle of our date.

94. The Eric whose confirmation bias made him convinced that he could not be influenced by confirmation bias.

95. The Eric who thought that he was somehow being original or intriguing by saying provocative things simply to get a rise out of people.

96. The Eric who couldn't get his act together.

98. The Eric who was an artist who painted with broad strokes and drew deep breaths.

99. The Eric to end all Erics.

45. Stet

So now you're probably thinking: Congratulations Kat, you have finally finished writing and editing your book!

If only.

Even after massively editing down my manuscript, and killing all my darlings (as they say), two arduous tasks still remained.

The first is copy editing. Unlike your editor (in my case, Mario)—who has read your book proposal and understands what you are trying to achieve—your copy editor is likely some independent third party who you'll probably never meet, and who is paid very little money to "clean up" your manuscript. You know, catch typos, fix grammar and punctuation mistakes, tweak the language slightly for clarity, and so on. They receive an electronic copy of your precious book, and are given carte blanche to make any changes they deem necessary.

One day, you receive an email from your editor containing this supposedly new and improved manuscript. You open it and, much to your chagrin, there are red marks *everywhere!* And while maybe 5 to 10 percent of these are worthy corrections, the rest infuriate you. Because the copy editor has capitalized all the instances of "god" in your book, even though you purposely spelled it with a lowercase "g" because you are agnostic. And every time you used the words "they" or "them" as singular gender-neutral pronouns, they changed them to "he/she" and "him/her." And they flat-out removed words like "monosexual" and "metaphorulations," presumably because they couldn't find any entries for these terms in their super-special copy editor's dictionary.

But worst of all were the commas. Because you are not a very visual person—you think in sounds. And as a recovering slam poet, in your mind, your prose has a very specific cadence to it, so you generously dole out commas to convey all of the necessary pauses and syncopations. But your copy editor seems to be your exact opposite: a predominantly visual person who is easily distracted by commas, and feels that they clutter up sentences, or worse, represent punctuation potholes that get in the way of readily reading a sentence.

So now you have to meticulously go through each and every one of these word changes and comma deletions, and type "stet," "stet," "stet" (proofreading speak for "let it stand"—aka, ignore the copy editor's changes).

Shortly thereafter, as you are still recovering from the whole copy editing ordeal, your publisher will send you a proof of your book. Which is exciting at first—to see the book in its final layout. But then it hits you that you have to *read your goddamn book all over again! For the umpteenth time!* What's worse, this time, you cannot just read it to simply appreciate your accomplishment. No, you need to go over this thing with a proverbial fine-toothed comb, trying to catch any remaining typos and formatting errors.

By the time you are done proofing your manuscript, you feel completely done with your book. You never want to read it again. You don't even want to look at it. Or think about it. Ever, ever again.

Which sucks for you. Because now you have to spend the next year of your life promoting it.

46. Book Tour

Whenever a musician releases a new record, or an author releases a new book, there is an expectation that they will do some kind of tour in support of it: performing songs or reading excerpts from their latest work in venues across the country, and possibly other parts of the world. Tours are a wonderful way to connect with your audience and spread the word about your latest creative endeavor.

Having said that, there is a notable difference between music tours and book tours. Namely, when musicians go on tour, audiences are happy to pay some kind of cover charge or ticket price to see the show, which helps offset the traveling and lodging costs incurred while on tour. In contrast, when you are an author who is not in any way super-duper famous, audiences are generally not willing to pay to see you. Instead, they will expect you to magically show up at their local bookstore and do a reading for free. And afterward, if you are lucky, perhaps they will buy your book—which is a good thing, to be sure, but this money does not go directly into your pockets. No, it will be divvied up between the bookstore and your publisher. And while you will ultimately receive a modest royalty for each book purchase, your publisher will hold onto your share for another six months or so, until your biannual royalty check arrives in the mail. Which, suffice it to say, will be long after this tour is over.

Come to think of it, you won't actually be receiving any royalty checks from your publisher until they recoup the modest book advance they gave you. Which you used to buy a really cheap used car, so that you could do your book tour in the first place.

Well, that's not the only reason you bought this really cheap used car. You also bought it because you will need a car to get around in the city that you will soon be calling your new home. Because you are leaving the Bay Area in the rearview mirror. The rearview mirror of your brand new used car.

You are not the first person to move away from the Bay Area. Not by a long shot. Many people, after having made boatloads and fistfuls of money as a result of relentless tech and/or housing bubbles, will eventually move on, and they can pretty much go wherever they please. If, however, you are someone (like me) who initially came to San Francisco as a youngling to discover yourself as an artist and/or to explore your newly found queer identity, and (given those priorities) you have not made enough money to fill up your fists, let alone load up an entire boat—well then, as mandated by law, you are only allowed to move to one of two places: Portland or Los Angeles. Because these are the two major cities outside of the Bay Area that are closest to you. And you really don't have the resources to move much farther away than that.

On the bright side, you will know people in each of these cities: friends who fled the Bay Area a year or two or more before you.

While I have friends in both of those cities, my decision to move to Los Angeles was sealed when Eric #3 mentioned that he and his partner David just bought a small house there, and it happens to have an illegal in-law apartment in the back. So they invited me to move in for relatively cheap, since they can't legally rent it.

So that's a big part of why I chose Los Angeles over Portland. The other reason is that Eric #97 lives in Anaheim. As you could probably tell from a couple chapters ago, we really hit it off. We've even visited each other twice since then. So by moving to L.A., we can continue to see one another.

And I know, I know, I can just hear some people complaining:

"Oh no, it turns out that Kat Cataclysm turns straight at the end of the book!" To which I respond: "Fuck you." Seriously, a person's sexual orientation doesn't just change because of who they are dating. I am still very much bisexual. Not to mention ethically non-monogamous, so I will still likely be dating people who are not of the male persuasion. But frankly, even if Eric and I got married, and I became Mrs. #97, and even if we lived monogamously ever after, *I would still be bisexual!*

Get it? Got it? Good.

99 Erics officially came out three weeks before I moved to L.A. My first two book readings—in Oakland and San Francisco—were very well attended, although I chalked that up to me being local and having lots of friends show up. Two days later, I drove my new used car up I-5 for readings in Portland, Seattle, and Vancouver. I had no idea what to expect, so I was pleasantly surprised by the decent-sized crowds awaiting me. (I later learned that some of these folks turned out because of positive reviews *99 Erics* received from *Fence Sitters,* and the wildly popular website *Math Jokes Anonymous.*) At those events, I read the chapters "Publisher's Clearing House," "Posers," and "Shopping Carts, Part One," respectively. And even though the audiences were mostly comprised of strangers, many were laughing along, and quite a few were downright cracking up. There is simply no feeling better than making a room full of people laugh. (Well, with the possible exception of gargantuan math-sex and dream orgasms.) That was the main reason why I wanted to be a stand-up comedian in the first place. But I suppose I'll have to settle for being an absurdist short fiction writer and faux novelist who occasionally makes people laugh during her book readings.

After returning home from the northwest leg of my book tour, I packed up all my things. I sold off most of my furniture, although I didn't get much money for it because it was all cheap Ikea stuff, although in my mind it was all partially hand-crafted, via my own hands and those weird-ass Ikea Allen wrenches.

Then, on an overcast Monday, I crammed all of my remaining belongings into the trunk and backseat of my new used car. Like many older vehicles, it sports a CD player, so I went all old school and burned a special mix-CD for this occasion. I popped it in. And as the first notes of Sebadoh's "Brand New Love" rang out over the shitty car speakers, I drove off into the sunset.

Verbatim. Because it was actually about mid-day, so the sun was pretty high in the sky. Plus you couldn't really see it anyway, on account of it being overcast. Also, the sun sets in the west, not the south—which was the direction I was heading.

The day after arriving in Los Angeles, I read at a queer bookstore in West Hollywood. Since both Eric #3 and #97 were in attendance, I read their respective chapters. I was pleased to see that Eric #97 was all smiles and not the least bit embarrassed when I described our math-sex/landlord debacle in front of a room full of people. And even though he's ostensibly straight (although I still think that math-sex plus dating a bisexual person makes you at least a little bit sexual-minority-ish), he seemed very comfortable hanging out with all the queer folks who attended the event.

After the reading, Eric #3 excitedly came up to me and tried to convince me that I should pitch *99 Erics* as a TV show: "It could be like *Girls* or *Sex in the City*, but with actual queer content and ethical non-monogamy!" he exclaimed. I told him that I was flattered, but then explained all my fears about having Hollywood producers cast actors to play me (as I expressed to Eric #17 back in Chapter 12). Plus, way back in Chapter 10, I signed a contract promising Mario that I'd write a second book—the YA dystopian novel *The Senses Ceremony*, published under the pen name Kathleen Kennings—so any TV or film adaptations of *99 Erics* would have to wait. At least for the time being.

After the reading, Eric #3 and David, and Eric #97 and I, all went out for drinks together. We had a blast. For the first time in almost a year, I was filled with good feelings about my life and where it may be heading.

I had a couple of days to unpack and start to settle into my new illegal in-law apartment before having to catch a flight out to the east coast. Once there, I would travel by Amtrak and public transit, doing readings in Washington DC, Philadelphia, New York City, and Boston. Albeit not in that order, as it's almost impossible to get all the cities to line up according to geographical location when you are booking a tour.

The final stop on my tour was New York City. Specifically, at Climax, an adult-bookstore-slash-sex-toy-shop in Brooklyn. I had been to Manhattan before, but never to Brooklyn, so I spent most of the day exploring its various neighborhoods. I even went to Coney Island, which turns out not to be an actual island. But I suppose I can't complain, because when I lived in Oakland, I spent a lot of time at Lake Merritt, which isn't even an actual lake. As I walked through all these neighborhoods, I recalled how, way back when I first moved to Oakland, people used to say that Oakland was to San Francisco as Brooklyn was to Manhattan. This was intended to convey the fact that Oakland, much like Brooklyn, was a relatively inexpensive nearby city where working-class folks, artists, and young people could actually afford to live. And it struck me how both of these places have since become extremely unaffordable too.

I arrived at Climax a half hour before the reading, and was greeted by Delilah, the store manager. She said that she had been following my *99 Erics* blog over the last two years, and she was excited to finally be able to read the whole book to find out how it all ends. After she went back to tend to the cash register, I decided that, for Delilah's benefit (plus also because this was my final reading on this book tour), I would read from this penultimate chapter and the final one. I sat down in a chair in the front row and rummaged through my now worn-and-torn copy of *99 Erics* in order to refamiliarize myself with those chapters. And just as I reached the part in the chapter "Book Tour" where I write, "And just as I reached the part in the chapter 'Book Tour' where I write . . ." I overheard someone in real life say (in a BOOMING MAN VOICE), "So, I take it you're going by the name Kat now."

I turned around and there he was: Eric #2. It felt like forever ago since the day when I left him (along with grad school) behind. But seeing his face and hearing his voice triggered all of those old feelings in me: of me being a pleaser, of wanting to avoid conflict with him at all costs.

I tried my best to keep my composure.

Me: Yes, my name is Kat Cataclysm now. Are you still going by Eric Anagnorisis?

Eric: Yes, of course. Why would I ever change my name?

Me: I don't know. Perhaps because you played in a punk rock band at some point? Or maybe to mark the fact that you underwent some kind of important life transformation?

Eric: Nah, I really haven't changed all that much over the years. I'm still the same old Eric. So how are you doing?

Me: Um, shocked. And stunned. Shocked and/or stunned. Can I ask what you are doing here?

Eric: Well, I live here. In New York City. I'm an assistant professor and run my own lab at NYU. How about you? I'll bet you are teaching linguistics somewhere . . .

Me: No. I was never able to get back to grad school to finish my degree. I'm mostly just a writer now.

Eric: Oh, what a pity.

Me: What do you mean, "what a pity"? There is nothing "pitiful" about being a writer! Other than the general lack of financial compensation.

Eric: Sorry, I didn't mean for that to sound like an insult. In fact, I made a New Year's Resolution to not make fun of other people. So instead of ridiculing others, I'm trying to simply pity them instead.

Me: That is bound to backfire on you. Much like my experience with trying not to be patronizing.

Eric: Anyway, once I surmised that you were going by this *nom de plume* . . .

Me: Kat Cataclysm is not a "nom de plume." It's my superhero-slash-weirdo name. It's also my legal name—it even appears on my driver's license. And can I just say, you're trying to act all fancy-schmancy by invoking what you presume is a French literary term, when in actuality the French don't even say "nom de plume." They say "nom de guerre." Which literally means "war name." And my war name isn't Kat Cataclysm; it's Kathleen Kennings. Even though neither of us have fought in any wars.

Eric: If you'll just let me finish, what I was trying to say is that, once I realized that you were going by this new name and doing a book reading here in New York, I thought it would be the perfect opportunity to finally introduce you to someone very special. Anastasia, why don't you come over here. I want you to meet your mother.

"MOTHER?!?!" I thought. This isn't the type of pickle that most women find themselves in. You know, suddenly learning that you have a biological child that you were not previously aware of having. I'm pretty sure that I would have remembered bearing a child somewhere along the way. Especially given the fact that I'm sterile. Plus the fact that I've never understood *WHY WOULD YOU TURN YOUR CHILD INTO A BEAR?!* But then I was struck by the name: Anastasia. It rang a bell.

Upon being beckoned by Eric #2, a girl emerged from behind a display of newly released atheist and agnostic erotica anthologies. She was wearing an oversized "Frankie Say Relax" t-shirt with lederhosen. And she looked eerily familiar.

Eric: Kat, I'd like you to meet Anastasia.

Anastasia: Hi Mommy.

Me: Hi . . . nice to meet you. But you aren't actually my child. You're my clone.

Anastasia: Clone?

Me: Yes, clone. You're an exact replica of me. Genetically speaking. I can tell because you're the spitting image of me when I was about your age. Although I'm not quite sure why we call identical images "spitting" . . .

Anastasia: I don't understand.

Me: See, way back when we used to be together, Eric #2 here promised to make a cloned version of me, so that she could take care of the baby we were planning to have, and so that I could spend my time focusing on my linguistics career. But I assumed it was all a joke. I never in a million years believed that he would actually go through with it.

Eric: It was relatively easy. You left your hairbrush behind, with plenty of DNA to harvest from your hair follicles.

Me: Are you sure you didn't use DNA from my saliva? Because if you did, that might explain the whole "spitting image" thing.

Anastasia: So you had a baby? Does that mean I have a sister? Or brother?

Me: No, I never had a baby. On account of me being sterile.

Anastasia: Sterile as in germ free? Or germ-cell free?

Me: Germ-cell free. And besides, even if I did have a baby, they wouldn't be your sibling. They would be your . . . um, child? I guess? I'm not sure how kinship terminology works for clones.

Anastasia: Why didn't you just adopt?

Me: Well, after finding out that I was sterile, I left Eric #2. To become a lesbian. Although I turned out to be bisexual instead.

Eric: Ha! I figured that you being lesbian was probably just a phase. So now that you're straight again, perhaps we can pick things up where we left off?

Me: *Oh my god, what is everyone's problem with not understanding the very basic definition of "bisexual"?!*

I could tell that my sympathetic nervous system was sympathizing with my current plight, as it began pumping adrenaline into my bloodstream, sending me into fight-or-flight response. I wanted nothing more than to flee this store in much the same way that I ran away from Eric #2 all those years ago. But I couldn't do that this time, on account of my impending book reading. Not to mention the presence of this young girl, who I never knew even existed, and who was the spitting image of me back when I was her age. The whole situation was way too surreal. Too surreal for me even—which is really saying something, given that I write absurdist short fiction!

In fact, this entire scenario reminded me of the penultimate scene in *Kill Bill: Volume 2*, which I had watched just a few months ago with Eric #97. The protagonist, Beatrix Kiddo, shows up at Bill's place with the intention of killing him for the horrible things he had done to her, only to find Bill playing with their daughter B.B.—who Beatrix didn't even know was alive. So, according to this analogy, Anastasia was like B.B., and I was like Beatrix Kiddo. Which basically meant that Eric #2 was the equivalent of Bill.

In the throes of my fight-or-flight response, plus all these unconscious connections and emotions, I jabbed Eric #2 with my fingertips. Five times. In the chest.

Eric: *Ouch! Why the hell did you just punch me like that?!*

Me: It wasn't a punch. It was the five-point palm exploding heart technique. From *Kill Bill*. Once a person is struck, they can only take five steps before they fall over and die.

Eric: But why would you fucking try to kill me?! After I created and raised your clone for you?!

Me: Relax, silly. I don't really know the five-point palm exploding heart technique. I highly doubt it's a real thing. Besides,

Bill doesn't actually die at the end of the movie.

Eric: Yes he does. He takes five steps then falls over.

Me: But there's this whole fan theory I read on Reddit explaining how Bill couldn't possibly have died, because he actually takes six steps rather than five. And if you watch the end credits, everyone Beatrix kills in the film has their name crossed off—except for Bill. Because he's not dead. He was just pretending, as foreshadowed by the earlier scene with B.B. and the toy guns, where Bill plays dead. In other words, Bill lets Beatrix run off with B.B. in the end.

Eric: Wow, fascinating, I never picked up on all that. I'm going to have to re-watch that movie now.

It was at that point in our exchange that the store manager, Delilah, approached me and suggested that we start the reading. For obvious reasons, I was feeling a bit shaken up, and my initial plan of reading this chapter seemed a little too close to home. Unsure of what to do, I made a snap decision to begin my reading with the first chapter of the book.

And as I read from "Eric Number One," I was reminded of how, at the start of this project, I was convinced that I could never become a real novelist, because I was no good at putting my characters into conflict. And how I imagined that, if I introduced conflict into my own life (e.g., by dating an indie rock guitarist), I might be able to overcome my conflict avoidance. And of course, that didn't work. But then it occurred to me that over the last third or so of this book, I've been through all sorts of conflict: from Matilda leaving me, to having a reality TV celebrity with authoritarian tendencies elected president, to dating the Worst Eric Ever, to losing my job at CliqueClick, to almost being run over by a Goober self-driving car, to being evicted from my apartment, and finally my experience today having to confront Eric #2, not to mention learning that I had been non-consensually cloned.

And as I recited the last paragraph of "Eric Number One," it dawned on me: *Holy shit, I have totally succeeded in putting my protagonist (aka, me) into all sorts of conflict! In almost each and every chapter! Perhaps I am capable of becoming a real novelist after all!*

After the reading, I answered audience questions and signed a few books. Folks slowly trickled out of the store, until the only people left (other than Delilah, who was stacking up all the foldable chairs) were Anastasia and myself.

Me: Did you like the reading?

Anastasia: Yes. Although I will never look at banana slugs the same way again.

Me: Me neither. Look, there is something that I need to tell you. Eric #2 is gone.

Anastasia: Gone? Did you kill him?

Me: No, no, nothing of the sort. I'm not a killer assassin, after all. But I am a writer. So I simply wrote him out of the rest of the story.

Anastasia: But why?

Me: Well, for starters, he's really bossy with that BOOMING MAN VOICE of his. He showed up here with the intention of hijacking my story and turning it into a happy ending for him, one where we ended up back together. And I couldn't have that. Plus, he's kinda sorta a mad scientist, if you really and truly think about it. On top of all that, look at how he dressed you.

Anastasia: (looking down at her "Frankie Say Relax" t-shirt and lederhosen) Yeah, he did dress me like a dorkball.

Me: Look, I don't have much money, but I'd be happy to take you to the thrift store once we get back to Los Angeles, and we'll get you some new used clothes.

Anastasia: Yay!

Me: Also, we're going to have to change your name. Because "Anastasia" was a joke name that Eric #2 came up with many years ago. And you are now going through a transformative life change: leaving behind the mad scientist with a BOOMING MAN VOICE who raised you and dressed you poorly, and moving on to live with an older version of yourself who will treat you way better than that. I promise to take you under my wing, show you the ropes, and other mixed metaphors.

Anastasia: Well, what will my new name be then?

Me: How about Kat? Kat Cataclysm. You know, since we're genetically identical and all.

Younger Kat: Although I'm pretty sure we still differ quite a bit at the epigenetic level.

Me: Good point. Nurture trumps nature! Way to be precocious!

Younger Kat: I'm looking forward to being Kat Cataclysms with you.

Me: Actually, I believe the correct plural form would be Kats Cataclysm. You know, like Senators Elect or Surgeons General.

Younger Kat: I'm starting to get hungry. Could we go out for ice cream? Or cookies? Or donuts?

Me: You mean "drunk food"?

Younger Kat: Yeah, I guess.

Me: Okay. But just so you know, when you grow up, you will completely lose your sweet tooth. And instead, you'll prefer more savory foods, such as anchovies and blue cheese.

Younger Kat: Ewww!

Me: But hey, before we go, let's help Delilah with the rest of the folding chairs. Then we'll be on our way.

47. Dénouement

FADE IN:

INT. KAT'S ILLEGAL IN-LAW APARTMENT—DAY

Me: How's it coming along?

Younger Kat: I'm on Chapter 5, during the scene in *The Senses Ceremony* when Katnip first discovers that she has fashion sense, and therefore transcends the Tactile division she was born into.

Me: I thought we had decided that Katnip's sixth sense was going to be a sense of humor.

Younger Kat: No. Fashion sense! Think about it: You can't have the protagonist in a dystopian universe cracking jokes all the time. It'll spoil the mood.

Me: Okay, good point. So tell me, how does her fashion sense manifest?

Younger Kat: She has a penchant for asymmetric haircuts. And rainbow tattoos.

Me: Hmmm. And what do rainbow tattoos signify in Katnip's universe? Queer people? Shopping carts? Macadamia nuts?

Younger Kat: Isn't it obvious that rainbows signify the refraction of light waves via airborne water droplets?

Me: Well, to some readers, it might. But other readers may have very different expectations. You should keep that in mind.

Younger Kat: Fucking expectations.

Me: Also, another thing you should remember is to put Katnip into conflict . . .

Younger Kat: I know, I know, in each and every chapter. But

I still don't understand why you are making me write your book for you.

Me: Well, first off, you aren't writing it for me. You're writing it for Kathleen Kennings. Which is our *nom de guerre*.

Younger Kat: But we haven't fought in any wars.

Me: But we have fought in wars verbatim.

Younger Kat: Oh, so the "war" part is not to be taken literally then?

Me: Exactly. Second, the reason why I have made you the lead author on our YA dystopian novel is because of my new theory about childhood.

Younger Kat: What theory?

Me: Well, I used to believe that children were drunk all the time. Like, naturally drunk. But you don't really seem all that drunk to me. In fact, you often seem way more sober than I am. Even on days when I haven't had any IPAs. So I've since abandoned that theory, and I've come to a brand new realization that children are like interns.

Younger Kat: Interns?

Me: Yes. Because let's face it, until the day you turn eighteen, you pretty much have to follow all of my rules and do all of my bidding—much like an intern would. And like interns, you are expected to do all this work for free, under the understanding that I will mentor you in exchange: teach you important life skills, allow you to accrue experiences that will be useful for your future, etcetera. However, the problem with this whole system is that most adults automatically assume that their children and/or interns are drunk all the time, and therefore incapable of handling any important tasks. This is why they only ever give them grunt work like fetching coffee or doing pointless errands in the case of interns, or washing dishes and taking out the trash in the case of children. This helps explain why so many children grow up to resent their parents, and why so many interns come to resent their bosses: because they are constantly given trivial busywork rather than real important work.

Younger Kat: So what does this have to do with me?

Me: I am giving you real and important work—aka, writing a YA dystopian novel. So that you don't resent me!

Younger Kat: This sounds potentially exploitative.

Me: But it isn't. Because we are combining all of our money—from both your writing and my writing—and splitting it fifty-fifty.

Younger Kat: Can I buy kitchen cabinets full of Oreo cookies with my share of the profits?

Me: Sure, if you wish.

Younger Kat: So what are you writing then? A sequel to *99 Erics?*

Me: God, no! That would mean me dating ninety-nine more Erics, bringing the grand total up to 198. I simply couldn't do it.

Younger Kat: But in the sequel, it doesn't *have* to be Erics. You could do "99" of something else instead. Like go to ninety-nine different baseball games. Or write ninety-nine different absurdist short stories. Or have math-sex to ninety-nine different numerical sequences.

Me: Math-sex? How did you learn about that?

Younger Kat: From reading this book.

Me: I think you're a little too young to know about math-sex.

Younger Kat: How can you possibly say that when you haven't even bothered to establish my actual age yet?

Me: Sorry. We will not be revealing that. Mario strictly instructed us to keep our ages vague, in order for this book to appeal to the widest possible audience.

Younger Kat: Hmph.

Me: Look, since you brought up the subject, I suppose you could be right: Perhaps math-sex could be a focus of my next book. I could maybe even try to convince Eric #97 to collaborate with me on a "how to" guide for math-sex.

Younger Kat: Sex sells! And "how to" books sell even more!

Me: Or perhaps I could turn it into an anthology: *Best Bisexual Women's Math-Sex Erotica*, for instance?

Younger Kat: I think that's a tad overly specific.

Me: Oh, wait a second. Scrap the whole math-sex idea. I just realized that now I *finally* have time to work on that graphic novel about the lives of barnacles that I always dreamed of writing. Like, ever since eight chapters ago.

Younger Kat: That sounds boring.

Me: No it isn't.

Younger Kat: Yes it is. BOR-ING! Barnacles don't do anything! All they do is just sit there on the sides of rocks, or boats, or whatever.

Me: Don't you dare stereotype barnacles as lazy! They lead very fascinating lives. Every barnacle starts out as a nauplius—a one-eyed larva that can swim around freely. Then they pass through five different larval stages until they become cyprids, at which point they stop feeding, and instead search around for a suitable place to live out the rest of their lives. And once they find that perfect rock, or boat, or whatever, they will glue themselves to it, then subsequently develop into adult barnacles. It's basically a Hero's Journey. Albeit for barnacles.

Younger Kat: But what about conflict? I'm not sensing any conflict in your story.

Me: Mussels.

Younger Kat: Mussels?

Me: Yes, mussels. Mussels are the mortal enemies of barnacles. Because they are constantly competing with barnacles for space on rocks, and boats, and whatever. Plus, mussels feed on the baby nauplii—in fact, they are one of barnacles' most feared predators! Along with whelks and starfish.

Younger Kat: Whoa!!!

Me: See, I told you barnacles live exciting lives.

Younger Kat: No, not your story. A circle of nothingness just materialized out of thin air behind you. Look!

Me: Holy cow!

Younger Kat: What do you think it is?

Me: I think it might be a Time Gate.

Younger Kat: Where does it lead?

Me: If I had to venture a guess, to the women's restroom in the basement of my favorite pub near my old apartment in Oakland. About a year and a half ago. See, I'm stuck in a Möbius-strip-like causality loop with a future version of myself. Although I suppose now they are "past me," and I am their "future me."

Younger Kat: You don't have to bother with explaining the whole situation. I read this book, remember? I've just never seen a Time Gate before, is all.

Me: Well, I suppose I have something to take care of then. Although I'm not exactly sure what to say to her to persuade her to write *99 Erics* . . . Anyway, why don't you just keep working on *The Senses Ceremony*, and I should be back very shortly.

Younger Kat: Wait, before you go, don't forget this.

Me: Oh, it's my tube of lidocaine. Thank you so much! This is the perfect piece of evidence—not too important, but not too trivial—to convince past me that I am coming from her future.

Acknowledgements

I am indebted to Amy Butcher, Anna Dickinson, Grace Allen Terwedow, Heather Gold, Jake Pyne, Jeffry J. Iovannone, Kate Mancuso, Leivahna Simcha Schector, Lizabeth Alexander, Marit Bosman, Minna Dubin, Sinclair Sexsmith, and a few anonymous others, for all of their feedback, editing acumen, and/or other forms of support offered along the way. Many thanks to all of my Patreon supporters who helped make this novel possible. This project began as lark, growing out of a 2014 workshop that I participated in, but which never had a formal name; I thank all the amazing writers who encouraged and inspired me there. I am very grateful to Juliana Delgado Lopera and Virgie Tovar for inviting me to read early excerpts from this book at Radar Productions and Sister Spit events in 2015–2016, and to Heather Gold for offering me the same opportunity at Yarn: Comedy Storytelling during 2017–18. Large swaths of this book were written at various dining and drinking establishments across Oakland, many of which are name-checked or alluded to in the book. But I want to give a special shout-out to the folks at (the now sadly gone, due to the latest "boom") Pacific Coast Brewing—I very much appreciated all of our random conversations, the tasty IPAs you served me, and the fact that none of you ever asked me what I was writing; sorry for turning your restroom into a Time Gate. No banana slugs were harmed in the making of this novel.

About the Author

Julia Serano is a writer, bisexual woman, and a longtime resident of Oakland, CA. She also just so happens to be a recovering slam poet, prog rock enthusiast, is fascinated by barnacles, has bicycled the Posey Tube, and may even share a few other attributes with this book's protagonist. But otherwise, her and Kat Cataclysm have very little in common. For instance, unlike Kat, Julia is the author of three non-fiction books about gender, sexuality, and/or social justice activism—*Whipping Girl, Excluded,* and *Outspoken*— and her other writings have appeared in numerous anthologies and in media outlets such as *The New York Times, TIME, The Guardian, Salon, The Daily Beast, Ms., Out,* and *Bitch.* If you enjoy Kat's quirky take on the world, then you might also enjoy Julia's lo-fi solo music project **soft vowel sounds** and her previous noise-pop band *Bitesize.* Information about these projects, and all of her other creative endeavors, can be found at her website: *juliaserano.com.*